ADVANCE PRAI

"With *Rabbit Rabbit Rabbit*, Nadine Sander-Green has written a wonderfully compelling novel about a young newspaper reporter who strives to form a meaningful bond with the people and politics of Yukon, while struggling to break free from a toxic man. I rooted and prayed for Millicent, the young protagonist, every step of the way. A rich rendering of Whitehorse and Dawson City, and of courage in the face of love gone wrong." —**Lawrence Hill, author of** *The Book of Negroes* **and** *The Illegal*

"*Rabbit Rabbit Rabbit* is an emotionally affecting, entirely believable portrait of a strong young person succumbing to and nearly losing herself in someone else. In its skillful braiding of the personal, the political, and even the ecological, this is a meditation on the potentially devastating effects of power and control." —**Gil Adamson, author of** *The Outlander* **and** *Ridgerunner*

"An engaging debut novel. Filled with flawed and fascinating characters, Nadine Sander-Green's coming of age story in the Yukon is a moving tale of how we experience harm—in human relationships, in politics, and on the land—and how we begin to move towards recovery and repair." —**Alix Ohlin, author of** *Dual Citizens* **and** *We Want What We Want*

"I love Nadine Sander-Green's decision to send a novice reporter to the Yukon. What is Millicent escaping, and what does she hope to find? This ain't Jack Nicholson exposing the underbelly of Chinatown—but something similar occurs, though what's uncovered is more inchoate and inside us all: the threat of loss. And loss—of love and land—is always startling. The wonder of *Rabbit Rabbit Rabbit* is there's room for an ending that makes sense of a friend's words: "you've turned into someone I don't know." The full gamut of life's ironies is here, from the absence of tundra swans to the ubiquity of dirty bird hot chicken. Nadine Sander-Green has managed to create a wise and powerful novel out of an achingly present portrait of an urban north that lies within all of us." —**Michael Winter, author of** *Minister Without Portfolio*

"Nadine Sander-Green writes with verve and clarity about life in the Yukon, a place not seen often enough on the page. We root for Millicent, a young reporter growing up fast, to find her agency, pull free of the vortex of her relationship, and take in the expansive complexities of life and land around her. *Rabbit Rabbit Rabbit* is a wise, exuberant, page-turning read." —**Catherine Bush, author of** *The Rules of Engagement* **and** *Blaze Island*

"*Rabbit Rabbit Rabbit* is raw and exquisite. A haunting story about the claustrophobia inherent in obsession and loneliness, and one woman's journey to find and create purpose. Sander-Green's intimate, atmospheric prose invokes a setting both unfamiliar and bewitching that readers won't soon forget." —**Deborah Hemming, author of** *Goddess* **and** *Throw Down Your Shadows*

Rabbit Rabbit Rabbit

a novel

Nadine Sander-Green

ANANSI

Published in Canada in 2024 and the USA in 2024 by House of Anansi Press Inc.
houseofanansi.com

House of Anansi Press is committed to protecting our natural environment.
This book is made of material from well-managed FSC®-certified forests,
recycled materials, and other controlled sources.

House of Anansi Press is a Global Certified Accessible™ (GCA by Benetech)
publisher. The ebook version of this book meets stringent accessibility
standards and is available to readers with print disabilities.

28 27 26 25 24   1 2 3 4 5

Library and Archives Canada Cataloguing in Publication
Title: Rabbit rabbit rabbit : a novel / Nadine Sander-Green.
Names: Sander-Green, Nadine, author.
Identifiers: Canadiana (print) 20230483275 | Canadiana (ebook) 2023048333X
ISBN 9781487011291 (softcover) | ISBN 9781487011307 (EPUB)

Classification: LCC PS8637.A538765 R33 2024 | DDC C813/.6—dc23

Cover and book design: Greg Tabor
Cover image: Galyna Andrushko / Adobe Stock

*House of Anansi Press is grateful for the privilege to work on and create from the
Traditional Territory of many Nations, including the Anishinabeg, the Wendat, and
the Haudenosaunee, as well as the Treaty Lands of the Mississaugas of the Credit.*

 Canada Council
for the Arts

Conseil des Arts
du Canada

 ONTARIO ARTS COUNCIL
CONSEIL DES ARTS DE L'ONTARIO
an Ontario government agency
un organisme du gouvernement de l'Ontario

With the participation of the Government of Canada
Avec la participation du gouvernement du Canada | Canadä

*We acknowledge for their financial support of our publishing program the Canada
Council for the Arts, the Ontario Arts Council, and the Government of Canada.*

Printed and bound in Canada

MIX
Paper from
responsible sources
FSC® C103567

To my mom and dad, who taught me to be brave.

1

PERFECT EQUILIBRIUM, TWELVE HOURS of light and twelve hours of dark. Soon night would pull its blinds over the city for the winter. For now, if you didn't look too closely, Whitehorse was like any small city down south. On the outskirts: a strip mall with Starbucks, Walmart and Canadian Tire. On the main street: some restaurants, cafés and bars; a few gift shops, businesses and hotels.

It was the end of September. Tourists who drove up the Alaska Highway in their RVs to see the vaudeville show and the old sternwheeler and buy eighteen-dollar Sam McGee Sours had fled to Florida for the winter. Locals, the ones who'd been lucky this year, had already skinned, butchered and packaged their moose. They were tucked safely back in their government offices. The streets were empty, like a movie set after hours.

The *Golden Nugget* newspaper was on Second Avenue, one of the main arteries that led out of town, a block away from the river. The office looked like a Western saloon:

pea-green exterior walls, dirty white shutters on either side of every window. Next door, the neon sign for the Mad Hatter bar flickered.

Across the street, a giant mascot dressed like a maple leaf, top-heavy in his silver tights and running shoes, waved maniacally at every passing car, gyrating his hips and pointing to the logo on his chest, Northern Tax Solutions. When there was a break in the morning traffic, he sat slumped on the curb, kicking pebbles or tilting his head back to stare in quiet contemplation at the sky, only to jump up again and start dancing the Macarena for the next set of cars.

Millicent paced on the sidewalk outside the door to the newspaper, her heart a wasp trapped in a glass jar, beating hard and wild against her rib cage. She couldn't believe she had arrived in Whitehorse not even ten hours earlier. In the cheap highway motel where she had spent the night, the people in the room next door blared cop movies until dawn. She tossed and turned in the cardboard sheets, until finally at six, unsure if she had slept at all, she hauled herself into the shower and used the little bottles of shampoo and conditioner to wash her greasy hair. For at least an hour, she agonized over which outfit to wear, posing in front of the mirror in the cramped bathroom, trying to ignore the bags under her eyes and the fact that whatever she tried on, she looked like a secretary from the 1950s.

A gust of wind from the river blew through her tights and billowed her jacket like a sail. The air had an edge, like a blade slicing into her lungs. Millicent swallowed the lump in her throat and unclenched her fists. A bell jingled overhead as she pushed open the door to the *Golden Nugget*, announcing her arrival.

Inside, the dark empty lobby smelled like office supplies and cigarette smoke. Most of the room was taken up by a long wooden counter that looked like it belonged in a nineteenth-century hotel. On top of the counter was a bell and a sign handwritten in jiffy marker that read *Ring if You Must*.

Millicent crept through the lobby, her Mary Janes making no noise on the floor. She paused at the stairwell. The smell of wet ink wafted up from the basement. From upstairs came the muffled sound of a radio, the only sign of life in the building. She took the stairs slowly, clutching the handrail.

The newsroom was a sprawling space that took up most of the second floor. There were lots of desks, but they had no chairs and were covered in stacks of yellowing newspapers. Two workstations were set apart towards a corner. One was scattered with notebooks and paper coffee cups. A Vince Carter poster was thumbtacked to the wall above it. The other workstation, which was clear except for a desktop computer and a red telephone, she assumed was hers.

On the far side of the newsroom was an office. The sign on the door said *Editor*. A wide interior window beside the door looked out over the newsroom. Millicent glanced through the window. Franc, her new boss, sat with his head bowed over the desk.

He was scribbling on a series of pink sticky notes. A boombox on the windowsill blared the CBC news report: *Up next on your morning news, Premier Jakowsky is expected to announce plans for the Vista at a press conference this morning. A Whitehorse daycare has shut its doors after several dog-biting incidents. And Dirty Bird Hot Chicken officially opened to a lineup three blocks long.*

Franc was older than he had sounded on the phone. Black hair covered the backs of his hands. He wore a faded jean jacket with a wool lining. Underneath this, she could just make out a T-shirt with what appeared to be a wolf howling at the moon, the kind she had seen for sale next to decorative shot glasses, postcards of the Arctic circle and canisters of bear spray in the string of identical gas stations along the Alaska Highway.

Millicent wished she had dressed more casually. Her stiff pencil skirt cut into the flesh of her stomach. The door was open just a crack. She knocked softly. There was no answer, so she opened the door wider, standing half in the office, half in the newsroom. Franc either didn't hear her or didn't care. Each time he finished a sticky note he slapped it on top of the desk, cleared his throat and started a fresh one.

Millicent stood still, one hand sweating on the door-knob. Where else was she supposed to go? The newsroom was empty. Morning light poured through the half-dozen tall, wide windows.

On the boombox, the weather cut in, a hushed voice reading through the temperatures for Dawson, Mayo, Carcross, Watson Lake and Old Crow. Franc looked up from his desk as though he had just noticed her. His face was blank. He motioned for her to come in.

Millicent forced a smile and sat down on the hard

wooden chair across from the desk. She shifted, waiting for him to say something. The head of a black bear was mounted on the wall behind the desk, next to a framed degree: Carleton University '85. Underneath these hung a series of certificates claiming Franc was the winner of Sourdough Sam's Log Toss in 1995, 1996 and 1999. The bear's chocolate fur and black glassy eyes gleamed under the office's fluorescent lights. From the large outer window she could see beyond the scaffolding of Riverbend Estate, the high-end condo building under construction next door, towards the crest of a mountain that seemed to rise right out of the river and cut off a slice of the endless sky. The peaks were soft, as if the cold, dry northern wind had humbled them.

"So what brings you to the majestic north?"

Millicent's face grew hot. She recognized his hoarse voice from the phone. It sounded like he hadn't spoken in days.

"Well, this job," she said.

She wondered if he knew who she was. Maybe he didn't remember she was starting today. Maybe he'd forgotten entirely that he'd hired her. After all, the phone interview hadn't taken any longer than setting up a hair appointment.

Franc tapped his fingernails against his desk. He looked out the window. "Most of you young kids come up here to add a notch to your belt, so you can say you did it. Lived in the Yukon. Saw the northern lights. Learned how to swing an axe. Drove a fucking dogsled team. I don't know." Franc shook his head. "Last about three months before running down home."

"That doesn't sound like me."

Franc glanced at Millicent. There were olive-tinged shadows under his eyes. She wondered if he had spent his entire career sitting at this very desk.

"Hope not."

Millicent straightened her posture.

"You'll write at least two articles every morning, three if you have time. The more words the better; don't listen to any of that bullshit they teach you in j-school about cutting down your words. That's great if you're at the *New York Times*. We have a paper to fill here. Every single day." *Two or three articles every morning.* Millicent thought back to the phone interview with Franc that hot evening in August.

Millicent had graduated from college that spring and was living at her parents' house. Her mother was in bed, reading through her stack of library books. Her dad was cooking dinner, following a recipe for prawn Pad Thai that used obscure ingredients like galangal root and kaffir lime leaves. He hummed to himself as he diced green onions with a Chinese butcher's knife. As soon as Millicent picked up her phone and Franc asked for her by her full name, she knew the call had to be about one of the far-flung reporting jobs she had applied for. She hadn't expected to hear back about any of them. Under the heading *Professional Experience*, her resume listed only her job at the school newspaper and a brief stint as a sandwich artist at Subway.

It had been so easy to get hired. Too easy. Franc had asked her three questions.

"Do you have a reliable car?"

"Sure," she said.

"Winter tires?"

"Um, yes."

"Can you write fast?"

Millicent thought for a moment and then spoke in her most confident tone. "Yes."

"I'd like to bring you up here," he said.

"For an interview?" she asked.

Franc laughed. "For the job. When can you start?"

She hung up the phone, unable to find the right words to explain to her dad what had just happened. She didn't need to. He rested the knife on the cutting board. *Go*, he said.

FRANC WAS STARING PAST Millicent at his half-open office door. She hadn't expected to be thrown in like this on her first day of work. He was still talking, something about covering Question Period when it was session, that most of the politics up here was bullshit talking-heads like the rest of the world, but the *Nugget* still had to cover it. Millicent realized she had stopped listening. She had no idea how much she had missed. Feeling guilty, she stared at the back of the door. Hanging on a hook were an umbrella and a plastic bag from Walmart that probably contained Franc's lunch. A metal fork had punctured the bag.

"When it's not in session you'll help Bryce out with the regulars. He's the *sports reporter*, Franc was saying, using air quotes, "but due to some capacity issues he does it all. Car crashes, high school graduations, parades, fires, suicides. You name it."

"Suicides," Millicent repeated.

"News is news."

Franc had risen from his chair and was leaning against the window ledge. Millicent could smell him: wood smoke and sweaty wool, as if he had been working outside all morning and neglected to shower. He jiggled the window open halfway and a cool draft entered the office. He pulled a fresh pack of du Mauriers from his back pocket and fumbled with the wrapping. He held out the box to Millicent, who shook her head, shocked that he was smoking indoors.

"Can't just cherry-pick what we cover," Franc said. "Would you agree?"

"I don't know."

"Yes, you do."

Behind his glasses, Franc's eyes were glassy and green like stones at the bottom of a river. Her heart began firing in her chest again. This was a test.

"I learned it's unethical, covering suicides," Millicent said. "For the family's privacy, but also because studies have shown that publicizing suicide can lead people suffering from depression to actually do it."

She was surprised that she remembered these facts from journalism class in such detail. Millicent was never sure if it was fair to call what she was learning "journalism." She attended an arts school that hired broke poets to teach students how to ask open-ended questions, and to bring pencils to press conferences, not pens, in case it rained.

"Is that right?" Franc said, trying to hide a smile.

"That's what I learned."

"I was just checking you went to j-school."

"Of course I did."

"Of course you did."

They were both smiling now. The transformation of nervousness into relief made Millicent feel brave, delirious almost.

"Did you not read my resume?"

"Just threw the whole lot down the stairs and yours landed at the bottom, so I dialed you up."

Now Franc turned his back to her. His shoulders were broad and curved inward. He inhaled and tapped the ashes out the window. The longer he stood there smoking the more Millicent questioned if she had imagined the playfulness. For a few moments she thought she actually might survive here. She wondered if this meet-and-greet was over, if this was her cue to leave.

"That's me and Charlie. Out on the trapline," Franc said just as Millicent was about to stand up.

She scanned the office until she found what he was talking about: a small framed photo on the wall, next to his university degree, that she had overlooked. She wanted to ask who Charlie was, but the way Franc had said his name made it seem like he was someone she should already know. A famous person, perhaps.

"Where's the trapline?"

Franc didn't answer. He finished his cigarette, put it out in a can of Folgers that sat on the window ledge and sat back down at his desk. Millicent looked at the photo: a younger, slimmer Franc with one arm tossed over the shoulder of a shorter man in a baseball cap. This man had darker skin and softer eyes. Clutched in Franc's free hand by its two hind legs: a frozen dead animal. White fur. A rabbit. The other man was reaching out his arm to take the photo. They were both beaming.

"Looks beautiful out there," Millicent said.

Franc kept his gaze on his half-open office door. He swallowed loudly. "When you're finished your story, yell out the headline. If it's cat stuck in tree, yell *Cat stuck in tree!* Loud enough so I can hear it, please. Then I'll comb through and send it off to production. Paper goes to print at noon. No exceptions."

Through the office window, she saw a lanky man wearing a backpack and a bike helmet come into the newsroom. He seemed to be moving in slow motion. Millicent watched as he slowly shrugged off the backpack. He took off his glasses and cleaned them on his hoodie. When he took his helmet off, she saw that his hair was so blond it was almost white. He settled into the chair under the Vince Carter poster.

"Bryce," Franc said.

Millicent opened her mouth to say something, but nothing came out.

"Jakowsky's making an announcement in half an hour. This could be the big one. You'll cover it."

Franc peeled one of the sticky notes from his desk and handed it to Millicent. She could barely read his hurried cursive. *Jakowsky. Vista. Rec Centre. 10.*

"The big one?"

"Could be."

"What do you mean?"

"You know who Jakowsky is, right? The premier? Our premier? Please tell me you knew that."

2

BRYCE'S KNEES PRESSED INTO the dashboard of Millicent's father's 1994 Mazda Protegé. Other than to mutter "Left here," or "Take a right," Bryce was quiet on the drive up to the press conference. The car smelled like musty, damp towels. Her boxes and bags, all her life's belongings, were still crammed into the back seat and the trunk. The car radio didn't work, neither did the back doors nor any of the windows. The windshield had so many cracks Millicent had to slump in her seat to get a clear view.

What a strange feeling to have another human in the car after the solo drive north. Bryce's presence seemed to take up the entire car. He smelled a bit like weed and a bit like something else, something comforting. Nutmeg, maybe. His hands were large and he rested them open on his thighs as if he didn't know what to do with them. He wore a friendship bracelet, the braided thread faded and soft, the kind an eight-year-old girl might make for her best friend.

"From my niece, back in Ontario," he said when he saw her looking at it.

"Pretty." Millicent forced herself to concentrate on the road that went up from town, the blur of big-box stores, the lights turning from red to green. Bryce stared out the passenger window.

"I'm assuming you don't know much about the Vista?" he asked.

Millicent squawked out a laugh. "Nothing."

Bryce smiled, holding his gaze out the window. "Here's the short and sweet. It's all you really need to know. The Vista is this huge chunk of wilderness, bigger than Scotland—that's what they say. Everyone up here has been fighting over it for a decade. The price of gold is ridiculous right now, something like sixteen hundred dollars per ounce, they're calling it the second gold rush. So of course Jakowsky wants to let this Chinese company, GoldPower, rip the land up and build a mine. The Gwich'in, it's on their traditional territory. They want to protect it. Always have, no matter how many jobs Jakowsky is promising. And now Charlie is running for premier and his whole campaign is about protecting the caribou herd, so obviously our old friend Jakowsky is feeling the heat."

Again, Millicent did not have the nerve to ask who Charlie was. The shame of her naïveté filled her gut.

"You don't want to know how many of these pressers I've been to," Bryce said.

Millicent's palms started to sweat on the wheel. She knew she hadn't graduated from a top-tier journalism school, but still, how had she never even heard the term "presser"?

It was the very gentle atmosphere of the Horizon Institute that drew her to it in the first place, the fact that 20th-Century American Poetry class could count towards her journalism credits. And the fact that in the spring, the main courtyard was filled with hundreds of baby rabbits that students, unwisely, cradled in their arms while sitting on their Mexican blankets studying for exams. It took most students five or six years to finish their degree; they were always taking time off to work on organic farms in Costa Rica, or moving back in with their parents when they ran out of money. Millicent had been surprised at her focus and determination. She graduated easily in four years, at the top of her class too. But what was it good for? Only now did she understand how unprepared she was to be a daily-news reporter.

"I've never actually been to one of these," Millicent said.

Bryce finally looked directly at her. "Well, of course you haven't. It's your first day of work. You'll catch on."

"No. A presser. Any press conference. This is my first one."

The city fell away behind them as they climbed a hill and crossed the Alaska Highway. They passed a sign that marked the distance to Anchorage, the nearest city, 1,133 kilometres away. Bryce peered out the window again as they passed a statue made of scrap metal, a horse rearing up on its hind legs. "I don't know how else to say this, but how did you get this job?" he asked.

Millicent could barely get the words out. "I honestly don't know."

"Sorry."

"It's a good question."

"I didn't mean it that way."

"I went to this college called Horizon. It was more like an art school disguised as journalism school," Millicent said finally. "Mostly I just learned how to write poems."

"That's chill," Bryce said.

"Super chill."

"I don't really get poetry."

"Nobody does."

They had reached the top of the hill and their destination, the Northern Lights Recreation Centre, a modern, light-filled building. Millicent parked the car. Bryce was already leaning over his backpack, rummaging through his camera equipment. He sat up and looked at her.

"Recite one of your poems," he said.

Millicent turned off the ignition with a grin. "Never."

Bryce laughed. His wire-rimmed glasses sat slightly crooked on his nose. They looked like the frames her grandfather wore. Millicent couldn't tell if he was trying to be ironic and cool or if he was just oblivious to style.

She got out of the car and closed her door. From the top of this hill, she felt as if she were seeing the north for the first time: the wide blue channel of the Yukon River coiling through Whitehorse, the surface of the water winking silver reflecting the sun. Behind the town and the clay cliffs was an endless stretch of boreal forest. Even the low-lying mountains, which rolled through the land like the back of a sleeping reptile, were carpeted in trees. The quiet was enormous, as if the vast expanse of land had swallowed the city's noise.

Bryce was leaning against the passenger door, arms folded over his chest, waiting for Millicent as she checked her purse for a second time: notebook, pencil, recorder.

"The newspaper is on its deathbed. I'm guessing Franc didn't mention that in your interview."

"No, he didn't. Should I be worried?"

Bryce shrugged. "It's just the *Golden Nugget*."

A Bluebird school bus was parked not far away. Faded orange curtains covered every window. Loud reggae music rattled the glass. Millicent slung her purse over her shoulder and paused to take in what looked like someone's home on wheels. She wondered if this kind of living arrangement was considered normal for Whitehorse.

She advanced a few steps to see around the front of the vehicle. The bus's headlights were the size of pancakes and spattered with dead insects.

"Does someone live in there?"

"Some guy. Everybody knows him."

"What's his deal?"

Bryce smiled.

"Let me rephrase. Everybody knows of him. Nobody seems to actually *know* him," Bryce said, using air quotes. "He parks all over town. Highway pullouts. Up here at the rec centre. The Walmart parking lot. No idea if parking this beast wherever he pleases is officially legal, but that's why people love it up here. It's the wild west. Or the wild north. Legal doesn't mean the same thing as it does in the rest of the country. Technicalities get swept under the rug."

A pair of hands yanked open the curtains, window

by window. There was a brief flash of human silhouette, then it was gone.

"Speak of the devil." Bryce turned away and walked ahead towards the entrance of the recreation centre. Millicent loitered for a moment longer, unsure why she was drawn to the bus. Maybe there was a story here for the paper.

The man opened the last set of curtains near the front of the bus, directly above where Millicent was standing. His black hair was held back by a bandana. He looked just shy of middle-aged. Even though he had a generous beard and a mess of curly hair, he was still clean-cut, not the dishevelled-looking creature she had imagined. When their eyes met, her feet wouldn't move. The man seemed unfazed by her breach of privacy. Was he smiling? He knocked on the window three times and lifted his hand into a wave. Millicent managed to return a weak acknowledgement before she turned around and jogged across the parking lot to catch up with Bryce. Her Mary Janes slapped against the pavement. The cold dry air cleaned out her lungs.

The party room was packed with plastic conference chairs set in neat rows. On the wall was a sign that read *Happy Eighth Birthday, Mitzi!* A glass wall looked out over a swimming pool.

A group of what Millicent assumed were government workers sat in the front row, whispering. They were smartly dressed from the ankles up in tailored pants and shirts. When it came to their footwear it was clear that comfort trumped style: faded Nike sneakers, sandals with wool socks. Bryce stood at the back of the room, looking through his camera lens at the empty podium. It was clear to Millicent that she couldn't just follow him. She was on her own now. She sat next to a man in jeans with a notepad open on his lap and tried to make eye contact, but he was busy, absent-mindedly pressing the palm of his hand against the tips of his gelled hair.

Millicent opened her notepad. On the first page, in her neatest handwriting, she wrote the date: *September 25th, 2011*. The room was filling up with more bureaucrats. A petite woman wearing a jacket with the CBC logo on the front strode through the door with a cameraman in tow. The man sitting next to her stopped grooming his hair and half-heartedly introduced himself as Kyle from 97.3 The River. "Native pride," he said. Millicent was unsure if this was the station's tagline or just something he said when he met people.

"Millicent," she said, reaching out her hand, but he was ignoring her again as a man in a dark blue suit and a goatee walked up to the podium. "That's Jakowsky," Bryce whispered as he squatted in the aisle beside Millicent.

The room grew quiet.

"Welcome everyone, and thank you for taking the time out of your busy schedule to attend this announcement. Today is a significant day for our territory. It's a day when we can all breathe a sigh of relief, knowing that our history, culture, environment, economy and community will continue thriving." The premier paused and looked down at his notes. He flashed a smile. "I like to think of these facets of our territory as threads on a rope. The more tightly they are wound together, the stronger the rope."

Millicent was scribbling down what the premier was saying, word for word.

"I'm pleased to announce that we've officially concluded a three-year study tracking the precise location of the Porcupine caribou's calving grounds. We are now certain that the location of GoldPower's mine is over 60 kilometres away from this site." Jakowsky paused. "This is great news for the entire territory. GoldPower will employ over 800 Yukoners, many of them Gwich'in. We can all rest easy now, knowing that industry and environment are working in co-operation."

Millicent glanced over at Kyle. His notepad was empty.

"Yukoners are a special kind of people," Jakowsky continued. "We have a connection to the earth, to our land, something those who live south of our borders cannot even fathom. The Porcupine caribou will be one hundred percent protected. The herd will continue to use its pristine calving grounds to maintain its healthy population, as they have done for thousands of years, if not millennia. This was, after all, their land first."

Kyle tapped his foot restlessly. "Is," he said under his breath. "Not was."

When Jakowsky finished his speech and left the podium, Kyle got up. He and the woman in the CBC jacket cornered him by the door and thrust recorders towards his mouth. A scrum. One more thing Horizon had not prepared her for, Millicent realized. Bryce collapsed in the chair next to her and began scrolling through his photos.

"Better get over there, tiger," he said.

"I will. I just …"

Bryce looked over at Jakowsky. The premier was speaking to the other reporters with dramatic hand gestures. Bryce glanced at Millicent, raised his eyebrows and smirked.

"You don't know what to think of all this?"

"What do you think?" Millicent asked, then laughed awkwardly. "I mean, seems like I'll get more of a straight answer from you than this Jakowsky character."

Bryce looked over at the swimming pool on the other side of the wall. The surface was so still it was hard to believe it was water, not glass.

"I think this is all just noise."

HALF AN HOUR UNTIL deadline. Millicent wrote the article so quickly she barely looked up at the words she was typing. Charlie, she had learned from her frantic Google search, was the first Indigenous candidate to run for premier in the Yukon. He was Gwich'in, from a tiny fly-in community in the Vista where it was illegal to buy alcohol. The community largely lived off the caribou they hunted every spring and fall. She wondered why she hadn't done any research before starting the job. She supposed it was because it hadn't even occurred to her that she might be reporting on day one.

Once she finished her 500 words, Millicent sent the article to Franc and yelled out, "Caribou press conference!" then leaned back in her chair, allowing the newsroom to come back into focus: the plush red carpet, the whirring overhead fan, the smell of cigarettes. She was surprised that Bryce didn't even look up from his computer.

A few minutes later she got up and walked over to Franc's office. She leaned against the doorframe, unsure if she was allowed inside.

"Is it okay?"

"Fine."

"I guess I just didn't have much to work from, being my first day and all."

"I said it's fine."

"I'm sure over the coming weeks—" Millicent started.

"I have five articles to edit before I get to yours," Franc said without looking up. "Get to production. The front proof is laid out, I need a copy editor."

Millicent looked around the newsroom. There was a door on the far side with a sign that read *Production*.

"Me?"

"Yes, you."

THE PRODUCTION ROOM WAS just as large as the newsroom—much too large for an editorial team of two, or three now, she supposed, including her. In it were two rows of chest-height wooden easels and a makeshift kitchen with a coffee maker and a toaster. A graveyard of computer chairs with faded fabric and broken limbs filled the rest of the space, along with a desk in the corner with half a dozen computer monitors, wires tangled and lights blinking. A middle-aged man sat behind the set-up, too engrossed in his work to notice, or care about, Millicent's presence.

She traced her fingers along the edge of an easel, imagining the room full of reporters thirty or forty years ago, back when the newspaper was the most trusted way to find out what was happening in the world. She could almost feel the buzzing energy: reporters drinking scotch and smoking cigars while tearing up the copy with red pens. Laughter. Tension. *The newspaper is on its deathbed.* She knew she had entered a fading industry. Still, staring at the layer of dust on the windowsill, she couldn't shake the feeling she had arrived decades late to the party. That she was walking amongst ghosts.

"Front page is ready for proofing," the voice behind the computer monitors said, snapping Millicent out of her daydream. "I'm laying out page three right now. Be done in two shakes."

Millicent stared at the empty easels. "Where's the, uh, front page?"

The man pointed towards a printer beside his desk and went back to squinting at his screens.

Millicent went over to the printer and took the legal-sized page from the tray, scanning it as she wandered back to the easel. The photograph on the front page of the *Golden Nugget* was of a regal-looking fox. The animal was perched on the edge of a clay cliff, staring directly at the camera lens. The day's headline: "Helicopter Crashes after Tangling in Wires." Did the fox have something to do with the helicopter crash? No, she realized as she read the photo caption: *Local photographer gets up close and personal with a red fox on hospital ridge.* She wondered if the photo and headline combination was a drastic

mistake but decided to let it go. If it was, surely someone else would see it.

With a red pen in her hand, Millicent scanned the
beginning of Bryce's article on the helicopter crash.

After dropping workers off at a remote mining camp,
a man in his thirties was nearing the Whitehorse airport
when his roter got caught in telephone wires. The helicopter crashed forty feet below.

She was afraid she wouldn't see any mistakes. What
if the paper went to print full of typos and grammatical
errors and it was all her fault? Where was Bryce? Why
was she the only one doing quality control on her first
morning of work?

Luckily, Bryce was a messy writer. In the third paragraph she spotted a "their" instead of "there," and in the
fourth she found a double period and a semicolon that
should have been a colon. As she scanned the rest of the
page, her red pen hovering over Franc's editorial, *Curling
Club's Finances on Thin Ice*, Bryce and Franc rushed in.
Franc grabbed the rest of the pages from the printing tray
and handed a stack of them to Bryce.

"Eight minutes," Franc said.

"Luxurious," Bryce said. He took his glasses out of
the pouch of his hoodie, slipped them on and winked at
Millicent. "All the time in the world, right?"

THE *GOLDEN NUGGET* WENT to print in the basement at
noon on the nose. Millicent waited on a cold plastic seat
in the lobby until a bald man in a blue jumpsuit dropped

a stack of newspapers on the front desk next to a sign that read: *$1.50, $1 for seniors.*

She grabbed a copy, still warm from the press and smelling of ink. She tucked the paper under her arm and, floating from adrenalin and the relief of knowing the stress of the day was behind her, pushed open the heavy door to the sunlit street.

Millicent turned away from Second Avenue towards the river. She shaded her eyes with her hand as she walked past a canoe-rental shop that was closed for the season, its yard a cemetery of red, green and yellow boats chained and locked to one another. The wafting aroma of hot bread was coming out of the log building across the street. A bakery. Even the sunlight was different here—sharp, like it could cut through skin.

Millicent wanted to be alone at this moment, to see her byline in print for the first time. She found a concrete bench on the Millennium Trail, a paved path that followed the curve of the Yukon River. She sat next to a sign that read *No Swimming, Dangerous Current* and a trashcan over-flowing with McDonald's wrappers and beer cans. Up close, the river was dizzying. It was wide enough for a cruise ship to navigate, and the water ran clear and fast. She wondered how deep it was.

The screech of bicycle brakes startled her. Millicent whipped her head around. Bryce. He hopped off his bike. A joint burning in one hand, he pushed his vintage red Norco down the path towards her with the other. He leaned his bike against the back of the bench.

"You found me," Millicent said.

"Wanna get high?"

"No, thank you."

Bryce took a puff of his joint and stared at the current.

"I smoke it for my back pain," he said.

"Really?" Millicent asked.

Bryce laughed. "No. I take a few hits after deadline every day. Gets me through the long afternoons."

Millicent flipped through the newspaper, searching for her name.

"He didn't print your story," Bryce said without taking his eyes off the water.

A heavy lump of dread formed in her throat. Millicent turned the paper over to make sure it wasn't on the back page.

"Like I said, it's just the *Golden Nugget*. Don't take it personally. Franc doesn't care what we write, he just needs to fill the paper. I find it easier to think of myself as a house painter or something. Just get in there, get the job done and get out. Tomorrow is a new day, a new house to paint."

"He really doesn't care what we write?"

"Well, I mean he does care. But first and foremost, he's got to get the paper out. And to get the paper out, every square inch has to be filled."

"Tell me the truth."

Bryce sat down next to Millicent on the bench, his nutmeg scent floating between them. He bit his bottom lip, then broke into a guilty smile.

"Okay. Franc asked me to fix up your story, then he'll run it in tomorrow's paper."

Millicent choked down hot tears. She would not cry. Not on her first day. She could tell Bryce didn't know what to do because he kept opening his mouth and then closing it again without making a sound.

"This shit is complicated," he said finally. "Franc shouldn't have thrown you to the sharks like that. You want the rundown?"

"Please." Millicent loosened a sharp stone that was wedged between the wooden slats of the bench and chucked it into the current.

"The problem is there's an election coming up next month, and every time anyone—reporters or the official opposition or even the Gwich'in—asks Jakowsky what he's going to do with the Vista, whether he's gonna let this big-ass mine go ahead, he's just silent. Totally silent."

"Like, he just doesn't respond?"

"No, he talks, of course. You heard him babbling away about nothing during the scrum. He keeps saying they need to finish consultations with the Gwich'in, but of course that's bullshit. Consultation. He's not doing anything, just sitting on his ass until the election is over. We all know what the Gwich'in want. They've been saying it for years. It's their territory. If anything happens to the caribou, especially up in Old Crow, they're fucked. It's the only town up there for thousands of miles. Caribou is their main food source. It's their everything. They're the caribou people. What are they going to eat? Twenty-dollar avocados shipped up by plane from California? Fuck no." Bryce was speaking quickly now. "Jakowsky just doesn't want to lose any precious voters. He won by twenty votes last time.

Twenty votes! And now he's up against Charlie, and Charlie is Gwich'in. Jakowsky knows he's holding on by a hair. He doesn't have the guts to say a word. End of story."

Millions of gallons of water slipped north. The river moved without effort, the only sound a faded hush, the kind of sound that existed only if you tuned in to it. A bird landed on a lone rock in the middle of the current, its black feathers gleaming a hint of blue.

"Hello, crow," Millicent said, to fill the silence.

"Raven."

She laughed. "Whatever."

Bryce took another drag. "I know Franc can come off a little cold at first, but just give him time."

"I guess."

"The *Nugget* is the only place he goes to escape his own life. Believe it or not, he's probably happiest there."

"What do you mean?"

Bryce leaned over and picked up a small round stone from the pavement. He held it above his eye, blocking the sun.

"He just doesn't have much going on," he said finally. "Lives by himself. Makes a tuna casserole for dinner every night and brings the leftovers for lunch. It kills me. Some days after work we go next door to the Mad Hatter for a couple of drinks. And all we do is talk about the ledge or city hall. That's about the extent of his social life."

The raven stirred and took flight, its wings ripping the sky's fabric; neat, audible strokes until it soared over the bridge and out of sight.

Bryce held out the joint between pinched fingers. "Sure you don't want some?"

"On my first day of work?"

"Fair point."

They sat in silence, watching the current, as if waiting for something to change.

"How did you end up at the *Nugget*?" Millicent asked.

Bryce stubbed the joint out on the bench and placed it in a Ziploc bag.

"Same old story. I was tired of the rat race down south. I was doing PR for some law firm down in Toronto, spending all my money on brunch and shoes and things I didn't need, just to distract myself. And guess what?"

"What?"

"I woke up one day and realized I was unhappy. Like, really unhappy. I could hardly get out of bed for weeks. When Franc offered me the job, I didn't think twice. Found a cabin in the woods on Craigslist, packed my old Ford Taurus, threw this old steed on the roof," Bryce nodded towards his bike, "and started driving."

He leaned back against the bench and stretched. The blond hair on his forearms glimmered in the sunlight.

"I actually left so fast I only brought three CDs with me for the entire five-thousand-kilometre drive. Didn't know I'd be out of radio reception most of the way. Ryan Adams, Lucinda Williams and Gillian Welch."

With that, Bryce began humming something with a country lilt. Millicent couldn't make out what song. She didn't care to ask, just let herself be carried away by the tune and the constant *hush* of moving water.

3

AFTER WORK, MILLICENT DROVE thirty kilometres down
the Alaska Highway towards her new home. Sophie had
described it as a two-bedroom apartment, on the edge of
an industrial park. She thought she would feel relief after
finishing her first day, but there was no lightness in her
body, not when she knew she would have to show up to
the *Nugget* the next morning and repeat the humiliating
day all over again.

It was getting dark. She switched on her headlights and
sank deeper into her seat. She fiddled with the radio dial,
hoping it had miraculously fixed itself while she was at
work. Nothing but white static. On her right was a sign
pointing towards the Sixty Below Brewery and Mount
Mackenzie, the local ski hill.

Millicent let off the gas and leaned forward into the
windshield. She could hardly believe it. Parked at the pull-
out was the school bus. The vehicle's curtains were all

open, the windows illuminated with light. A small red machine sat on the pavement outside. A generator, she guessed. Millicent remembered the way the man on the bus had knocked on the glass to say hello, and how the abrupt movement had, for a moment, paralyzed her. She had imagined she was invisible in this new land, but there was something in the way the man had stared at her from the window that made her realize the town was smaller than she realized, in a way she didn't yet understand. She couldn't hide, even if she wanted to.

Millicent looked at the bus in the rear-view mirror. She wondered how many people lived like this up here. Away from society. On their own terms.

A semi-truck pulled out from behind her to pass, honking. Millicent looked at her odometer. She had slowed to 40 to look at the bus. She pushed the clutch from fourth to fifth and accelerated back to the speed of traffic.

MILLICENT SLOWED AGAIN WHEN she came up to a gas station. Beside it was a decrepit-looking restaurant with a sign that read: *The Northern Dragon I* and *Off Sales*. She turned off the highway, and the smell of deep-fried chicken and gasoline seeped into the car. *Turn right at the gas station and Chinese restaurant and follow the dirt road till you hit the end*, Sophie's email had said. This had to be it.

When Millicent had emailed Sophie to say she was moving north, she didn't expect a reply. The gossip at Horizon was that Sophie had moved to the Yukon the day she finished her last exam and started working as a barista at some café in Whitehorse. Her reputation with men had got the better of her, that's what the girls from the "clan" said. She needed to get as far away as possible, start fresh. Millicent didn't have any reason to believe differently. She and Sophie hadn't talked in years.

But Sophie had written back immediately. *Your timing is perfect*, she wrote. *My roommate just moved out. The apartment has this old cast iron bathtub. Five hundred dollars a month, heat included, if you can believe that. You have to move in! It'll be just like old times.*

She passed an abandoned field lit up by a sea of pink. She remembered seeing these plants in pictures; it was fireweed, the last flowers to bloom before winter. A building with a sign that read *Dave's Mechanics* came into view. Millicent experienced a moment of panic as a pack of dogs ran out from the back and leapt up against a wire fence, only a few feet from her window, flashing snouts and teeth.

"Fuck," she said, accelerating until the barking faded. Sophie hadn't warned her about the dogs. Why was she even living out here?

The sky had turned, instantly it seemed, from twilight to a sheet of black. Her headlights shot tunnels of light on the bumps in the road. Millicent jerked the wheel left, then right, to avoid the deep gouges. The engine whined as she crested a hill and arrived at the end of the road, a gravel pit of a parking lot behind a two-storey clapboard building.

In the empty lot, Millicent sat with the engine running. Her headlights shone on a red door. She wondered what

Sophie looked like now, if she still kept her hair long. Sophie had thick ginger hair that she was always fussing with. "Feel it," Sophie would urge, guiding Millicent's hand to the finer hair on the nape of her neck. "Still wet. I showered three hours ago!" She used to have a way of flipping her head upside down and raking her fingers through her hair that fascinated Millicent. When she lifted her head, her hair was piled into a perfect loose bun.

They'd been inseparable during Millicent's first semester at Horizon. Sophie lived in the room next to hers. She was the only second-year student who still lived in the dorms. After her night class, she would bang on Millicent's door and insist she come over for a drink.

"Bienvenue, ma chérie," Sophie would say. She had decorated her room to look like a bohemian club, with silky scarves draped over the lights and an antique cabinet for her liquor. She had taken the batteries out of the smoke alarm to burn jasmine incense. What a foreign feeling to be immersed in indulgence. Millicent's parents had never bothered with simple pleasures. They didn't drink booze or listen to music or heat the house above 17 degrees. Their bookshelf was packed with hardcovers about acid rain and invasive plants.

Millicent and Sophie would sit on the carpet with their backs against the wall. They sipped their cocktails and Sophie would tell her about her childhood. She had grown up in downtown Montreal and her parents took her to museums and cafés on the weekends. When she was still a teenager they brought her with them to jazz clubs.

Sophie was always interested in Millicent's courses,

especially her poetry classes. One night she asked her when she had first known that she wanted to be a writer. Sophie always listened so intently that Millicent found herself giving answers she had never said out loud before. "I don't know. But I always felt that poetry was just the closest thing to the truth," she said.

Sophie grabbed Millicent's hand and held it. Her hazel eyes grew wide when she had something urgent to say. "Promise me you won't forget that."

Millicent nodded. "I promise."

She felt as if she'd stepped into a magical realm when she was in Sophie's room, as if there was a more inter- esting part of her that emerged, a part of her she didn't even know existed.

The other girls in the dorm—the rich girls from the "clan," as Sophie called them—would gather every night to watch shows like *Grey's Anatomy*. Sophie and Millicent tried their hardest to ignore the bursts of high-pitched glee from their rooms. Every few minutes the clan erupted into hysterical laughter, as if someone had broken into the room and was trying to tickle them to death.

These girls, whose names all seemed to be variations of "Katherine," clung together as a single organism. They went everywhere together—to class, to the cafeteria, even to the mailbox. Millicent didn't consider them potential friends, more like a group she orbited around and watched from a safe distance. It wasn't that she didn't like them; she had just never found a way into their sphere. Sophie, on the other hand, wouldn't even make eye contact with them. "You know that our society is in crisis when it raises young girls who are too afraid to take a shit without holding someone's hand," she'd say, twisting the stem of her cocktail glass between her thumb and her finger and looking at Millicent with a smile that was coy and sad at the same time.

MILLICENT TURNED OFF THE CAR and unbuckled her seatbelt, full of nervous dread at the reality of seeing Sophie again. When she opened the door, the smell of cold, damp soil and the sweet musk of pine needles rushed into the car. The night was so black she could hardly make out the outline of trees. The faint hush of moving water from the river, not that far away, sounded like the drone of a distant highway. The world seemed to be composed only of sounds and scents: the crack of branches in the wind, a rustling in the underbrush, the smell of evergreens.

Millicent approached the building. Sophie had said the apartment was the one closest to the parking lot. It must be the one with the red door. There were windows on either side of the door, and dim light filtered through the curtains. There was no doorbell, just a brass knocker and a peephole. Millicent knocked, arranging her face into a pleasant smile. She knocked again. When no one answered, she considered getting back into her car and driving away. But where else could she go? She didn't want to go back to the motel.

She jiggled the handle; the door was unlocked. Millicent pushed open the door to the familiar smell of jasmine and something ripe and fruity—kitchen compost, maybe. She stood in the small hallway, taking inventory: to the right she could see a kitchen, to the left a living room. She moved into the kitchen. A colander of limp spaghetti sat in the sink and a spider plant wilted on the windowsill. A ten-pound bag of beets lay on the counter. There was a small table and four kitchen chairs.

Millicent floated through her new apartment as if it were a museum, too scared to touch anything. In the living room was a red velvet chaise longue that looked like it belonged on the set of a community theatre production. On a small coffee table sat Zadie Smith's *White Teeth* and a half-empty bottle of Jameson's whiskey. She pressed her forehead against a patch of uncovered window. The moon had cut a milky hole in the night, and the stars had shattered across the bowl of sky. The shards hung low, billions of them. When was the last time she had spoken to Sophie?

AFTER THAT FIRST SEMESTER at university, Millicent had turned inwards. She lost track of the social life at Horizon. She spent every night on the third floor of the library trying to write poems for workshop, sitting in the corner desk by the Contemporary American Poetry stacks. Most of her poems came out flat and reeking of effort. It was embarrassing to think that her professor had to spend his evenings editing these poems. She knew how bad they were. But Millicent could feel the muscles in her chest seize when she wrote a line that sang, when she let go of effort. This was rare, but when it happened, she trusted it. She went back to her dorm and lay on her bed, staring at the ceiling, unable to sleep, her brain firing new lines as if it had been rewired. She had to convince herself to keep her laptop closed, get under the covers and breathe. There was always music seeping in from Sophie's room on those nights, accompanied by the sound of a man's voice; a low, serious tone as if he was discussing philosophy with her. Millicent would bury her head under her pillow to block out the sound.

UPSTAIRS, SHE COULD HEAR people having sex. At first there was just the squeak of a mattress, followed by low moaning. It sounded as if one was performing surgery on the other without an anesthetic. Then, silence. A few minutes later the smell of something sweet and salty wafted into her apartment, grilled cheese maybe.

Next to the living room and another room with a closed door, Millicent found a bedroom she presumed was hers. There was a mattress on the floor and a small chest of drawers. A closet held a handful of old hangers.

Millicent hauled some of her boxes and bags from the car and dropped them on the bedroom floor. She spread a fitted sheet onto the bare mattress and covered it with her flannel comforter. She hung a bath towel over the window as a makeshift curtain and stood in her doorway to admire her work. Under the harsh light of the ceiling fixture, the room looked as sterile as a hospital.

In the bathroom, she turned on the tap of the claw-foot bath and sat on the toilet lid watching the hot water thunder into the cast iron tub. She wished she had rented her own place so she didn't have to experience this feeling of nervous anticipation. Not that she could afford to live alone on the fourteen dollars an hour the *Nugget* was paying her. And not that she actually wanted to be alone. But who knew how long Sophie would be out? Would it be like this every night, tiptoeing around, wondering where her roommate was?

In the bath, Millicent perused a dog-eared copy of *In Search of Duende* by the Spanish writer Federico Garcia Lorca. She hadn't picked it up since her professor had assigned it for her poetry workshop. She didn't normally read a book more than once, but there was something about the way Tim talked about *duende* in class, pausing to close his eyes every few minutes, as if he was summoning a spirit, that made this slim book vibrate with significance. Tim was her favourite teacher. He made her feel like her writing was urgent, and nothing else she had done up to that point had felt urgent. It was a strange feeling that was both thrilling and overwhelming.

Alert to any sound that might be Sophie, Millicent settled deeper in the bath. The apartment was eerily silent. She told herself to focus on Lorca, to transport herself somewhere else, anywhere else. The words on her page blurred into ants.

Her mother had read the Lorca book too, probably more carefully and slowly than Millicent had. Her mother had devoured all the assigned readings from Millicent's creative writing classes: *The Art of the Personal Essay*; *Letters to a Young Novelist*; *Sylvia Plath, Collected Poems*. At the start of every semester, her mother would ask Millicent to email her the course syllabus. Millicent's father would find the books at the library. Her mother would read the stack over the next few weeks.

When Millicent came home for breaks between semesters, her mother always wanted to talk about the books, to pretend she was in the workshop too. She said university was wasted on young people, that if she could go back she would take every elective in the course calendar. Millicent found this heartbreaking—not that her mother was so hungry for knowledge, but that she refused to confront the truth: she wouldn't be able to go back to school.

Millicent would never dare to say this out loud. They did not speak of her illness. Instead, she would organize her mother's closet, plucking nightgowns from the floor and slipping them on hangers, while her mother lay in bed, analyzing lines from Lorca or Plath, the window open so she could feel the breeze on her face.

Her mother would frequently pause mid-sentence, close her eyes and fish inside her brain for the right words. When this happened, Millicent could feel impatience seeping into every cell of her body. She knew that her mother could not control the fog that obscured her once-articulate brain, that she was dealing with a disease that couldn't be cured or even treated. Her mother had essentially disappeared from society, and Millicent couldn't even wait one minute for her to find the right word? The guilt gnawed at her as she continued to organize her closet.

WHEN MILLICENT HEARD THE door open she scrambled out of the lukewarm water. She wrapped her towel around her torso and fastened it tightly, cleared her throat and slammed the bathroom cabinet to make sure Sophie knew she was there. Clutching the doorknob, she mustered the courage to leave the bathroom.

In the living room, sweet earthy jasmine incense burned on the windowsill. A jacket, a scarf and a purse were splayed haphazardly in the entranceway, as if these items had been strangling Sophie, as if she could not have waited one more second to remove them.

And there she was, lying on her belly on the velvet chaise longue, reading *White Teeth*, legs bent, bare feet sunny-side-up to the ceiling, her small frame drowning in an oversized orange T-shirt that read *Take Back the Land, Vote Charlie!* Her thick ginger hair hung in a bob at her jawline. As Millicent came into the room, Sophie tilted her chin up. Her hazel eyes looked even bigger than Millicent remembered.

"Milli Vanilli. Oh my god!"

"Soph."

Sophie dropped the book on the floor and ran to greet her. They held each other as water dripped from Millicent's hair and pooled on the hardwood at her feet. Sophie pressed her face into Millicent's neck and inhaled deeply. Millicent stiffened, remembering how casual Sophie was about touching, how she just melted into people, even people she hardly knew.

When Sophie finally let go and stepped back, Millicent saw that she hadn't changed. She had the figure of a lamppost, all knees and elbows and shoulder blades. Sophie had the unpredictable beauty of a model, with delicate features and dewy skin. With the right light and angle, she turned heads. At other times, however, especially when she was in a bad mood, Sophie's looks were unremarkable. Still, her effortless beauty had always made Millicent self-conscious about her own looks.

Standing face to face, neither of them knew what to say. Then Sophie laughed, and Millicent felt such enormous relief she wondered if she was going to cry.

"I cannot believe it's you, in the flesh," Sophie said.

Millicent placed her hands on her hips and grinned. "Here I am."

"I'm making you a drink to celebrate. My specialty." She picked up the bottle from the table and went into the kitchen. Pushing aside the dishes in the sink, she filled the kettle with water from the tap and placed it on the stove.

"Negroni?" Millicent asked.

"I'm a whiskey girl now," Sophie said. Without asking Millicent if she was hungry, she slipped two pieces of bread in the toaster. "I've been at the campaign office every night this week until an ungodly hour. They keep bringing in these cheese pizzas to keep us fed and happy. I haven't had a vegetable in weeks."

Sophie pinched the skin on the inside of her forearm, frowning. "How do you tell if you have scurvy?"

"I think literally all your hair will fall out first. I wouldn't worry about it yet."

Sophie laughed her charming laugh, her head thrown

back. She had a way of making anyone feel that they were funny.

She turned her back on Millicent and picked up a jar from the counter. She shook what looked like dried red berries out of the jar into a clay teapot.

"Rose hips. Picked and dried them myself," she said, unscrewing the cap from the bottle of Jameson's. Sophie poured some of the golden liquid into the teapot, lifted the bottle to her eye, frowned, then poured in another slug. "It'll be worth it, though, all this campaigning," she continued, serious again. "Charlie is going to win. This is going to be big. I can feel it in my bones." When the kettle was boiling, she poured the water into the teapot.

The sting of hot whiskey filled the air.

Millicent watched Sophie dig a knife into a block of butter she took from the fridge and spread it on the toast. Then she carried the two pieces of bread and the teapot into the living room. Millicent, carrying two empty mugs, allowed a thought to settle into her head, the thought she had been trying to keep at bay: everyone knew more about the Yukon than she did. Why was she writing for the local newspaper?

Sophie sat close to Millicent, even though there was room on the couch for both of them to sit with space in between. She sat cross-legged, her spine straight, as if she had just remembered to work on her posture. With one knee pressed into Millicent's thigh, she launched into a monologue about the apartment complex.

"Totally illegal suites, something to do with zoning in this industrial park, but bylaw can't be bothered to come all the way out here. That's why rent is so cheap at the Pit."

Millicent watched the salty icebergs of butter dissolve into the toast in Sophie's hand. "What's the Pit?" she asked.

"This apartment complex, your new home," Sophie said, smiling.

Two lamps with mismatched shades—one a deep maroon circular shape from the 70s, the other a Victorian-style design with gold tassels—spilled pools of light like phosphorescent lakes on the hardwood floor.

"Are you still writing poetry?" Sophie asked.

"Not really."

"Mill."

"What?"

"You have talent."

Millicent spoke quietly, "C'mon." She took a sip of her tea and whiskey, avoiding Sophie's gaze.

"What? I've read your poems. You know how big of a fan I am."

Millicent didn't respond. The curtain was open now and she stared out the window into the black night. The stars seemed so close to the glass you could almost reach out and touch them.

THEY REALLY HAD BEEN inseparable at the beginning. All those nights in Sophie's room, sitting on the carpet, listening to the clan cackling down the hall. How hard they'd both pretended that they didn't care, that they preferred to be left out.

One night, when the sound of their joy had become unbearable, Sophie stood up and announced, "Milli-Vanilli, we're going skinny-dipping." And they did, running down the hill to the rocky beach, braving the frigid ocean and breast-stroking naked away from the light. Had she ever experienced freedom before that night? Real freedom? Once they reached the buoys, they floated on their backs, staring at the moon. The darkness tricked them into believing the water was almost warm. The silence of the ocean was enormous. It felt as if they were the only humans on the planet.

MILLICENT PUSHED THE MEMORY out of her mind. That was years ago. When she finally spoke, her voice sounded overenthusiastic. False. "So tell me everything. You're a real Yukoner now. Do you hunt and fish and dogsled?"

Sophie crossed her arms over her chest and raised her eyebrows, making Millicent feel she had just asked the dumbest question.

"It's called mushing, and no, it's not really my thing."

"I was just kidding."

"You probably want to know why my last roommate left," Sophie said.

"I don't really—"

"She moved in with her boyfriend. Same as the one before."

"Bad luck, I guess."

Sophie leaned towards the coffee table, grabbed the bottle of whiskey and began peeling off the label.

"Is it bad luck, though? I didn't do anything wrong. Or is our society obsessed with pushing the hetero-normative relationships down our throats? So that we all pair off out of a deep-seated fear we'll be the last single people left?" Sophie paused. She eyed Millicent, then kept going. "Like in elementary school when kids were picked for red rover. Nobody wants to relive that childhood trauma. I mean, the guys are nothing to write home about. It's all government and mining up here, let's be honest. Tons of educated, hot-as-fuck women, but the dudes want to hunt and fish and have their women cook up fresh meat at the end of the day."

"Depressing."

"But it's not. That's what I'm saying. Why can't we be single and happy? Look at me. I've finally found peace up here, alone."

Millicent looked towards the kitchen with its wilting spider plant and the colander of old spaghetti in the sink. She wondered if Sophie was really happy.

"I missed you," Sophie said.

Millicent swallowed. "I missed you too."

"It's been too long."

"It has," Millicent said.

"I really have missed you," Sophie repeated. "Really."

Millicent didn't know how to reply. She put her hand on Sophie's arm and said, "I think I've got to go to bed."

"No! Not yet. Tell me, what are you going to write for the *Nugget*?"

"The election, looks like. Who's running. The Vista."

Sophie nodded. "Charlie needs more coverage. We're

always talking about that at the campaign office. He's media-shy. Maybe not shy, exactly, more like he thinks the way to victory is knocking on doors, winning people over one by one. He forgets all about the PR side. Maybe he's right. But still. I don't know why the paper's always printing propaganda about Jakowsky."

Millicent tilted her head, giving Sophie a half-serious, half-teasing look. "Is it propaganda, though?"

"Well, either way, the paper's lucky to have you. I've read the other reporter's stuff. What's his name?"

"Bryce."

"He's a bore. He writes like Hemingway. Worse, like Hemingway on Xanax."

Millicent let out a squawk of laughter.

"And you can tell all he cares about is sports," Sophie continued, clearly enjoying her friend's reaction. "Sports sports sports. The paper needs more colour. More life. Someone to tell the real stories of the Yukon."

Her words hung in the air between them, electric. Real stories of the Yukon. That's exactly what Millicent wanted to write.

"Do you know the man who lives on the school bus?" she asked.

Sophie was still trying to pick the label off the whiskey bottle, rolling pieces between her fingers and dropping the mangled bits on the floor.

"Not really. I've just seen his bus parked all over town. Nobody seems to know him. He's some kind of hermit. Why do you ask?"

Millicent hugged her knees to her chest. "I was thinking

it would be cool to write a feature about this school-bus lifestyle. Like living off the grid. Or affordable housing." When she spoke her idea out loud, it sounded more half-baked than it did in her head. "Or I don't know, whatever comes from the interview, you know?"

When Sophie didn't answer, she said, "This place is just full of eccentrics, isn't it?"

"That's one way to put it."

"What do you mean?"

Millicent watched her friend's chest rise and fall. There was something about this new Sophie; it seemed that the energy, the life inside her could turn off like a lamp. The North seemed to have hardened her. Millicent could tell she was choosing her words carefully.

"The thing you need to remember about Whitehorse is that it's the end of the road," Sophie said. "People up here do surprising things when they're away from the rest of society."

"What exactly are you saying?"

"The guy in the school bus is probably harmless, most of the eccentrics up here are. All I'm saying is that I remember what it's like to arrive here, all fresh and ready to suck the marrow out of life. You can't just trust everybody."

With that, Sophie heaved herself off the couch. She went to the bathroom and closed the door behind her. When she emerged a minute later, she had changed into pajamas.

"Sorry. You know me, I'm just protective of my Millie." Sophie opened her arms wide. She was waiting for another hug. "I didn't mean to scare you."

4

SUNDAY MORNING. HER OLD Dell laptop purred on her belly like a sleeping cat. Millicent lay in her clammy sheets with her head propped up by two pillows, skimming the news archives on the *Golden Nugget*'s website, trying to ground herself in her new reality.

Franc had gone easier on her for the rest of her first week, thank god. While Bryce ran around town reporting on a fire at a gas station and a boating accident in Miles Canyon, she was assigned a 250-word story on the weather prediction for the coming winter from a senior government meteorologist named Jim. Colder than average, she learned, but with less snow pack. Franc also asked her to tweak a press release from the youth indoor soccer league to make it less "press release-y." She completed both assignments carefully and well before the 11:30 deadline. Still, every morning as she walked through the jingling front door of the office and up the stairs to the newsroom, it felt as if a large, sharp stone was lodged at the bottom of her throat. It was just a matter of time before Franc threw her into a story that was way over her head. Before everyone found out she was a fraud.

In the kitchen, Sophie banged around, grinding coffee beans and slamming cupboard doors. The headlines on the front page of the *Golden Nugget* blurred on the screen. Millicent watched her computer rise and fall along with her breath. She had been avoiding the living room and the kitchen since she moved in. Sophie took up all the space in the apartment. She was always busy with some task, strumming her guitar with a pick in her mouth or pacing the living room with her cell pressed to her ear, trying to convince whoever was on her phone list why they needed to vote for Charlie.

Sophie had spent all Saturday in the kitchen, canning the ten-pound bag of beets while listening to a murder-mystery podcast on her headphones. She boiled the vegetables in a stockpot, peeled and chopped them, then pickled the beets in a concoction that smelled like vinegar, sugar and cloves. Whenever Millicent emerged from her bedroom, Sophie wiped her stained hands on her faded overalls, took one earpiece out and explained any new developments in the murder case, as if Millicent should be just as absorbed in the story as she was.

Millicent did try to spend the afternoon out of her bedroom. She read Lorca on the chaise longue and made herself her signature tomato, cucumber and mayonnaise sandwich, but she couldn't quite relax. Everything she touched belonged to Sophie.

MILLICENT PLACED HER LAPTOP beside her on the bed, flipped over and lay curled on her side. Light pressed into her bath-towel curtain, begging to come in. She looked at the time on her phone. It was only 9:30 a.m. How awful it was to dread Sunday, the day of rest, the day everybody else looked forward to.

This listless feeling was not new. It seemed to follow her everywhere. After graduating from college that spring, Millicent had moved back into her parents' house while she searched for a job. Her dad left for work at 7:00 a.m. and didn't return until 6:00 p.m. Alone with her sleeping mother, Millicent would drift through the house in her flannel pajamas, eating peanut butter with a spoon, forcing herself not to look at the clock on the stove. At noon her mother crept down the stairs in her nightgown to eat day-old porridge from a pot in the fridge. She preferred clumps of cold oatmeal to anything hot or less simple. She always said that if there were a pill she could take instead of eating a meal, she would be quite happy. Imagine all the time you would have if you didn't need to cook! You could use that time to do anything. Learn to play the violin. Write letters to politicians. Practise Russian!

This was ironic, since her mother had nothing but time on her hands. Millicent never said this out loud. She never said much about her mother's illness. It was as much a part of her as her brown hair and the freckles that were only visible in the summer. She had no memories of her mother being any other way.

She had been sick since Millicent was a child with a disease that baffled doctors and left her with only enough energy for the simplest tasks: opening the curtains, brushing her teeth and—on a good day—showering. It was as if she was allergic to using energy. The more of it she used, the worse her flu-like symptoms became. But this was much worse than a flu. Sometimes her arms could not hold up a book in bed. At other times it took her half a minute to remember Millicent's name. She would frantically search her brain for the three syllables as if she were searching for a set of keys in the morning.

Her mother didn't go to doctors anymore. What could they do for her? They had a label for her condition, one that Millicent still found hard to pronounce: myalgic encephalomyelitis. That's all doctors could offer. Millicent knew all the stories from when her mother first got sick. One doctor insisted she wasn't getting enough mental stimulation caring for a young child and suggested that she take up chess. Another doctor's main concern was with her husband: was it fair that he had to work at the office all day and then make dinner too?

In the kitchen, the kettle whistled, high-pitched and angry. Millicent listened to Sophie's footsteps patter across the living room and into the kitchen. The way Sophie moved through the apartment with such purpose reminded Millicent that she herself had none: not here, not at her parents' and not at Horizon—not anymore.

Millicent picked up her phone, dialed the first three numbers, then paused. Did she really want to do this? Her mother had tried calling her half a dozen times in the last week. It wasn't that she didn't want to speak to her, not exactly, it was that she knew hearing her voice would crack her open, force her to see the truth. She was lonely already.

Her mother picked up on the first ring.

"Millicent, sweetie," she said, her voice both urgent and tired. "How are you?"

"I'm doing fine, Mom," Millicent said.

"What's it been like at work?"

"I mean, it's a lot. But I'm getting the hang of it." The sharp stone had lodged back in her throat, and it grew more painful with each word.

"Are your stories getting printed?"

"Every day," Millicent said.

"And are you making friends?" her mother asked.

Millicent paused. "Sure, a few."

"That's wonderful," her mother said. "I knew you would."

And with the relief of knowing her daughter was safe, her adrenalin began to wane. This is how it always worked; she expended energy and then she crashed. Millicent imagined her mother in bed. Her hair would be tangled, her body hidden in the oversized nightgown that smelled sweet and rancid like a baby's milky breath. As she spoke about her latest relapse—she had been trying to chop onions and she should have stopped when she felt her arms grow weak—Millicent placed her laptop on the floor and burrowed deep into the tangle of sheets, listening to the slow music of her mother's voice.

5

MILLICENT'S SECOND WEEK of work went by in a blur of government press conferences, city council meetings and a bewildering number of locals making the announcement that they were running for office. Franc would pluck a press release from the fax machine, toss it on Millicent's desk and walk back to his office without saying a word. She would read through paragraphs littered with typos, take a deep breath and, when she had arranged the list of questions in her mind, pick up the red telephone receiver to make the call. There was the famous dog musher; the woman who owned the second-hand bookstore; the man who had been arrested for smuggling a small amount of cocaine into the territory twenty years earlier.

Once she had the candidate on the phone and was asking the questions, her nerves calmed down a bit.

"Why should Yukoners vote for you?"

"What sort of political experience do you have?"

"If you were to win, what do you see our territory looking like in five years?"

The candidates didn't seem to care who Millicent was or how long she had worked at the *Nugget*. They didn't have that luxury, she realized. There was a desperation in their voices as they rattled off their key message, knowing it was their one chance to have their platform heard. This gave Millicent a strange and unexpected sense of power. She held on tightly to this feeling every time she picked up the receiver. These people, she realized, needed her.

Jakowsky, the premier himself, had even called Millicent to welcome her to the territory. He explained his platform's slogan—*economy and the environment, a balance we all deserve*—in detail and how his four years in office had given him the kind of "experience, integrity and humility necessary to lead our territory through this time of change and prosperity." He paused after the words *integrity* and *humility*. It took Millicent a moment to realize he was waiting for her to write them down.

"Right, yes, gotcha," Millicent found herself repeating over and over.

From all these phone calls—hunched over her keyboard with the insides of her thighs sweating—Millicent managed to pump out 500-word articles that Franc buried in the back pages next to the horoscopes and cartoons. Of course he buried them. Where was "Keno City"? What did "self-government agreements" mean? She barely understood what she was writing. Why would Franc want anyone to read her stories?

Every day, after the adrenalin high of filing these stories by deadline, Millicent snuck down to the basement. The smell of ink and paper and the warmth from the printing press were a sedative for her fried nerves. She said hello to Steve, the press operator, a man in ripped blue coveralls who spent the hour hauling stacks of freshly printed papers to the loading door. He offered her a flat smile and a nod and continued working. Steve didn't seem to care that Millicent hid in the basement to eat her lunch. They had a silent agreement to leave each other alone, and Millicent was grateful for his unassuming presence.

The chugging silver press spat out a sheet of newsprint every half-second. Behind the machinery were shelves upon shelves of back issues of the *Nugget*. Millicent would slip papers halfway out so she could see the date and headline, choose one at random, then lie on the ratty orange corduroy couch in the corner of the basement with her tomato sandwich and begin reading.

September 15th, 2001. This issue was filled with stories about Korean Air Lines flight 85, a commercial aircraft headed to Anchorage. Just before 11:00 a.m. on September 11th, the pilot texted the letters "HJK" to airline headquarters. The code was assumed to mean "hijackers aboard" and the plane was ordered to land in Whitehorse because it would endanger fewer lives than landing in Alaska's capital. The prime minister authorized the plane to be shot down if it did not co-operate. Schools and government offices were evacuated. Locals were certain that their tiny northern city was the next target of the infamous terrorist attacks. Turns out it was just a translation error. There were no hijackers on board.

One day, Millicent noticed a stack of laminated sheets of newspaper on a shelf. She picked one up and, without taking her eyes off the tiny, antiquated-looking text, shuffled to the couch. Under the laminate, the page was yellowed, the ink faded. The *Golden Nugget* nameplate looked identical to what they printed today. Millicent squinted at the date in cursive. *1898.* She had never really considered how old the newspaper was. She knew that the *Nugget* used to be delivered to Dawson, Fort McPherson and Inuvik by dogsled back before the Alaska Highway was built. Franc had told her that on her first day.

1898, Millicent pondered. That was during the famous gold rush. She couldn't believe it. The banner headline read *Mr. Piano Man.* The photo underneath was of a group of showgirls on a stage, wearing corsets and feathers, heads cocked and smiling provocatively. The story was about a Quebec farmer who carried a piano up the Chilkoot Pass on his way to find gold in Dawson City. He was paid $3,000 to haul the instrument over the infamous pass, as well as to escort the Saucy Swinging Sextette, six sisters from San Francisco who were on their way to perform a dance show for the prospectors. At that time, the article explained, Dawson City had sprawled to 40,000 people. The prospectors were "hungry for gold and lonely for women." But the Canadian customs official wouldn't allow the party to pass over the mountains. The officer thought it was too dangerous and they would all certainly die on the trail. The six sisters and the farmer returned to Skagway, abandoning the piano at the top of the pass, right on the border between Canada and the United States.

ON FRIDAY AFTERNOON, MILLICENT came up from the basement, through the empty lobby and up to the newsroom. She took the stairs two at a time and was out of breath by the time she reached the top. There was the sound of men laughing coming from Franc's office. It was a boisterous laughter, the kind that happens late at night in a bar. She paused, her hand on the railing. Millicent had never heard her boss laugh.

She gave a quick glance through Franc's window on the way to her desk, but neither Franc nor the man in the cowboy hat and striped shirt noticed her. They stood next to the exterior window, smoking and looking out. Fresh snow had settled on the top of the mountains. The river snaked through town, steaming like a hot spring.

Millicent sat down in front of her computer and opened a blank Word document. She squirmed in her chair with no idea what to write. Afternoons in the newsroom were the opposite of the energized mornings. They were long and lazy, like a hangover, especially Fridays, it seemed. She could sense that everyone in the building was just waiting for time to pass so they could go home.

Millicent could hear a murmur of conversation coming from Franc's office. The man in the cowboy hat was talking, something about the trapline. A wolverine. How Franc had screamed like a girl. It had to be Charlie, Millicent realized, the man who Franc used to live with out on the trapline. The man who was now running for premier. She had tried calling his campaign office to set up an interview twice, but he hadn't called back. She had even asked Sophie why Charlie was avoiding her, considering all the other candidates had picked up on the first ring. Sophie mumbled something about Charlie having "strong boundaries" when it came to media and promised to get her an interview with him soon.

Millicent wrapped the phone cord around her finger, wondering if she should introduce herself. But by the time she worked up the nerve to get out of her chair, Charlie was already on his way out of Franc's office. She started to berate herself for her lack of assertiveness when Franc spoke.

"Wait," he said. His cheeks glowed as if he had been drinking wine. "Charlie, I want you to meet our new legislative reporter. Millicent." He waved a hand in her direction.

Millicent rose from her chair and walked over to the men as they stood just outside of Franc's office. She raised her hand and Charlie shook it. His handshake was firm.

"Nice to meet you, Charlie," Millicent said with an even voice. "We should sit down for an interview soon so I can learn about your platform."

Charlie had the kind of teasing eyes that implied every-thing was a joke. His jeans were so worn in, they fit his body like a second skin. He grinned at Millicent.

"No need. Gonna win this election, seeing as the editor of the goddamn newspaper is one of my oldest friends.

Just write an editorial singing my praises, won't you, Frankie-boy?"

Millicent assumed he was teasing, until she noticed the colour had disappeared from Franc's cheeks. "Charlie!" he said sharply.

"What?" Charlie lifted his shoulders and looked confused.

"You know we can't talk like that. Technically, you shouldn't even be in the newsroom."

Franc looked at Millicent, then at Charlie, then back at Millicent. Was he waiting for her to back him up?

"Absolutely," Millicent said firmly. "We're all about giving each candidate a fair chance to tell their story."

Franc nodded approvingly, and warm blood rushed to Millicent's heart—she had finally said something that impressed him. Now his voice was even and professional. "Charlie, as you know, the media can sway an election. We have an ethical responsibility to provide fair coverage and we will stick by that, regardless of who gallivants into our office expecting nepotism to do their work."

Franc maintained his poker face. Millicent had never heard him use that tone and she couldn't tell if he was serious or not. Charlie kept smiling, as if Franc's responsibility and the whole newspaper were a joke.

"Maybe that's true for the big media down south. Aren't you giving yourself too much credit, Frankie-boy? You're just the *Golden Nugget*. I've seen people wipe their ass with your classifieds."

Franc's face crumpled into a smile. He shook his head, mumbling something about putting up with a dimwit.

"I'm not too worried about getting all this coverage my team talks about," Charlie said. "Nobody believes what they read in the paper anymore. But if I go knocking on doors and get invited in for tea to tell my story, that's real trust now, isn't it?"

"Media coverage is just part of the game, Charlie, you know that."

"Why do I have to play the game?"

"You don't. But it's your loss if you don't get free coverage."

"You're quite the salesman, Frankie-boy."

Leaning against the doorframe, Millicent waited for a pause in the conversation.

"How do you two know each other?" she asked, trying not to sound too eager.

"Charlie's my professor," Franc said matter-of-factly.

"Your professor," Millicent repeated.

"Franc's the one with the fancy university degree. I only got a degree in bush smarts."

"Probably more useful up here than that old thing." Franc said, nodding towards the wall behind his desk and his framed degree.

"Here's the story," Charlie said, taking a step closer to Millicent. She could smell his breath: Orange Crush soda, cigarettes. "I met this fool at the Mad Hatter when he was just twenty-five years old. He was fresh all right, straight from the white picket fences of the big-city suburbs. Said he wanted a real adventure, and I happened to need help with my family's trapline. I didn't realize my mistake till he got into my canoe wearing brand new sneakers and this god-awful cologne."

Franc gazed out the window, perhaps embarrassed at the memory. "But I learned, didn't I?"

"For a white man, I guess you did."

Franc drew another cigarette from his back pocket.

"Yeah, for a white man," he repeated, lifting the cigarette to his lips.

Charlie tipped his hat to Millicent. "I gotta get back out to the property. Firewood season. That cord of wood isn't going to stack itself."

"So, the interview?" Millicent asked.

"I'll call you," Charlie said, and he headed towards the stairs without looking back.

Franc watched him disappear into the stairwell. Without another word, he went stiffly back into his office, closed the door and lit his cigarette. Millicent hadn't noticed that Bryce had returned to the newsroom from lunch. He was reclining in his chair, earbuds in, chewing on the end of a pen and watching a YouTube video of an Aretha Franklin performance.

6

ON THE WEEKEND, SOPHIE took Millicent blueberry
picking at the summit of a nameless mountain above Fish
Lake where the berries were rumoured to be good that
year. It was a kind gesture, Millicent thought, considering
she had been holed up in her bedroom every day after
work and had made little effort to reignite their friendship. She could sense that Sophie wanted her to be more
social, was expecting it to be like old times that first year
at Horizon. But after the waxing and waning of adrenalin
rushes all day at the *Nugget*, Millicent was too worn out to
match Sophie's energy. It wasn't that she didn't want to
spark their relationship again; of course she did. Who else
was she going to be friends with, up here in the middle
of nowhere? But something about the sound of Sophie's
quick, intentional footsteps moving through the living
room kept Millicent sequestered in her bedroom watching mind-numbing reality TV, making small talk only

when she emerged to pour herself a bowl of Cheerios for dinner.

After a half-hour hike up a well-worn path, they reached a summit at the top of a rolling hill. Sophie found a patch of berries fifty feet away. She squatted in her hiking boots and yellow windbreaker, her fingers working quickly and methodically, while Millicent wandered the summit in slow circles, looking for another patch.

With an empty ice-cream pail clasped in her fist, she tilted her head back and gazed up at the massive dome of sky. It was a milky, hazy kind of day, with the kind of flat light that strained the eyes even though there wasn't a spot of sunlight in the entire valley.

"Snow's coming soon," Sophie said, speaking to the ground. "I can just feel it."

Millicent pulled the hood of her jacket over her head to block out the wind, then bent her knees and stared at the ground. She couldn't find a single blueberry. She glanced over at Sophie and watched her fingers move swiftly from berry to berry, humming something to herself. When Sophie sensed that Millicent was watching her, she lifted her head and looked at her roommate with amused eyes.

"It's a new way of seeing, Mill. Just relax into it."

"I am relaxed," Millicent said.

Sophie stood up and carried her bucket towards the patch Millicent was staring at.

"No, you're trying too hard. They're right there. It's like those magic-eye books we used to read as kids, remember those? Just let your vision adjust and you'll see them."

Sophie wandered towards the far slope of the peak to find another patch. Millicent lowered herself onto her hands and knees, the wet earth soaking her jeans. She listened to the rhythmic gusts of wind. Then when the entire valley grew still, she listened to the sound of her own breath. Gazing at the tiny, delicate leaves crawling over the soft alpine floor, Millicent followed Sophie's instructions and let her eyes relax, her vision blur. There they were: constellations of tiny blueberries. They were everywhere.

Now that she was consumed by the repetition of her simple task, her senses seemed to sharpen. She heard the sound of berries plunking into the plastic bucket and her jacket flapping like a sail in the cold alpine wind. Millicent tightened the drawstring at her waist and pulled her jeans higher to keep out the cold air. She plucked a blueberry from its stem and popped it in her mouth. The tartness was an electric jolt to her tongue.

As she picked, her eyes methodically darting towards the next spot of blue, Millicent's mind drifted to questions she would ask when Charlie called for the interview he had promised. *So Charlie, what does it mean to you to be the territory's first Indigenous candidate for premier? What does Jakowsky's gold mine really mean for the caribou's calving grounds in the Vista?* And, to add real depth to the piece, the human-interest element: *Why did you enter the world of politics, anyway? What is it about you that is drawn to leadership?* She imagined her cool-toned reporter's voice asking these questions with a mix of authority and curiosity. She imagined Charlie nodding and looking off into the middle distance as if no other reporter had taken the time to ask these kinds of questions, as if she was breaking open new territory.

Sophie and Millicent must have stayed at the summit for hours. It seemed impossible to stop picking when the ground was a carpet of fruit. Every time Millicent thought she was too cold and ready to go back to the car, she found the motherlode of a patch and disappeared again into the spell of harvesting and daydreaming.

"I can't feel my fingers anymore," Sophie said, hovering behind her. She dumped all her berries into Millicent's pail, then pulled out a slender Thermos from her backpack and unscrewed the lid. A billow of steam dissipated into the mountain air. Peppermint tea, with a bit of cream. Millicent didn't even know Sophie had packed it. They passed the Thermos back and forth. The tea was still too hot, but they drank it anyway, wincing with every gulp and waiting for the blood to return to their fingers.

Sophie's nose was red and running from the cold. A single snowflake landed on the tip of it.

"Told you," she said, screwing the lid back on the Thermos and sliding it into her backpack. She slung it over one shoulder as the sky began cautiously spitting snow like the first kernels of popcorn in a pan of sizzling oil.

She stared at Millicent for a minute, as if searching for something.

"What?" Millicent asked.

"I'm taking you out tonight," she said. "You need to socialize."

Millicent snapped the lid on her ice-cream pail and

stood up. Her legs cried out from squatting for so long. "I do?" she asked. She knew Sophie was right.

"Yes. We'll go to the Mad Hatter. Wear lipstick. See where the night takes us."

SOPHIE WENT TO WASH her hair as soon they got home. She only washed it once a week, she explained to Millicent as she wriggled out of her dirt-stained jeans, the bathroom door wide open.

"Who am I trying to impress? I live in a fucking industrial park next to mechanics who operate illegal shops. Other than that it's just me and the coyotes."

In the kitchen, Millicent stared into the fridge, searching for something to eat. Picking berries in the mountains had made her ravenous. "You mean you're not after an old mechanic trying to dodge the tax man?" she yelled over the sound of running water.

"Good point!" Sophie yelled back. "I should widen my perspective!"

After blow-drying her hair, Sophie applied a vivid plum-coloured stain to her lips. She begged Millicent to wear some too, claiming it would bring out her eyes. Millicent knew she'd be self-conscious all night in a colour that obnoxious. She did resign herself to wearing one of Sophie's size-small spaghetti-strap tank tops that squeezed her breasts together and clung to her belly, a pair of hoop earrings and some clear lip gloss. Millicent stared at herself in the mirror.

"I look like a late-nineties R&B singer."

Sophie tucked a loose strand of hair behind Millicent's ear. "You look practically edible."

LIKE THE *GOLDEN NUGGET* building, the Mad Hatter looked like a saloon. The entranceway was graced by a stuffed albino moose with a handmade sign around his neck: *Please do not ride me*. A large brass bell hung over the bar. Ring it and buy the whole bar a round, was the old Yukon rule.

Customers were lined up to order at the bar. When Sophie reached the front of the line, she leaned in. "Two Jägerbombs and two pints of the cheapest beer you have on tap." She handed the bartender a twenty-dollar bill and tipped him two quarters with the change.

The girls tipped the shots into their mouths, left the tiny glasses on the bar and found the only vacant table, at the back of the room next to the washrooms. The tables were tall and they sat on wobbly stools, gulping their lagers and talking about old times, about the girls in the "clan." Millicent could feel the alcohol softening her nerves and she relaxed her lips into a lazy grin.

"What was their name again?" Sophie asked.

"Whose?"

"All of them, they all had the same name."

Millicent's grin grew wider.

"The Kates."

"Oh yes! Kate, Katie, Caitlyn, Katherine and Katy-Lynn!"

"Don't forget Casey," Millicent said.

Sophie shook her head, her face serious. "Casey doesn't

count. I saw her wearing regular jeans once, not yoga pants."

They both erupted into a cackle. Sophie put her head on the table, her shoulders heaving with delight. When their laughter died down, Millicent took her last gulp of beer. She placed her empty glass on the coaster. "So what do you think they're all doing now?"

"Getting married, having babies, unknowingly taking on one hundred percent of the emotional labour in their heteronormative partnerships, I suspect."

"I heard Katy-Lynn actually started a vegan restaurant in Vancouver."

Sophie's voice was cool. "Wow, good for her."

"Supposedly it's pretty successful, something about vegan chicken wings," Millicent said. Sophie changed the subject.

"What about the guy you were dating at Horizon? Whatever happened to him?"

Sam. Sophie had never liked him. She always said Millicent was out of his league. Mostly she couldn't stand the way he wore his five-finger toe shoes at the beach. He called it his "minimalist footwear," claiming they made him more connected to the earth.

"That was a long time ago."

"Right."

"I never even think about him," Millicent added.

She stared at Sophie's plum lips. Sophie was looking at her with that irritating, all-knowing expression. Maybe, Millicent pondered, Sophie never liked Sam because *she* never really liked him. It was the way he kissed her twenty-five times a day. How, when he met her mother for the first time, he crawled into bed beside her as if he were a lifelong girlfriend. Sam was loving, eager to please and excitable, like a small dog. He adored her, which seemed like enough until he left for a semester in France and she couldn't muster the energy to reply to his 2,000-word emails.

"You were so much better than him," Sophie said. "You were out of everyone's league, Milli Vanilli, and you never even knew it."

When Sophie finished her beer they ordered another round, yelling at the bartender over a Guns n' Roses track.

"Millicent!"

Bryce was perched on a stool at the end of the bar. A paperback lay next to his half-empty glass of beer.

Millicent jabbed Sophie in the ribs.

"There, that's Bryce."

Brave from the alcohol, Millicent insisted that Bryce join them, which he did, but only after explaining that the reason he was here was that the bartender was one of his best friends. He didn't go to bars alone.

They couldn't find another stool, so Bryce stood at the table, towering a foot above Sophie and Millicent. He put his book on the table: *The Sun Also Rises*. Sophie looked at Bryce and back at Millicent, beaming. "Hemingway," she whispered into her ear, her breath boozy and hot. "I told you!"

Millicent bit her lip to keep from laughing.

The presence of this seemingly sober man clutching a Hemingway novel, unsure where to look, transformed the energy of the table. They became more serious and slightly awkward. Sophie looked at her phone, uninterested in playing along.

"Sophie is volunteering for Charlie's campaign," Millicent offered.

"Good for you," Bryce said.

"I don't have much choice, do I?" Sophie responded, slipping her phone back in her pocket.

"Well, I don't know about that—" Bryce started to say.

"Jakowsky is trying to steal the land from our Indigenous people, who have lived here—no, who have thrived here—" she corrected herself, "for thousands of years. And for what, all for money? So Jakowsky and his Conservative buddies can continue golfing and patting one another on the back while a whole species is at risk of becoming extinct?"

"But is it really that black and white?" Bryce asked.

Millicent felt an anxious desire to chime in, to say anything. "Well, I mean, I'm sure it's more nuanced than that," she added.

Sophie shot her a hard look. "Yes, it is that black and white."

Bryce spotted an empty stool at another table and carried it over. He took off his toque and laid it next to his pint, then scratched his head as if deciding what to say.

"Jakowsky isn't the only one stealing," he said. "We all are. And we won't even acknowledge it. Look at us three, naively driving up to the Yukon with all our belongings from down south and calling this home, staking our flag."

Sophie frowned, "That is a completely different story—"

"But it's not," Bryce interrupted. Millicent had never seen him so assertive. She wondered if she had misjudged him. "We come up here, take jobs, take land, take stories. We call it our home. We just take, take, take, and in our off time, we come to the Mad Hatter and get loaded to forget about it all."

"That is the exact reason I'm volunteering for Charlie's campaign," Sophie protested.

"Sure, I get that, but you can't just cancel everything out by doing one good deed. You can't just say Jakowsky is evil and the rest of us don't have blood on our hands."

Sophie downed her beer, took her phone out again and slid it across the table towards Bryce. "I like you," she said with a coy smile. "Give me your phone number."

Bryce looked at the phone with a startled expression, as if he had never seen one before.

"Don't worry, I'm not hitting on you. I'm on a man hiatus—ask Milli. I just like that you don't bullshit."

AFTER TWO MORE BEERS and a gin and tonic each, along with a stint of dancing to Robyn's "Call Your Girlfriend" beside the table—even Bryce joined in for the main chorus, moving his long arms with awkward jerks—Millicent and Sophie took a taxi back home, urging the driver to keep going down the dirt road, insisting that they weren't that drunk and indeed there was an apartment complex right next to Dave's mechanic shop. Yes, they lived there. Yes, they had money to pay for the ride.

"We're not trying to kidnap you, man," Sophie said,

leaning forward in the seat to make sure the driver could hear her. "Isn't it supposed to be the other way around?"

They stumbled into the apartment at 1:30 in the morning and ate pickles straight from the jar, too lazy to make the sandwiches they were craving. Sophie was wearing her jacket indoors. Her lipstick had faded and smeared across her mouth. Under the fluorescent light of the kitchen, her skin looked pale, sickly even. It hit Millicent then how much practice Sophie had putting on a brave face.

"Sleep in my bed?" Sophie offered.

Millicent screwed the lid back on the pickle jar. "I don't know, Soph. I just need to crash hard."

"Please, please? I have Egyptian-cotton sheets. And I'm excellent at staying on my side of the bed."

"Alright, alright," Millicent said. "At this point I could pass out on top of a wet log."

Sophie's room had the familiar smell of jasmine incense and a hint of rotting fruit. Fairy lights were strung on the ceiling and a picture of Frida Kahlo hung above the queen-sized bed. Ketchup-smeared plates and empty mugs were strewn on her bedside table and dresser.

Millicent's body sank deep into the soft mattress like she was falling into a dream without even being asleep. She flipped onto her side and curled into herself while Sophie fiddled with her phone.

"Mill."

"Yeah?"

"Have you ever been truly lonely?"

"Of course."

"I mean painfully lonely. So lonely it hurts your bones."
Millicent fought the pull of sleep.

"Are you that lonely?" she mumbled into her pillow.

Sophie started a soundtrack of gentle ocean waves on her phone. "I can't sleep without this."

Did she eventually admit that yes, she was that lonely? Millicent didn't know if the words had come from Sophie's mouth or they were fabricated in Millicent's dream, all she knew was that when she woke up in the morning, Sophie was spooning her from behind and she seemed so peaceful Millicent didn't dare to move.

THE NEXT MORNING, HUNGOVER and starving, they took Sophie's truck into town for breakfast at the Sunridge Café, where Sophie worked during the week.

Sophie cracked open the windows and turned on CBC radio. Millicent stuck her hand out the window to feel the air on her skin. The snow from the day before had already melted, giving the air a fresh, damp smell charged with possibility. Sophie turned off the Alaska Highway towards town. They passed the historic sternwheeler, permanently dry-docked at the edge of the river; an organic grocery store that claimed to be open twenty-two hours a day; and the brown legislative building where Jakowsky's office was.

Millicent had always thought there were two types of hangovers: depressing and relieving. Today's hangover was relieving, as if the part of her that had been wound up and stuck in worrying mode had suddenly gone slack and she could relax and gaze out the window, taking it all in.

After a few minutes, she turned her attention to Sophie. She was wearing overalls and a plaid flannel shirt, driving with one hand on the wheel and one knee pressed into the dash. She hadn't brushed her hair. Her concentration was not on the road but on the radio, which featured a call-in show about tips for insulating your home to reduce heating bills.

Sophie cut the engine in front of the café. It was the only breakfast joint open on Sundays and it was packed and loud. They ordered coffee and bagels to go (Sophie got a 35 percent discount) and brought the food back to the truck.

"Let's go for a Sunday drive," Sophie said. "I'll take you out to Lake Laberge—you know, where Sam McGee was cremated?"

She crinkled her grease-soaked parchment paper into a ball and stuffed it in the glove compartment. Millicent closed her eyes. The fatty perfection of the BLT melted in her mouth.

"You are my captain," she said with her mouth full.

"There are strange things done in the midnight sun," Sophie said as she pulled back out onto the street. "By the men who moil for gold, the Arctic trails have their secret tales, that would make your blood run cold."

As they passed the Walmart, Millicent saw it again: the bus.

"I know, Millie, you're more onto contemporary poetry," Sophie said in a parody of a snotty English accent. "But this is Yukon history."

It was parked at the very back of the lot.

"Soph, that's the bus I was talking about."

Sophie swerved sharply into the Walmart parking lot. She pulled up beside the bus but kept the engine idling.

"Soph!" Millicent whispered, as if the occupant of the bus could hear her.

"There's something written on the side," she said. "I want to see what it says."

Millicent craned her neck out the back window. Sophie was right. The word *Asshole* was spray-painted in bright red on the side of the bus.

"I wonder why he's an asshole," Millicent said.

"Probably because he parks this monstrosity wherever he likes, and people are sick of it," Sophie said.

"Maybe he can't afford a real place."

"True," Sophie said. "We are in the middle of an afford-able-housing crisis. It's horrible. The tent city down at the legislative building is so sad. It's almost winter, for Christ's sake. Are we just going to let people freeze to death? I mean, look at us even, we're two educated women with full-time employment and all we can afford is an illegal apartment in an industrial park thirty kilometres out of town."

The front door of the bus opened. A man emerged, his head a mass of black curly hair, stretching his arms as if just waking up. Millicent slapped Sophie on the knee. "Go, go, go!" she yelled. Sophie gunned it and the truck spun out of the parking lot.

7

ON MONDAY MORNING, FRANC leaned over Millicent's shoulder and placed a sticky note on her keyboard with the word *Jim* and the last four digits of a phone number.

"Who's Jim?" Millicent asked.

"The meteorologist," Franc said.

"Didn't I just interview the meteorologist?" Millicent asked.

"Yup."

"And you want me to interview him again?"

"Yup."

"Okay," Millicent said slowly.

"The only story I've got today is Bryce's feature on the Filipino Ping-Pong team, and I'm not being racist here or anything, but that's not exactly news. Jim was just on CBC talking about permafrost and the highways. Ask him about that. Or ask him anything you want. All I know is I've got a completely blank page two to fill by noon."

Bryce was sitting at his desk next to Millicent, his forehead still glowing with sweat from his morning bike commute. He was wearing grey sweatpants and a Toronto Raptors jersey. This seemed to be his office uniform. He rolled his chair away from the desk and spun around to face Franc.

"The Filipino population is exploding right now. There's like a thousand of them in Whitehorse," Bryce said. "That's on par with the French Canadians."

"Your point?"

"It's news, Franc. Sports isn't all jockstraps and bloody knuckles. Athletes have feelings too."

"You're tender, Bryce."

Bryce pulled a lighter out of his pocket and flicked it on. "I can go burn a building down if you want."

"I'll let you know if it comes to that," Franc said.

Millicent got up from her desk to stare across the street at the liquor store's neon sign. "There's nothing happening on the Vista, nobody announcing that they're running for office, nothing on any election issue at all?"

Franc shook his head. "Dead air."

Millicent hadn't planned to say anything, but the words spilled out of her unbidden. "What about a feature? It could fill the whole second page if we had a photo."

Franc laughed. He looked at the clock. "Good luck finding a story for a feature, doing the interview and writing the thing in less than three hours."

Millicent kept looking out the window, not daring to meet Franc or Bryce's eyes. They were waiting for her to say something more.

"There's that guy who lives on a school bus. I keep driving by it. You know the bus I'm talking about, Franc?"

"Everybody knows it," Franc said, looking at the clock again.

"Well, I noticed yesterday that it had been vandalized. Someone had spray-painted 'Asshole' on the side ..."

"That's not exactly a story," Franc interrupted.

Millicent's face flushed. She forced herself to continue. "That's just the jumping-off point. Why was it vandalized? Is someone frustrated with people who live in vehicles all over town? Why does he live there? Can he not afford an apartment?"

Franc stared past Millicent out the window.

"We do have an affordable-housing crisis," she added. "I think this could really add some depth to that issue."

Franc raised his hands, palms open. "Fine. I want seven hundred and fifty words plus a photo by deadline. Today."

Bryce opened his mouth. He stuffed his lighter back in his pocket.

"Are you serious?" he asked.

"Great, I'm on it," Millicent said. She was already shoving her notepad and the *Nugget*'s DSLR camera into her backpack.

"Dead serious," Franc said, staring hard at Bryce. "Where do you shit when you're living on a school bus in the Walmart parking lot? Whitehorse needs to know."

Franc laughed at his own words, then returned to his office and pulled his door three-quarters closed, as he did every morning before deadline.

Bryce heaved himself out of his chair, followed Franc

and yanked his door back open. He stood there with one hand on the doorknob and the other on his hip.

"I think this is a bad idea."

"I have a completely blank page two," Franc said. "What do you want me to run, that very poetic rant about the lack of public transportation that you wrote when you were high in your cabin, Bryce? The one you sent me at two in the goddamn morning last weekend and asked me to run as an editorial?"

Bryce's face turned sheepish. He bowed his head and shook it, muttering something about Whitehorse needing better bus service on Sundays. He looked back up at Franc, his eyes serious.

"It's Millie's second week and you're sending her out alone to interview this weirdo?"

He had never called her Millie before.

Franc gave them both a weary look that told them he was done. "I'm sure he's not that weird. Just a hermit. There's a difference, Bryce," he said. He looked up at the clock on the wall of the newsroom again. It was already 9:30. He took his glasses off and rubbed his eyes. "What do you think?" he asked Millicent.

"I'm on it. Like you said, I'm sure he's just a harmless man who has lived an interesting life."

Without waiting for any further discussion, she ran down the stairs, her backpack flopping against her jacket.

MILLICENT PULLED INTO THE Walmart parking lot. The morning was a headache kind of grey, cold but not so much that she could see her breath. She had never seen the clay cliffs from this angle. They rose jagged above the parking lot, full of scraggly spruce trees that jutted out at a forty-five-degree angle.

The bus was parked exactly where it was before. She pulled up beside it and got out of her car. Up close, it was clear someone had taken their time spray-painting the word *Asshole*. The writing was in a neat cursive. Millicent felt a tingling sensation in her chest; she was tempted to get back in the car and leave. Instead, she reminded herself that the story was her idea. She had made a commitment. What would Franc run if she came back with nothing because she had been too scared to even try?

A low pulse of music could be heard coming from inside the bus. Millicent rapped her knuckles on the door three times. The music stopped and the door folded open. The man wore Carhartt overalls and a faded bandana in his hair. He stood at the top of the three steps in bare feet. He was older than she had expected, in his early forties at least.

"Oh hi, I'm a reporter with the *Golden Nugget*," Millicent began.

"Hello, reporter from the *Golden Nugget*," he said, smiling. He had a faint French accent.

"Right, sorry, my name is Millicent," she continued. "This might sound a bit odd, but I'd like to talk to you. My editor wants a human-interest story."

"And this is me, the interesting human?"

Millicent smiled. "Yes."

"Wonderful! Well, hello then. My name is Pascal."

"Pascal, would you be open to an interview?"

"I would be honoured," he said. *Haw-noured*. His Québécois accent was not thick, but it was there.

"Millicent, oui?"

"Oui."

"Parles français, Millie?"

"Oui, mais juste un peu."

"Your accent is good." Pascal didn't move from the top of the stairs. She wondered if he was going to address the obvious vandalism, but he said, "So you're here to make me famous?"

Millicent smiled. "I'm not exactly the paparazzi, but I'll do my best."

"You're funny," he said. "Come in, let me show you my palace." He moved out of the way so Millicent could squeeze by.

Millicent waited for her eyes to adjust to the dark. There was a comforting smell of oatmeal and bacon.

"Sorry," Pascal said, yanking open a set of orange curtains. Daylight spilled in. "Forgot to do this."

He moved along the rest of the bus opening all the curtains. Millicent looked around. She couldn't believe it. The bus was not at all what she had expected. She was standing in a small kitchen. A table made of gold-coloured hardwood was on one side of the bus just behind the steering wheel. The two bench seats looked freshly upholstered. Across from the table was a stainless steel counter and a shiny chrome sink. A Mason jar filled with sprouts sat in the sink. More Mason jars lined a shelf above the sink, strapped against the wall with bungee cords.

They were filled with flour, lentils, rice, raisins and chocolate chips. In the wall space between the windows there were photos. In one of them, a young woman looking deliriously happy swung a hula hoop in a grassy field. In another, Pascal was knee-deep in a river, grinning as he held up a silver fish.

"Make yourself at home, Millicent," he said. "Would you like coffee?"

"Yes, thank you," Millicent said. She sat in the driver's seat and placed her hands on the giant steering wheel, imagining what it would feel like to drive down the highway with forty feet of steel behind her. She closed her eyes for a moment as the idea made her dizzy.

On the bus's dash, directly underneath the windshield, where the sun would soak through on a clear day, was a long, narrow planter box full of herbs. The soil was damp, as if Pascal had just watered it. Millicent took hold of a sprig from the closest herb, rolled it gently between her fingers and lifted her hand to her nose: thyme. She couldn't believe he lived like this. He had really made a home for himself, on a school bus.

The bus quickly filled with the sharp aroma of coffee. Pascal pulled his sleeve down over his hand to grab the handle of the pot. He carried the coffee pot to the table and motioned for Millicent to sit on one of the benches as he settled in across from her. She looked past the kitchen, wondering where he slept.

"Cowboy coffee," he said. The skin on his forehead, cheeks and neck was golden. She could see the tan line on his chest where his skin met his T-shirt. Millicent watched him pour the contents of the steaming pot into a mug. His fingers were stained black with engine oil, his nails bitten short.

"Thank you."

"You know what that is? Cowboy coffee?"

"Of course," Millicent said.

Pascal smiled down at the pot, content with this answer.

"So, how did you find this bus?" Millicent reached into her backpack and pulled her notebook out, maintaining eye contact in case Pascal got skittish when he realized she was going to write down what he said, but he just leaned back and slung his arm over the back of the bench, basking in the attention.

"I didn't find it. I reassembled the whole thing myself from a wreck in the scrapyard. A 1992 Bluebird. Diesel engine."

1992, diesel engine, she scribbled.

"I built the bedroom and the kitchen. Did the wiring. And the woodwork," he continued. Millicent kicked something plastic underneath the table. She looked down and saw a bin stacked with pots and pans and greasy plates.

"Forgot to do your dishes last night?"

Pascal held her gaze with faded blue eyes. He didn't take them off her, even when Millicent looked down at her notebook, pretending to be reviewing her scribbles. He looked at her as if he was trying to make her laugh but also wanted her to feel uncomfortable. When Millicent met his gaze again, he smiled. He brought the clay mug to his lips and took a sip of coffee. She watched his Adam's apple as he swallowed.

"What was your question again?" he asked.

"I was just wondering about this bin of dirty dishes," she said.

"We only have so much time in a day. Why waste it on something boring like dishes? Some people have called me, how do you say it, a hedonist?"

"Yes."

"I think it's just a simple philosophy: spend your time on the parts of life you find beautiful."

Millicent scrambled to write as fast as Pascal spoke. When he finished, she swallowed nervously. She had to ask him.

"How did your bus get vandalized? Is someone upset with you?"

At this, Pascal looked away. "That is just—" he started. "It's nothing."

"Okay," Millicent said, waiting for more.

Pascal stayed silent, gazing out the window at the still empty parking lot.

"Have you found that Whitehorse residents are frustrated because you park your bus all over town and use your generator?" she asked.

"No, no, it's not that," he said quietly. "I need to paint over that. This is my plan for the day."

"So you have no idea why someone would have done this to your bus?"

Pascal's voice was suddenly sharp. "It really is not important."

Millicent wondered if this was her cue to leave. She clutched her backpack on the bench beside her. Outside, the parking lot was filling up with morning shoppers. A grocery cart rattled behind the bus. A child screamed as his mother tried to coax him from his car seat.

She couldn't leave yet. She didn't have a story.

"What's all the equipment for?" she asked. Beyond the kitchen table was a plywood desk. On it were two computer monitors, wires, microphones and video cameras of different sizes.

At this question, Pascal regained his enthusiasm. "I'm a filmmaker. I make documentaries, reality TV shows, that sort of thing."

"How did you get into that?"

"I was a ski instructor when I was younger, and I saved for years to buy all the equipment. I wanted a wild life, wilder than what Quebec could give me, so I renovated the bus. Moved up north. Started the business. That was a long time ago now. I must have been twenty-five. Now I'm about to get my big break."

"Oh yeah?"

Pascal rubbed his jaw.

"It's a reality TV show. I'm calling it *Cribs with Engines*. I will be travelling around the country on this bus, helping people convert their vehicles into living spaces. Semi-trucks, buses, vans, trucks with canopies, even big cars could all have bedrooms and kitchens built into them."

He paused. "Do you like that name? *Cribs with Engines*?"

"Sure," Millicent said.

Pascal smiled. His eyes shone. "It's been my dream for a long time. I know it sounds … what's the word? Narcissism?"

"Narcissistic."

"Yes, narcissistic, but ever since I was a kid I knew I should be in front of a camera. Not behind it."

Millicent listened to him as if he were talking on the radio, soothed by the steadiness of his voice. When he spoke she felt strangely calm, like she had known this man for years.

Pascal leaned forward. Now he was vibrating with excitement.

"I met this producer from Montreal last month at a film fest down south. He was very happy about my idea. He said I just had to write a pitch for the pilot episode and he would sign on. He said he had not seen anything like it. Or met anyone like me."

"Wow. That's big," Millicent said. She wondered what he did to make money since the show hadn't taken off yet. "So when does filming start?"

Pascal leaned back against the bench seat, ignoring the question. "Now I want to know about you, the reporter with ..." he stalled for a moment, searching for the right word. "The *turkwiss* eyes. Is that how you say it?"

"Turquoise." Her throat tightened. She could barely get any sound out.

"Turquoise," she repeated.

"Turquoise." Pascal took off his bandana and ran his hand through his hair, a mess of black curls with the odd streak of grey. He was waiting for her to say something about herself. Millicent wiped condensation from the window with her sleeve. A pickup truck had parked diagonally across from the bus. It had one of the

I Value the Vista bumper stickers Millicent was seeing everywhere.

"The Vista," Pascal said, following her eyes. "Hippies have been crying about this since I moved up here."

"You're not a hippie?"

"I'm a businessman."

Millicent could see his bare feet under the table. "Really," she said, in a teasing voice that seemed not her own.

"People think I'm a hippie because I live on a bus, but I live on a bus because it's just smart." Pascal spoke seriously now. "It has nothing to do with putting flowers in my hair or how much granola I eat."

Millicent knew she should be writing this down, but she also knew that if she moved even an inch, she would ruin the moment. She could see the story forming now.

"How much granola do you eat? Off the record, of course."

Pascal smiled. He had pulled out a phone and was fiddling with it.

"That is a very personal question," he said as a sad, slow song suddenly crackled through the speakers.

"You're too young to know this band. Massive Attack," Pascal said. He plucked a set of keys from his pocket and swung them around his finger. "Want to go for a ride? It's the only way I can really show you my life. We'll finish the interview out there."

"Out where?"

"It's a surprise."

Millicent wondered what would happen if she actually

agreed to go with him. She still didn't understand the lay of the land. She was constantly getting turned around and disoriented. He could take her anywhere and she wouldn't know where she was. Nobody would know where she was. It was a crazy idea.

"I can't," Millicent said. "I have to write this story by noon."

"I'll have you back long before then, I promise."

Millicent thought about this. Part of her wanted to just give in. She hadn't even gotten into the politics part of the interview. What did he think of the affordable-housing crisis? Did he live on the bus because he couldn't afford a real place? Plus, there was an easiness between them. He didn't feel like a stranger.

Pascal didn't wait for her to say anything more. He grabbed a rag and used it to wipe condensation from the windshield. Then he sat down behind the wheel, pulled the seatbelt across his chest and started the engine.

Millicent sat frozen at the kitchen table. The Mason jars above the sink rattled as the bus made its way down Second Avenue. Her heart beat loudly in her ears. Franc and Bryce would be wondering where she was, what was taking her so long. She knew she had to go back to the office, to stop this momentum before it took her too far.

She got up and slung her backpack over one shoulder, clutching the kitchen counter for balance.

"Just drop me off here," she said. Pascal obediently pulled over in front of the newspaper office. The engine idled loudly. She could see Bryce's head and shoulders through the newsroom window.

"I have enough for a story. I'll give you a call if I have more questions."

"I can have you back by eleven."

"Deadlines, you know," she said with a tight smile.

Pascal nodded. He stared flatly at the traffic. She needed him to pull the lever to open the door. She knew by now Bryce was watching.

"I wanted you to see what it's really like," he said, his eyes wide and hopeful. "So you can put it in the article."

Millicent clutched the strap of her backpack even tighter. He was harmless, she knew he was. This was journalism: going deeper, breaking down boundaries. This was why she had come to the Yukon in the first place. She still had time. She would type fast.

8

THEY TOOK THE BRIDGE out of town and turned onto a gravel road that cut through a forest of white spruce and lodgepole pine. The sky had cleared. Millicent was back at the kitchen table. She watched Pascal as he reached for his sunglasses on the dash and settled deeper into the driver's seat. He kept one hand on the wheel, the other rested on the edge of the open window. Her father drove like that during road trips. By the end of the summer, his left forearm was always darker than his right. He and Millicent had taken trips together, just the two of them, because even stretched out in the back seat with a sleeping bag and pillow, these trips had been too much for her mother's sick body.

Millicent watched as the forest turned into clay cliffs. Then the clay cliffs disappeared and they could see the Yukon River. Behind it was Whitehorse: grey government buildings lining the water, Main Street with its colourful storefronts, a smattering of houses, the hospital, the big-box stores, and beyond that, the sea of boreal forest.

Her thighs jiggled as the bus rocketed over a washed-out section of road. She could feel the vibration in her throat, her ears and her elbows. Then the road surface was smooth again. Pascal picked up speed. She closed her eyes and her body felt weightless. Sunshine leaked through the streaked windows. The light seeped through her eyelids and the engine was too loud for her to do anything but rest in this in-between state. She felt that until now she hadn't had a single moment to just *let go* since she arrived in the north. She wished she could forget about her deadline, the newspaper, the fact that she would have to do it all over again the next morning.

They were approaching the edge of a lake. The bus pulled into an unpaved parking lot with a sign that read *No Overnight Camping*. Pascal backed up the bus, twisting his head and chest out the window, until the wheels were inches from the water. Millicent dug around in her backpack for the camera and slung it around her neck. Pascal got up from the driver's seat and patted her shoulder as he headed for the back of the bus. "Follow me, paparazzi," he said with a laugh, the creases around his eyes deepening.

Beyond the kitchen and the plywood desk, a curtain rod divided the front and the back of the bus. Pascal pushed aside the orange curtain, revealing a bedroom. It was spare and clean. A narrow bed was covered by a brown comforter, and a watch and a sleeping mask lay on a flat brown pillow. Millicent could smell laundry detergent. A small wooden bookshelf was attached to the wall, and she could see the titles of the five books that sat there: *The 7 Habits of Highly Effective People*, the *Kama Sutra*, *Tintin au Tibet*, *One Hundred Years of Solitude*, and *Filmmaking for Dummies*.

Pascal got on his knees on the bed. He removed a plywood panel from the wall above the bed and crawled in through what looked like a cupboard door.

"Come on," he called to Millicent.

The insides of her wrists began to sweat. She felt a hundred miles away from the *Golden Nugget*, from anything familiar. But she had come this far; she couldn't stop now. Millicent got on the bed and hoisted herself through the door.

She was in another small room. There were no windows back here, but in the light coming from the bedroom she could make things out. There was a workbench and a scroll saw. A shelf held what looked like more video equipment. Hanging on the wall were cross-country skis and snowshoes and a bunch of hula hoops.

"What is all this? Why are we in here?" Millicent asked, feeling nervous.

"Hold on one second," Pascal said.

He was fiddling with something. Suddenly, the back doors of the bus groaned open, revealing the lake. It stretched down the valley as far as she could see, the water wrinkled by the wind. Low-lying hills were cloaked in trees.

"Bear Lake," he said happily. "It's a zoo in the summer, but nobody is ever here at this time of year."

Millicent inhaled and exhaled slowly, calming her wild heart. She was okay. She was fine. This was beautiful.

Noticing the stiffness of her body, Pascal reached out and touched her arm. Millicent wondered if he was like this with everyone.

"Do you like it?"

"I do," she said.

"Sometimes I stay here for days."

They sat on the floor of the bus, legs dangling out the back, staring at the stretch of water. Millicent wedged her hands under her thighs. A woodpecker drove its beak through the bark of a nearby pine, the *knock knock knock* the only sound breaking the silence. The land seemed to have calmed her. Listening to Pascal's quiet breathing, Millicent felt like she could ask him anything.

"Can you not afford an apartment? Is that why you live on the bus?"

Pascal laughed. "Oh, Ms. Reporter. You are always working."

Millicent couldn't stop herself from smiling. "I am at work right now, remember?"

"Of course I could afford a place, but I know that kind of life would not make me happy."

"Does it get lonely?"

Pascal kept his gaze on the water. "Of course," he said.

"So why don't you just live like everybody else?"

"I love my bus. It's living, how do I say it ..." Pascal paused and scrunched up his face at the sky. "It's living outside the box that can get lonely."

Millicent wished she hadn't left her notebook on the table. "What do you mean, 'outside the box'?"

"The box of comfort."

She waited for him to continue.

Pascal's voice tightened. "Everyone says, Oh, what a beautiful life you have, no mortgage or bills or anything tying you down. Then they go back to their government jobs and heated houses with three bathrooms and I'm here on my bus. Alone. But I know their life will not make me happy, so this is the only choice for me."

Millicent willed Pascal's words to burn into her mind so she could remember them back at the office.

He sat slumped over now, looking down at his bare feet. "Is this too much to tell you?"

"Not at all." Millicent lifted the camera to her eye. "Can I get a picture?"

"Of course, paparazzi," Pascal combed his fingers through his hair, then looked at the camera. Through the lens, he looked even older. He didn't pose or look away. He gazed directly at the camera, not smiling but not frowning either, waiting for Millicent to press down on the shutter.

9

SOPHIE HAD MADE THE announcement the night before: she would make a roommates brunch. They would drink too much coffee and stuff themselves with hash browns and bacon and laze around all day.

Millicent lay in bed smelling roasting potatoes, her mind drifting to the one memory she had been trying to avoid: Pascal. His intense gaze. The narrow space of the bus. The way he had touched the base of her spine to move her gently out of the way. It was stupid, and she hated herself for thinking this way. Her first interview with a reasonably attractive man and she couldn't stop daydreaming about him. He had probably forgotten her now that the article was published. She knew she should forget about him too, but ever since the interview she felt as if she was floating, as if she had swallowed a balloon.

She opened her door and looked out towards the kitchen. The sun poured honey-thick light onto the floor.

The table was set with plates and cups that looked like they had come from a church basement. There was a bowl of scrambled eggs, a platter with hash browns and bacon and a Bodum of coffee. Sophie sat with one heel on the seat of the chair, her arms wrapped around her knobby knee. She smiled coyly. "Well, well, well, if it isn't my Milli Vanilli."

"Bonjour, roommate." Millicent closed the door of her bedroom behind her and crossed the living room to the kitchen. She sat down across from Sophie and clenched her feet in her slippers to rein in her energy. She wondered if Sophie could read her, but her roommate just said "Let's eat. I'm starving," piled a mountain of eggs onto her plate and passed the rest to Millicent.

Sophie squeezed a pool of Sriracha onto her plate. Her short hair was pulled into a high ponytail that barely fit into the elastic, the tuft of hair sticking out like the bristles of a paintbrush. She scooped eggs onto her fork, grinning maniacally at her food. "Come to mama."

Millicent scooted her chair closer to the table so she could reach all the steaming plates.

"This is just incredible, Soph. Really. Thank you."

Sophie chewed, wide eyed and amused.

"Somebody spike your drink this morning?"

Millicent bit her lip to hold back a smile. "Just happy it's Saturday, I guess."

Friday's edition of the *Golden Nugget* was under Sophie's mug of coffee. The bottom story on the front page was Franc's predictions for next month's election. Millicent had heard Franc and Bryce talking about the editorial just after deadline the day before in Franc's office. His door was half-open, and their voices carried into the newsroom.

"It's going to be close, but I really think Charlie is going to take it," Bryce said. "People are starting see how such a tight-lipped government is toxic for democracy. They want transparency and change, and they know Charlie is going to give them that."

"You live in a fantasy, Bryce," Franc said. "Nobody cares about that."

"People are smarter than you think," Bryce said.

"People are not smart, they're greedy. They want GoldPower and they want the eight hundred new jobs Jakowsky's promised. They don't know what will happen if Charlie is premier and that scares them. And if they're scared, they'll vote for that status quo. Trust me." Franc paused. The newsroom fell quiet. That familiar acidic sensation filled her chest. I'm the political reporter, Millicent thought. I'm supposed to be part of these conversations. She rolled her chair over the floor closer to Franc's office, sensing he was about to say something important.

"Charlie is my friend. I know he comes across rough, but he understands this place more than anyone I know," he said. "Yes, Charlie would lead this territory with integrity and respect. Yes, it would set a precedent for Indigenous leadership in our country. Yes, we're dumb as nails not to elect him. But it's never going to happen, so let's just drop it."

"Maybe you've been doing this job for too long, Franc," Bryce said, his voice teasing.

"Maybe you haven't been here long enough, Bryce," Franc said flatly.

Millicent was just about to stand up and join them, but it was too late. Bryce stalked out of the office, threw on his jacket and his bicycle helmet and left for lunch.

"EAT, MY LITTLE BABUSHKA," Sophie said, motioning to the food on the table.

Millicent plucked a piece of bacon from a paper towel saturated in fat. "Going out canvassing today?" she asked, hoping to steer the conversation away from the *Golden Nugget* and the story on the next page. She hadn't told Sophie yet about her interview with Pascal. Sophie would make a big deal about it; she knew she would.

Sophie reached blindly across the table and poured coffee into Millicent's teacup, her eyes on Franc's editorial. "I don't care what your boss says," she said, tapping her finger on the editorial. "That's what stories like this do. They confirm people's fear that change can never happen."

"It's just Franc's opinion. Probably like four people will read it in total," Millicent said.

Sophie hung her head back, the xylophone bones of her chest exposed. She spoke to the ceiling. "But media has the power."

"I guess."

"Just wildly throwing around your opinion during election period can have direct consequences on who we vote into office. The media really is the problem." Millicent had forgotten this about Sophie: how her eyes grew distant when she got going. How she talked so fast her speech was impenetrable, no matter what she was arguing about.

"And don't get me started on large corporations buying out practically every outlet on earth. The days are long gone when we could actually call a newspaper unbiased—"

"We're actually independent," Millicent interrupted.

Down the road, the pack of dogs barked at a passing car. Sophie gulped down the rest of her coffee. "I don't mean that you're the problem, Mill."

Millicent reached for another piece of bacon. "I know how you get," she said.

Sophie smiled down at her empty cup.

"Yeah. You do."

Sophie licked her finger and flipped the page. Millicent's feature took up the whole of page two. "Local Filmmaker Finds Freedom Living without Permanent Address." Actually, Franc had wanted a different headline—"Middle-Aged Man Squats Year-Round in School Bus in Walmart Parking Lot"—and Millicent had asked him to "water it down" because she knew how much Pascal would hate it.

Sophie slammed her fist on the table. "What the fuck, Mill?"

"What?" Millicent said, trying her hardest to keep a straight face.

"You met the school bus guy? How could you not tell me?"

"It appears I did."

Millicent explained what had happened, about Franc

and the Walmart parking lot and Bear Lake, while Sophie skimmed the article. Even upside down, Millicent could see Pascal's eyes in the photo, amused although his mouth was serious. He looked older in black and white, more refined somehow.

Sophie's mouth twisted into a smile. "So he wants a reality TV show? Starring him?"

"I guess he's—"

"About renovating cars into homes?" Sophie interrupted. "That is too hilarious. Slow news day at the *Nugget*?"

"I think it's more about, like, living outside of the box. Giving people the chance to really look hard at their lives and see if it's what they actually want," Millicent said, embarrassed as soon as she finished. These were not her words. They were Pascal's words. Why was she defending him?

Sophie raised her eyebrows, waiting for Millicent to continue.

"It's stupid, I know."

Sophie's face grew serious. "Your article isn't stupid," she said. "I'm not saying that. I just think this Pascal man comes off as a bit of a cliché."

Millicent stabbed her fork into a potato and smeared it in ketchup. Across the table, Sophie waved her knife in the air and went on about Pascal, how preaching that we should all just live outside the box was a bit "much."

"Like, not everyone has the ability to just upend their lives and move into a school bus."

"That's true," Millicent said, staring down at her plate. Then she was suddenly overcome by the sharp memory of how they had fallen out at university. It was a memory she had taught herself to repress, but here it was again, surfacing like a bloated dead fish in the sea. It was the way Sophie waved her knife in the air as she spoke that triggered the memory, the way her confidence took up all the space in the small apartment, the way Sophie was completely oblivious to this, just as she had been completely oblivious to the fading of their friendship.

It was after the first semester at Horizon that their relationship began to crack. Sophie was volunteering for whatever organization or cause might make the front page of the university newspaper. It was the student union when the free bus passes were being revoked; Greenpeace when seabirds were choking on plastic; a pro-choice group when the Children of God began distributing pamphlets explaining how early a fetus can feel pain. If there was a cause, there was Sophie.

And if it wasn't a rally she was motivated by, it was a grad student she'd picked up at a bar, a different man every weekend. She would push the end of her single bed flush with the window so they could blow cigarette smoke outside while lying in bed. Sometimes they would laze around like that until dusk, four feet dangling from her open window. Millicent would walk underneath the window on her way back from the library and stare at the combination of Sophie's purple nails and the hairy toes of a Russian literature grad student. If by any chance Sophie noticed Millicent, she would offer a small wave and then shut her window, as if to keep all the fun inside.

They would still have negronis in Sophie's room every few weeks. Sophie would ask about her poetry and about her mother, but Millicent couldn't help wondering if she was boring her, sitting on the floor in her ridiculous Costco tube socks while Sophie pranced around the room, switching on lamps because "lighting is everything," trying different shades of lipstick and talking about her latest conquest, how she made him coffee and Baileys on her hot plate after they made love, or how he promised to take her to the new oyster bar downtown. By then, their whole friendship seemed false. Millicent wondered if she had been a mere stand-in until Sophie found what she was really looking for: extravagance, men, sex. Had she been the only one in the dorm gullible enough to fall for Sophie's fleeting charm?

In the kitchen, Millicent pushed her plate away and focused on Sophie again. The rich morning light highlighted her jawline. Sophie's beauty was still there, it always would be. She leaned forward in her chair and began playing with the loose threads of her cloth placemat.

Sophie was inspecting the photo. Now her face split into a big grin. "He is *hot*."

"I hadn't really noticed," Millicent said.

Sophie tossed her head back and laughed.

"C'mon Mill, you don't always have to be so straight. I mean, he seems like a little out there, yes, but he is fuckable."

"I'm not really in the market for a man," Millicent said, staring past Sophie at the front door. She always stopped breathing when she was caught in the beginning of a lie.

Sophie put her hand on Millicent's forearm. "Are you okay?" she asked in a softer tone.

"What do you mean?"

Sophie appeared to think about this for a moment,

then she rose slowly, stacking the sticky plates before putting them in the sink.

"It can be lonely," she said. "I remember when I first moved up here, I didn't know a soul." Sophie turned the faucet on. She squeezed a long line of green soap into the hot water. The kitchen filled with the scent of fake apple. "It was as if the land could swallow me whole," she said to the wall, "and nobody would notice."

Millicent thought back to the enormity of Bear Lake, how piercingly quiet it had been out there, just her and Pascal. She thought about how close she had felt to him then.

"So why did you stay?" Millicent asked.

"Same as everyone else, I guess," Sophie said. "I got comfortable."

BACK IN HER BEDROOM, Millicent refreshed her email. One new message.

From: Pascal Gagnon. Subject line: *Thank you!*

Her heart throbbed in her throat. She couldn't believe it.

Hello Ms. Reporter.
I saw the article in Friday's paper. You are a great writer! You seem to really understand the freedom of living on a bus. This is rare. But this photo that was printed! I need to get my hair cut, no?
Xoxo,
Pascal

*PS—I shot a ptarmigan out at Bear Lake yesterday
and need to eat it before it spoils. It's too much for one
person! Would you like to come by my bus later today
for dinner? I am 15 kilometres north of town, at the
exit by the river. Six o'clock.*

Millicent stared at the words *Six o'clock*. Her body
broke into a sweat. She began pacing the bedroom. Was
he crazy, she wondered? She had given him her address
in case he had anything to add to the interview. But now
this, inviting her to dinner?

Millicent pressed her forehead into the cold windowpane
and closed her eyes. Maybe this was some sort of northern
hospitality she didn't understand. Maybe this was perfectly
normal. She imagined the two of them alone on the bus,
at night. She imagined his teasing eyes and the way he had
refused to take his gaze off her. No. She couldn't fool herself.
Inviting her to dinner on his bus, somewhere out of town
along the highway was not only out of line, it was dangerous. Her instinct was to be too trusting. She did not know
this man. And she didn't know anyone who knew him.

Millicent sat back down on the bed and hunched over
her computer.

*Dear Pascal,
I'm glad you liked the article. I won't be able to make
dinner tonight. Thank you for the kind offer.
Sincerely,
Millicent*

She let the cursor blink over her name, looking up at the bare white walls that boxed her inside her bedroom. Without allowing herself to second-guess herself, she deleted the entire email and began again.

Dear Pascal,
Thank you for the kind words. Dinner sounds lovely.
I'll bring wine. See you at six.

10

MILLICENT CRACKED OPEN the car window. The rush of fall air calmed her nerves. The Alaska Highway was a long, grey carpet runner unravelling over the land. That's what the locals called it, Millicent had noticed: the land. Not the specificity of a forest or river or mountain, but a term to encapsulate everything outside of Whitehorse. There was town and there was land.

Millicent passed a weigh-in station for semi-trucks travelling between Whitehorse and Alaska. She glanced at the row of idling trucks, drivers on their hands and knees, tinkering with the wheels. Some were gathered in a circle, smoking and laughing.

A bottle of wine lay in the passenger seat. She wore a simple black dress that was scooped low on her chest, a pair of slippery tights and a knee-length parka to cover it all up. She had lined her lips—a frightening deep red that belonged to Sophie—and then immediately rubbed the colour off with a piece of tissue.

What a relief to be out of the apartment and on the open road. She had tried to get out before Sophie got back from canvassing so that she wouldn't have to explain where she was going, but Sophie's truck had peeled into the parking lot as Millicent was locking the apartment door.

"Where ya headed?" Sophie called out, slamming the driver's door. Millicent pressed her purse closer to her body, praying that Sophie couldn't see the outline of the wine bottle.

"Just to the movies with some people from the *Nugget*."

"Look at you go, making friends," Sophie said, winking at Millicent as she passed her on her way to the apartment.

"It's really not a big deal," Millicent said, opening the door to the Mazda. "Just a dumb movie to pass the time."

The lie had just slipped out. But once the words were out, she couldn't take them back. She knew what she was doing was risky. And she knew Sophie was protective. She'd ask Millicent to text her every half hour. She'd make her feel embarrassed about going. *So are you actually into this guy? But he lives on a fucking school bus! Millie, I can't believe it!*

On either side of the highway horses roamed the barren hills. Maybe it really wasn't a big deal. She would eat ptarmigan for the first time in her life, have a glass of wine and be home in a few hours.

Her excitement had turned into a thrilling dread by the time Millicent spotted the bus, at 15.3 kilometres on the odometer. She turned off the highway and into the pull-out, then killed the ignition. Nobody, she realized, had any idea where she was. Not Sophie, not anyone at the *Nugget* and not her mother. Hands still clutching the wheel, she waited for Pascal to emerge from the bus. Surely, he must have heard her engine. He must be waiting for her. Millicent checked her reflection in the rear-view mirror. Then, in what felt like slow motion, she took her seatbelt off and reached for the wine bottle.

She slammed her door and walked around to the front of the bus, noticing that the graffiti had been painted over in a slightly lighter yellow tone. The smell of wild sage, spruce needles and diesel filled the air. The curtains on all the windows were closed. She knocked on the door. A semi-truck passed on the highway and then there was nothing, a silence so intense it rang, like a mosquito lodged in her ear canal.

An outhouse with green, peeling paint perched on the edge of the pullout with a sign nailed to the door that said *Closed for the Season*. Millicent circled to the back of the outhouse. From here she could see the Yukon River, glittering like a snake basking in the sun. Maybe he was down by the water, somewhere she couldn't see. She thought about calling out his name, but she couldn't muster any sound.

Millicent turned around and walked stiffly back to her car. He hadn't read her email. He hadn't thought she would actually take him up on dinner. Why had she? How embarrassing to be clutching a twenty-four dollar bottle of wine like this was a formal date. He wasn't even here! Millicent wanted nothing more than to be back on the highway, driving home. Sophie would drink the wine with her. She would tell her the whole story. Millicent didn't bother with her seatbelt, just started the car, the tires spitting gravel towards the highway as she remembered Sophie's words. *You can't just trust everyone.* She didn't know Pascal, not at all.

She sensed his presence before she saw him, a clamping in her gut. His body grew larger in the rear-view mirror. Pascal was jogging after her. He was shirtless, with a towel draped over his shoulder and something in his hand. As he drew closer, she saw that it was a beer. Millicent did not think. Her body behaved on impulse. She left the engine running and the car in neutral and lifted her hand to her eyebrows to block the sinking evening sun.

"Where are you going?" he laughed, coming to a stop by her door.

She had forgotten his face: the grooves in his forehead, the grey in his beard, his teasing eyes. "I don't know," she muttered. Millicent tried not to stare at his bare stomach, at the thin line of hair that ran from his belly button to the top of his shorts.

"Weirdo," he said. Pascal took a swig from the bottle and, mouth full, held it out to Millicent. She got out of the car once more, closed the door and grabbed the bottle. She took a sip, allowing the beer to slide down her throat. The cool liquid calmed her. She handed the bottle back to Pascal.

"Thank you."

He stared at her as if he knew something about her that she didn't. Like why she was here.

"You're welcome." Pascal pulled her into a hug. "Really though, where were you going?" he whispered in her ear. His bare skin was warm. She could smell deodorant, maybe cologne. With a stab of pleasure to her heart, she wondered if he had put it on for her. Pascal finished the beer, wiped his lips with the towel and handed the bottle to Millicent.

"Hold this for a second? I'll park your car out of the way."

With the towel still draped over his shoulder, he folded himself into the driver's seat. She hadn't processed how tall he really was; he made the Mazda look as small as a toy. Pascal put the car in reverse and it shot into a narrow wedge of space between the bus and a stand of spruce trees. He slammed the door and tossed Millicent the keys.

"You can drive stick!" he said, disappearing into the bus. When he returned, he had another towel. He handed it to Millicent. "Come with me. I want to show you something."

She could still leave. She could turn around and get back in her car without a word. Instead, Millicent picked her way down the steep bank, through prickly rose bushes that scratched her tights. Pascal walked quickly, as if they might miss whatever it was he wanted to show her. Every few minutes he stopped and looked back to see if she was following. The sun threw orange light over the river, a wide channel barrelling north as if trying to outrun itself. When Millicent caught up, Pascal started telling her about the fish he had caught in this section of the river: trout, Dolly Varden, Chinook.

They had reached the open valley and the river. "So what did you want to show me?" Millicent asked. In front of them, the water was perfectly still, a pool of calm compared to the raging current beyond. She clenched her fists inside her parka. It was colder out in the open, where the wind tore freely.

"This." Pascal was looking at the pool.

"The water?" Millicent asked.

"The eddy."

"What about it?"

"Probably the last time we can go swimming this year," he said, looking towards a mountain in the distance, its peak dusted with snow.

"Are you serious?" Millicent said. "It's barely two degrees out here."

Pascal didn't answer. He balanced on one leg to remove one shoe, then the other. In nothing but his briefs, he bent over and folded his clothes neatly on a flat rock. He had a solid body, not overly muscular, but with the kind of mass that could not be pushed over. He wobbled over some sharp rocks, muttering to himself.

"Viens viens," he said, without looking back.

Millicent exhaled loudly.

"I can almost see my breath!" she yelled after him.

Pascal stopped and stood with his back to her, staring at the current. The waistband of his boxers cut into his flesh. Millicent wondered if he was angry, if he was the kind of man who could flip moods in a second. But he turned towards her with an easy smile. "Trust me, this will be good for you. Like a northern baptism."

"I'm not Catholic," Millicent retorted, trying to stall.

"Me neither." Without further hesitation, Pascal dove into the water. He broke through the surface with a loud whoop, his hair slicked to his head. Watching him, Millicent was suddenly filled with a desire to be outside of her own body, to be anyone but herself. She scrambled out of her clothes and stood shivering in her red underwear with her arms wrapped around her soft stomach.

"Come in!" Pascal yelled.

Millicent approached the pool and stepped into it. The water was so icy it didn't feel cold, just painful. Pascal was lathering his hands with a sliver of soap that slipped through his fingers like a live eel. "Want some?" he asked. Millicent shook her head, too shocked to speak. He scrubbed his stomach and his armpits, then dunked under the water again. When he emerged, his lips were the colour of a bruise.

"You're freezing," Millicent said through chattering teeth.

"Stage-one hypothermia," Pascal said, grinning. The creases around his eyes deepened. "After a few minutes you can't feel anything."

THROUGH THE WINDSHIELD, DAYLIGHT was fading into a hazy blue. Millicent slipped her dress over her head and draped the towel Pascal had given her over the back of the driver's seat. She took her phone out of her purse to check the time. She had no idea how long they had been down at the river. But the screen was black; her phone was dead. After an initial jolt of fear, realizing she was really, truly alone with Pascal, she forced herself to let it go. Who cared if Sophie tried texting her? She deserved this.

Millicent inhaled deeply and closed her eyes, taking in the scent of the bus. It smelled just like it had the last time: porridge, bacon, diesel. She ran her fingers through her wet hair. The endorphins from the cold surged underneath her skin. Pascal was right, the swim had been worth it. She felt relaxed, like she was floating a foot above the ground, like nothing else mattered except for this moment.

Millicent hovered over Pascal as he knelt on the floor in his wet boxers to turn on the propane heater. He held down a button and leaned his ear against the heater as if trying to detect breath in an unconscious person. There was a clicking and a *whoosh*, and then a rush of warmth blasted out from the heater.

"Magic!" Pascal exclaimed. His knees cracked when he stood up and he mumbled to himself in French. Something about being old.

"Well," she said. "How old are you?"

Pascal leaned back against the kitchen counter and smiled. "Twenty-two."

"So you've just had a rough life?"

"Exactly."

Millicent glanced at the photos on the wall. The woman hula-hooping in the grassy field smiled at her.

"Who is this?"

"My last girlfriend. I don't know why it's still up there."

Pascal reached behind her and peeled the photo from the wall. He folded it in half and threw it under the table.

"What was she like?"

"She was a beautiful soul, but she didn't understand me. Not like you, Ms. Reporter."

Millicent raised her eyebrows. "I understand you?"

Pascal locked eyes with her. "Yes," he said. "You ask all the right questions."

He went behind the curtain and re-emerged wearing jeans and a flannel shirt. He put on Mazzy Star and took the ptarmigan from the small refrigerator under the counter. Millicent watched him roll the sleeves of his flannel shirt up to his elbows.

A contented ease fell over them as he began cooking. He fried the breast meat in a wok with garlic, kale and red pepper flakes. The meat sizzled, warming the bus with a sweet, fatty scent as the dreamy chords of "Fade Into You" played through the speakers. Millicent's job was to drink wine and slice cantaloupe for dessert. She chose a paring knife from the cutlery container at the end of the table. When Pascal saw her using the weight of her body to slice through the hard rind, he abandoned the sizzling wok and came over.

"Non non non." He handed her a different knife. "Use this."

The blade sliced through the fruit like it was a moist cake. There was a sense that they did not need to talk, and without this pressure, conversation flowed effortlessly. Millicent wanted to know everything she couldn't ask about in the formal interview.

"Do you have any brothers or sisters?" She dug the seeds out from the melon and licked the juice from her fingers, the sweetness a shock after the chalky wine.

"One, Marie. She was an acrobat in Montreal."

"Wow."

"But then she had three babies and let her dreams die."

She asked him his middle name. François. His favourite food? Lobster. His biggest fear? That people would think he was crazy.

"Why would they think that?" Millicent asked.

"Maybe you're crazy too, if you can't see why."

He asked her about her parents, and when she told him that her mother was sick he asked all the logical questions: For how long? Was it fatal? Then he asked, "Is she happy?" Millicent had to say she didn't know. Nobody had asked her that before. Nobody thought a sick person could be happy.

Pascal turned off the propane burner on the stove and carried the steaming pan to the table. He drained the last of the wine. "Chin-chin," he said, lifting his mug.

"Cheers."

"To a beautiful evening with a beautiful woman."

Pascal chewed, staring at Millicent in that intense, amused way, as if he could read her thoughts. She swallowed.

"So what's going to happen in the first episode of *Cribs with Engines*?"

"Is this the interview still, Ms. Reporter?"

Millicent could feel herself blush. She willed her body to stop.

"*Cribs with Engines* is dropped," Pascal said.

"Oh, I'm sorry," she exclaimed in surprise.

"Don't be."

"Aren't you sorry?"

"The universe is aligning."

Millicent's mouth twisted into a wry smile. "Really," she said, her voice teasing. Pascal leaned forward. He had never looked so serious.

"The producer, this man from Montreal I was telling you about? He wrote me an email and said he doesn't think turning vehicles into homes is what the viewers want. I don't agree with him, but he is the expert, you know? But he loves my personality, this is what he said. And he said to keep throwing him ideas, that we would find something that worked. I mean pitching, which of course is what I did." He was speaking rapidly now, tripping over his own words. "Now the show will be about driving around the Yukon on my bus, learning about Québécois people who have made a life for themselves up here, just people living outside the box, you know? My kind of people. Dog mushers, brewmasters, musicians, trappers."

The bus windows were fogged up from cooking. Pascal stared at the foggy glass, lost in his own fantasy.

"I sent the producer an email about my new concept. My guess is I'll get about twenty grand for the pilot episode. This is industry standard."

"Amazing," Millicent said. She wasn't sure what to think. It seemed bizarre that Pascal could just upend his reclusive life and start filming a reality TV show—starring himself. On the other hand, here was a man who had spent years renovating a shell of a school bus into something that could be featured in a home decor magazine. Anything, it seemed, was possible.

Millicent brushed her hand over the fabric of the kitchen bench, a blue floral upholstery from the '80s that Pascal had sewn into cushion covers. As he explained to her how hard it was to break into the film industry, Millicent had the strange sense that she was on a boat far out at sea. Like she had exited her own life. She swore she could feel the bus rocking.

Pascal slipped their empty plates and glasses under the table and into the plastic bin.

"What do you want to do?" he asked.

"Right now?" she said, startled.

With surprising grace, Pascal moved across the table to sit beside her. "With your life."

"I'm a reporter. You know that."

He placed his hand on her thigh, just below the hem of her dress.

"And then what?"

"I don't know."

"No?"

"I guess I'll slowly work my way up." Her heart banged in her ears. "Maybe move to a bigger city. A bigger paper." She didn't know what she was saying.

"Is this what you really want for your whole life?"

Millicent considered this. Nobody had asked her that before. An image of Tim formed in her mind: her professor sitting at the end of the table during those three-hour poetry workshops, chewing on the end of his pen, reading Millicent's work with such tenderness and care.

She wiped the condensation from the nearest window with her fist, avoiding his eyes.

"I write poetry." She realized she was whispering.

"What?"

"Poems," she said, louder. Pascal slid his hand under her dress and up the side of her thigh to her belly.

"Of course you do," he said.

Soon Millicent was telling him everything about her poetry class at Horizon.

"I had this professor named Tim—he made us all call him by his first name. He was humble, never talked about all the poetry awards he had won or books he had published. He just had this way of teasing apart our poems with such care that made us feel like, I don't know, like ..." Millicent trailed off.

"Like what?" Pascal asked.

"Like real artists."

Pascal traced his finger along the frill of her red underwear.

"The workshop was three hours long in this window-less basement, but by the time it was over, I could have sworn only fifteen minutes had passed." Millicent couldn't stop talking now; she didn't know what would happen with his hand and her body if she did. "It was this crazy time warp. And if Tim didn't think we all had talent, he was a good actor. The first few classes I doubted his sincer-ity, but the longer I watched him at the end of the table, how he chewed on the end of his pen until the ink bled in his mouth, the more I wanted to be like him. All that empathy and wisdom, you know?"

Pascal nodded.

"When class ended, I would push open the door into the sunlight and the salty air and just feel ..." Millicent paused and looked out at the sliver of moon rising above the hills across the river. "Electric or something."

He cupped his palm on the soft flesh of her inner thigh. The temperature of her blood rose to a boil.

"What does this feel like?" he asked.

"It's like the very opposite of boredom," she said, whispering now, because real sound would not come out of her mouth.

"So, we are both artists."

Millicent laughed. "I'm not an artist."

Pascal removed his hand and a sharp feeling took over her body, as if she had snapped out of a dream. Pascal spun the empty wine bottle in two full circles on the table, smiling to himself. "Just imagine," he said.

"Imagine what?"

"I can't tell you. You'll think I'm crazy. It's too soon."

"Tell me."

"Imagine the two of us living on the bus, travelling the country, making art."

Millicent scanned the bus: the Mason jars strapped in by bungee cords, the herbs on the dash, the hum of propane.

"You're insane," she said quietly.

"I tell you my deepest fear and you already poke me?"

"Would it help if I told you my biggest fear?" she asked.

"Yes."

"Death."

Pascal got up and fiddled with his phone, choosing a new album. The music pierced the silence. Then he pulled Millicent up from the table and drew her to him so that they were dancing.

"'You can't be scared of death if you live fully.' Massive Attack, remember? From our interview," Pascal whispered in her ear.

"When you kidnapped me."

"I didn't kidnap. You wanted to come."

"Were you surprised?"

"A little."

At first he kissed her softly, as if he were unsure if she would kiss him back. Millicent cupped the back of his neck.

Her dress on the floor.

His tongue on the back of her knee, moving up her thigh.

The condom package ripped open.

It was not a question, entering her, filling her. Her head emptied of thoughts. When the Massive Attack album finished, the only sound was transport trucks heading to Alaska, their headlights pouring white light through the bedroom window.

PASCAL WAS DEAD TO the world. Millicent could taste him on her tongue, sweet and earthy. He lay on his side behind her, one arm slung heavily over her hip. He did not move when he slept. She had to pee but she didn't want to disturb him.

The night was as dark as a well. She remembered her phone was dead. Millicent thought about Sophie and how, if she was still awake, she'd be wondering where her roommate had gone after the "movie." Every other night, Millicent had been tucked in bed by nine. That person already seemed like a hazy memory.

It seemed that hours had passed without a car going by on the highway.

Millicent thought about all the nights in the dorm at Horizon, listening to the sounds from Sophie's room next door, the moans, her flirtatious laugh after the deed was done. Millicent heard it all.

She banished any thoughts of Sophie and Horizon, forcing herself to float in the surreal moment of the present. She didn't have to report to anyone. She deserved this.

The minutes passed until Millicent knew she couldn't hold it in any longer. Pascal didn't stir as she hoisted herself to a sitting position. Her bare feet were cold on the floor. Millicent found her dress on the ground and wrestled it over her head. She felt her way past the stove and the kitchen table. She knelt on the driver's seat and grabbed the metal lever that opened the bus doors. It wouldn't budge. She tried again, this time with both hands in quick jerks. Slow down, breathe, she told herself. She was not trapped. She was fine. When she tried for the third time the door squeaked open.

She heard the steady, comforting sound of moving water. Millicent peed on a patch of fireweed by the generator as she looked at the shape of her car, nestled beside the stand of spruce. She tilted her head back, taking in the ceiling of stars, the billion pricks of light, the smell of spruce pitch and diesel and the acidic tang of her urine.

Back in bed, Millicent curled into Pascal. She placed his arm over her hip again as if he were a rag doll. He kissed her neck and mumbled something about sleep. She wished morning would never arrive.

11

MORNING, OF COURSE, DID ARRIVE. How long did they spend in bed with their limbs entangled, their breath syrupy from the wine? Pascal kissed each eyelid. Millicent formed a pair of scissors with her free hand and pretended to cut off the ends of Pascal's hair, like a hairdresser.

"What are you doing?" he said with his eyes closed.

His forehead shone like sunlight on steel.

"Giving you a haircut."

"I need one. Haven't had a real one in ten years."

Millicent cocooned deeper into his chest, her cheek flush with his collarbone. "How do you cut your hair then?" Her voice was muffled. It was hot under the comforter and it smelled like the night before. The insides of her thighs were sweaty underneath the covers.

"I just cut it myself with my sewing scissors."

Millicent came up for air.

"How did you learn to sew?"

Pascal stared at the roof of the bus with a look of delight, as if Millicent should have known the answer.

"I taught myself," he said. "How else would I learn?"

They spent the morning talking about their childhoods with a kind of urgency. How could they have seen each other naked but not know the names of their parents? Millicent did not say this out loud, but she could tell that Pascal was thinking the same thing. He wanted her to know him.

His were Marie-Claude and Pierre. They came from a farming town and got married straight out of high school. She was an alcoholic who suffered from depression. He worked full-time, took care of the children and dealt with her mood swings. He had left her only last year, although he should have done so decades ago, Pascal explained.

"He is finally free. But now he's in his seventies. What can you do with freedom in your seventies?" Pascal spoke with one hand on Millicent's stomach, as if she were a helium balloon that might float away.

They lazed around in bed until the sheets were damp and the afternoon's washed-out light slanted through the bus windows. Eventually Pascal sat up, ran a hand through his hair and pulled on his shorts. Millicent listened as he made his way to the kitchen. She waited in bed, afraid to move even a millimetre and let the warm air trapped beneath the comforter escape. There was a hiss of boiling water from the kitchen. Pascal hummed to himself. A few minutes later, he came back to bed and set a cup of cowboy coffee on the blanket on top of her belly.

HER BACK WAS PINNED against the yellow steel, just beside the word *Bluebird*. She took in his lips, his hands, the smell of his beard. He wouldn't let her go.

"We will see each other again," he said in her ear.

"Yes."

The Mazda hit the highway just as sun began to set, the day gone in a woozy second. It was the time of hazy blue dusk when moose and elk might dart across the highway. Millicent told herself to concentrate, but her mind kept drifting back to the wildness of the past twenty-four hours. The bus. Pascal. His body. She shook herself out of the trance as the Chinese restaurant came into sight. How, she wondered, was she was still on the road?

The smell of deep-fried chicken felt familiar by now, as did the ruts in the road that led back to the Pit. The engine whined as she crested the steep lip.

What would she tell Sophie? She wondered if she would be able to smell sex on her. She could say she'd had too much to drink with the *Nugget* crew and slept on Bryce's couch. That was simple. Believable. She would tell Sophie soon enough about Pascal, just not today. She wanted to float in this daze for a while longer.

MUSIC MUTED THE SOUND of the door as she came in, and she closed it as quietly as possible. The apartment smelled like freshly baked bread. In the entryway she saw a pair of scuffed white Nike sneakers, and she heard a deep voice coming from the kitchen. Millicent hung her keys on the wall quietly, trying to decode the man's voice before the people in the kitchen noticed her. The voice was cut off by Sophie's high-pitched laughter. Maybe the man was a date. Maybe Millicent could say hello and slip into her bedroom.

Bryce. It was Bryce's voice. Millicent felt her stomach drop. What was Bryce doing in her apartment? She moved numbly into view of the kitchen. A cribbage board, a bottle of Jameson's and a burning stick of incense sat on the table. She barely had time to observe that Bryce looked out of place surrounded by Sophie's vintage lamps and silk scarves before she was set upon.

"Millicent, thank god!" Sophie exclaimed, laying her cards on the table.

"Hey," Bryce said. He laid down his cards too, but after a quick glance at Millicent he looked away.

"Hey," Millicent said, trying hard to sound casual. "What are you … doing here?"

"Just came over to play some cribbage," Bryce said, still not looking at her.

"Sophie, can you explain this card party?" Millicent asked.

"I don't know how to start," Sophie said, looking at the ceiling.

"What do you mean?" Millicent said. A hot lump had formed in her throat.

"I was worried about you."

"Why?"

"You didn't come home last night."

"And?"

"I didn't know what to do."

Millicent's throat grew so tight she thought she couldn't swallow her own saliva. "Right."

"And you didn't reply to my texts. I couldn't just sit around and do nothing." Sophie's tone grew soft, her eyes pleading. "Mill, you're like a sister to me."

Millicent felt the weight of her dead phone in the pocket of her coat. She didn't want to hear the rest of the story. She wanted to disappear.

"You told me you were out with your co-workers, so when I woke up this morning and you still weren't home, I called Bryce." Sophie's voice was steady but her hazel eyes looked afraid. "Anyway, I called him and he said he didn't know anything about going for drinks." Sophie paused. "That's when we got really worried."

"We?"

She would not cry.

"Yeah. Bryce and I."

Bryce had plucked a coin from his pocket and he was setting it spinning on the table.

Millicent addressed Bryce. "I'm sorry you had to come all the way out here."

"It's fine. I wasn't doing anything."

The faded friendship bracelet on his wrist was covered in white dust. Millicent noticed that his elbows and his shirt were dusted as well. Bryce seemed to be sensing her stare.

"Actually, I had just finished making blueberry scones." He glanced at a plate on the counter. "I should have saved you one. Sorry."

Now it seemed that he couldn't stop talking.

"Really, Mill, I needed to get out of my cabin. And I

had just made all these scones, and when Sophie phoned I asked if she liked scones ... so I thought I might as well bring them over ..."

Sophie threw Bryce a sharp look, and he shut up.

"So anyway, when Bryce got here we saw your laptop open on your bed and ..." Sophie trailed off. Bryce leaned forward and spun the coin again. The conversation seemed to be causing him physical pain.

"And what?" Millicent demanded.

The coin fell flat on the table. Bryce pushed his hands into his pockets.

"I feel horrible about it, Mill, but we looked at your email. We didn't know what else to do," Sophie pleaded.

"Jesus."

"I didn't want to—" Bryce started to say, but Sophie shot him another sharp look.

"I was about to call the police, Mill. I know you. It just seemed so unlike you to disappear for a weekend."

Millicent ignored Sophie and stormed over to the fridge. She grabbed the big jar of pickles on the top shelf. It was unbelievable. She couldn't believe they'd had the guts to look at her emails just because she spent one night out of the apartment.

Sophie hovered by the sink next to her. "I am sorry."

"Me too," Bryce said.

Millicent struggled to loosen the lid on the jar. She knew Bryce and Sophie were watching her, waiting for her to say something, but she had nothing to say. Millicent slid a pickle from the jar. She crunched it and swallowed, her embarrassment hardening into something cruel: so they knew she had lied, that she had spent the night on a school bus with the elusive bus man. So what? The only thing Millicent could feel clearly was a sharp, raging anger. The one time she tried to be brave and live freely, Sophie yanked her back as if she were a marionette.

"You're mad. I get it," Sophie said. "I was just looking out for your safety, going alone out to his bus and all."

"I'm not a child, Sophie," Millicent spat.

"Of course not!" Sophie took a step towards her. "You just don't know many people up here, so I feel responsible for you."

When Millicent spoke, it was as if her throat was stuffed with cotton balls. "You can relax," she said. "You're not responsible for me. You're really not."

"You don't have to be embarrassed," Sophie said softly.

Millicent closed the fridge. She walked numbly over to her bedroom, avoiding further eye contact with either of them.

"I'm glad you're okay, Millicent," Bryce called after her.

Then he stood up, went to the entranceway to put on his shoes and left, slamming the door. As Millicent crawled under her comforter, she heard the sound of Bryce's tires as he drove away from the parking lot.

MILLICENT LAY IN BED with a pillow clamped between her thighs, listening to the clink of clean dishes being put back into the kitchen cupboards. So, Sophie was concerned for her "safety." Everyone in Whitehorse, it seemed, had an opinion about this man whom they had never met.

Millicent was tempted to text Pascal to ask if she could spend the night with him again. Wu-wei, she thought. Do not resist. Let go of control. Live your life with ease, as if you are being carried by a river's current. It was an ancient Chinese philosophy that Tim brought up during workshops when students were upset about their classmates' feedback. Write another poem, he'd say. Discover what else is inside you. Don't grow attached. If Millicent stopped clinging to the bank and rode out into the current of her life right now, what would that look like? She would get in her car, drive out to the bus and see what happened. She wouldn't stay like this, pillow clenched between her thighs, barely able to breathe.

There were three soft knocks on the door.

Millicent curled onto her side. If Sophie opened the door, she would see that she was asleep and leave.

"Mill ...? Millicent?"

"Yeah?"

"Can I come in?"

Millicent didn't answer, wanting more than anything for the evening to end.

"Sure," she said.

Sophie turned on the light. She was clutching a bag of salt-and-vinegar chips. It was the first time Millicent had seen Sophie step into her room. Now Sophie scanned the room, her gaze flitting from the window to the floor, trying not to show what she was thinking. Millicent suddenly saw her bedroom from Sophie's perspective: her bath-towel curtain, the unpacked duffel bags in the corner, her clothes vomited onto the floor. You couldn't even see the floor.

Sophie perched on the edge of the mattress. She licked the salt from her fingers one by one and wiped them on her jeans. "Want some?" she asked, holding the bag towards Millicent. "I brought them for you."

"I'm fine."

Sophie paused. "Can I come in with you?"

Millicent opened the duvet. Sophie used her arm as a pillow, careful that no part of their skin made contact, but Millicent could still smell the lavender scent and feel the warmth trapped between their two bodies. She lay on her back, staring at the ceiling.

"Can I meet him?" Sophie asked.

"Who?"

"You know who," Sophie said.

"We just spent one night together."

"If you like him—"

"I do."

"That's great," Sophie said.

Millicent recalled her woozy memories of the night before. *To a beautiful night with a beautiful woman.* What she remembered about that moment was his eyes, and how confidently he had stared at her, in her, through her. How she was forced to look away. Was she actually developing real feelings for Pascal, or had she been in some sort of a trance?

"What I was going to say," Sophie continued, "was that if you like him, he must be great."

Then Sophie folded her glasses and placed them on the nightstand. Millicent felt a rush of tenderness towards her roommate, an urge to take care of her. She'd forgotten that without glasses Sophie looked like a child. The toilet flushed in the apartment upstairs. Water snaked through the ceiling pipes.

"Here. Lift," Millicent said, placing a flat pillow under Sophie's head.

"Are you still mad?" Sophie asked.

Millicent cracked a small smile. "Just embarrassed."

"Please, Mill. Don't be. You have nothing to be embarrassed about." Sophie began nibbling her thumbnail, her nervous tic. Millicent rolled onto her side so their bodies mirrored each other, face to face.

"You know I've always looked up to you, right?" Sophie said.

"Not really."

"At university, you had this confidence," Sophie said.

"I really didn't—" Millicent began.

"But you did!" Sophie cut her off. "I, on the other hand, was obsessed with my own image, and what others thought of me. I desperately needed to come off as this sophisticated, intelligent and, like, sexually confident person." She rolled her eyes. "Remember how I had a red light bulb screwed into that lamp? Like, was I running some sort of underground brothel in the dorm room? Jesus."

"You are sophisticated and intelligent," Millicent said.

"I'm not fishing for compliments. I really had no idea who I was back then. No idea ..." Sophie's eyes glassed over as she choked on her next words. "Sometimes I still have no idea who I am."

"Soph."

Sophie closed her eyes and drew in a long breath, exhaling through pursed lips. She spoke with her eyes shut.

"The thing about you, Mill, is you've never cared what other people think. You have real confidence," Sophie said. "Like in university. You spent all your time writing, tucked away in the library and focusing on what mattered."

Millicent let out a real laugh.

"I wasn't confident. I was so shy I didn't know what to do with myself, so I hid in that library for four years. It was painful."

Sophie opened her eyes and spoke in a steely tone. "I spent every weekend drinking myself into oblivion."

"I know," Millicent said softly. Sadness filled Sophie's eyes. Millicent fished for her hand underneath the comforter. It was hot and clammy. Her skin looked as pale and fragile as tissue paper. Still, she was beautiful. She had the kind of beauty that could never been stolen from her.

"I would latch on to any guy," Sophie continued. "As long as he had a heartbeat and had the faintest idea who Dostoevsky was, I'd bring him home. Let him fuck me however he wanted. If it hurt, all the better. There must have been fifty of them. Maybe more. Did you know that?" Sophie didn't wait for an answer. "After a while, I was so ashamed I couldn't even look at you when you walked by. I started ignoring you. After the weekend, and the booze and the attention had worn off, I couldn't get out of bed for days. I locked my door. I ate dry crackers and made ichiban soup on my hot plate, totally numb until the next weekend rolled around. I didn't even get it together to graduate."

"I had no idea," Millicent whispered.

Sophie unclasped her hand from Millicent's and wiped a single tear from her cheek.

"Well, there you have it, you're all caught up," she said, forcing a smile.

"So that's why you came all the way up to the Yukon," Millicent said. "To escape."

"Everyone comes here to escape something, Mill."

Sophie seemed, suddenly, to be suffocating under the blanket. She threw it open and sat up, her bare feet on the floor, and gazed numbly at the bath towel draped over the curtain rod.

Millicent pulled the blanket up to her neck. A gust of wind rattled the window. "Soph," she said softly again.

"I made a promise to myself when I moved up here," Sophie said. "That I would learn what it felt like to be alone, really alone. And now? Sometimes I'm so alone I'm afraid I will just disappear."

12

PASCAL TEXTED MILLICENT the next morning. The message woke her like a hand on an electric fence. *Good morning Ms. reporter, I miss you already.* Their relationship flowed effortlessly from there. One week later, and Millicent had already fallen into the routine that she had been craving.

At work, she spoke to electoral candidates and asked them questions for a daily article called *Meet Your Next Representative*. During afternoons she interviewed candidates, asking if they supported the proposal for the new two-million-dollar penitentiary; how they would repair highways damaged by permafrost; how they planned to mitigate—she loved using this word—the affordable-housing crisis. And what about climate change, and creating Yukon-specific species-at-risk legislation? She spent mornings writing the stories. Bryce and Franc fed her some of the questions, but more often they came from a deep dive into back issues of the *Nugget,* which she read in the basement over lunch.

She learned that the Alaska Highway, which ran north out of town, had just been rebuilt four years ago, with a price tag of over 1.5 million dollars. Millicent remembered driving that stretch of road to see Pascal the night they ate ptarmigan. The highway was already damaged, undulating like a roller coaster in several stretches, so much so that she had to slow down to ten kilometres an hour. No candidate seemed to have a good answer for how to move forward, other than digging into government coffers and spending millions again to repair the road, knowing full well that the thawing earth would damage it again.

Millicent spoke to Jakowsky frequently. His PR person, Sunshine, called her every morning to ask if she'd like a five-minute interview. Millicent accepted because it felt wrong to decline a phone call with the premier. It didn't matter what question Millicent asked; Jakowsky found a way to twist his answer into another funding announcement: a new tennis bubble, state-of-the-art MRI machine for the hospital, a new airport runway to accommodate airbuses from Asia.

"We are a rich territory in so many ways, Millicent. When you've got something so rich, you just want to share it with the world. Do you know what I mean?"

"Sure," Millicent said.

One morning she asked him about GoldPower and why he was being so secretive about his plans for opening the Vista to mining. Jakowsky just laughed.

"Did I say something funny?" Millicent asked.

"I was just thinking that you're becoming like all the other reporters around here, behaving like the official opposition."

Millicent imagined him smiling condescendingly. A hot jolt of anger ran through her. "I asked you a simple question and readers deserve an answer."

"Well, Millicent, I'll tell you what I've been telling the other reporters. Politics doesn't work on your timeline. Our job is to serve the territory, not the media. Our job is to do the most thorough research before making any decisions. That means science. That means economic forecasting. That means consultations with the people who have been living on this land for thousands of years. I'm not going to make a hasty comment just so you can sell papers."

Millicent had no idea what to say to this, but she knew she needed to respond.

"Well, the people of the Yukon deserve to know before they elect—"

"Thanks so much for your time, Millicent," Jakowsky said, and hung up.

EVERY DAY AT FIVE o'clock she turned her computer off, ran down the stairs and drove to Walmart. Pascal parked in the same spot, at the very back. He would cook: wild game and vegetables she was unfamiliar with—bok choy or okra or radicchio—or whatever was on sale at the Superstore because it was about to spoil. He was careful with his money. After paying for groceries he always looked through his receipt, scanning for errors. He kept all his receipts in an envelope.

"When I sign the contract for the show we will celebrate with lobster and the best French champagne," he said one night, kissing her on the forehead. He smelled of sweat and faintly of wood smoke, even though he hadn't been near a fire. After dinner, Pascal put a pot of water on the stove to wash the dishes. They didn't negotiate the chores; they could communicate what needed to be done with a glance or a touch: she washed, he dried; she swept, he turned off the generator. Millicent couldn't believe how easy it all was. Maybe when a relationship was right, it was always this easy. After the chores were done, they would cuddle in bed, fully clothed. The propane heat didn't reach the bedroom.

One night Pascal showed Millicent clips from the pitch he was working on for the *No Permanent Address* show. With the laptop on her belly, he squeezed his eyes shut and nuzzled his face into her neck, mumbling that he didn't usually show people his work before it was finished, especially not a girlfriend.

Girlfriend.

Millicent ran her fingers through his hair, allowing the word to seep into her bloodstream. *Girlfriend.* In the few clips she saw, Pascal stood somewhere beautiful, on top of the clay cliffs or overlooking Bear Lake. He talked with his hands, explaining the concept of the show. Pascal was right: he was born for the camera. Millicent couldn't put her finger on exactly why, all she knew was she couldn't take her eyes off him, his real-life magnetism was amplified on the screen. He spoke with confidence and charm and a self-deprecating humour. When she craned her neck to look at Pascal watching himself on the screen, she understood how badly he wanted this show. With an eagle-eyed expression, he silently mouthed the words in time with the script.

When the video ended, Pascal closed the laptop and began circling her nipple with his finger. There was no question about sex; there were no nights without it. The act, it seemed, was as vital as food or water. *Look me in the eye*, he said as he entered her, and she did.

Millicent did not sleep on the bus. She told Pascal it was because she wanted to shower before work. The first few nights he begged her to stay, saying she could take a "birdie bath" in the Starbucks bathroom and no one would know the difference. When he realized she wouldn't budge on this, he let it go.

"You are a hero," he would say, half-asleep as she hoisted herself out of the warm nest of entangled limbs and blankets and into the cold night.

A drunk feeling flooded her body once she was on the ice-slicked highway, and the entire night blurred into a single sensory memory: Pascal's tongue, the smell of his skin, a fistful of his hair. She wished the Pit were farther away. She wished she could keep the spell and drive all night. The real reason she didn't sleep on the bus, Millicent realized one night as she catapulted dreamily through the darkness, was Sophie. She wanted to maintain some semblance of balance. She didn't want Sophie to think she was just throwing herself at Pascal. Because she wasn't.

Sophie was always awake when Millicent got home, even on those few occasions when she pulled into the parking lot well past midnight. Sophie would be sitting on the chaise in an oversized T-shirt, picking at her guitar, squinting at a sheet of music. Millicent would come in without interrupting her and flop down, jacket and hat still on, sweltering in the overheated apartment. Eyes closed, she listened to her roommate attempt to play "Zombie." Sophie could never make it to the end without messing up the chords and collapsing in despair.

"You're so close," Millicent would say encouragingly.

"If it isn't the lady of the night, back from the magic school bus," Sophie would reply. She would place the guitar back on its stand.

"Drink?" she offered.

"Please."

They would eat buttered toast and drink tea with whiskey in one of their beds, laughing about their younger selves, recalling how Sophie used to wash her hair with baking soda to save money to buy the best gin; how Millicent phoned a radio show to try to win concert tickets but got so nervous she breathed onto the live airwaves and hung up. Some nights they fell asleep together; other nights one of them would crawl out of the cozy nest and go to her own bed.

One night, a mug of boozy tea balanced on her chest, Sophie turned her head to look at Millicent with serious eyes. "Let me meet him."

"Who?"

"Who do you think?"

"Pascal?"

"He's clearly an important part of your life. That makes him important to me. So, I should meet him. Yes?"

"Yes." Millicent acquiesced. She didn't like thinking about her two worlds colliding. She didn't like wondering what Sophie would say about Pascal afterwards, or what Pascal would say about Sophie. But she knew she had no choice. She could tell by the firmness of her voice that Sophie had made up her mind.

"We'll have him over for dinner. I'll make quiche. Easy," she said, then rolled over on her side to sleep.

13

SAVE A COW, EAT A VEGETARIAN: Those were the words on Franc's bumper sticker. He leaned over and unlocked the door of his 1985 red Toyota Tacoma. Franc didn't make any effort to clear the passenger seat, so Millicent shoved a stack of last week's newspapers into the middle seat and hoisted herself into the truck. The cab smelled like cigarettes, oil and the yeasty tang of Subway. She tried to ignore the slivers of firewood and the dog hair that were ground into the seat fabric, and the feeling that she was invading his personal space—that nobody other than Franc had seen the inside of the truck in a long time.

The ignition coughed and coughed and finally spit into life. Franc yanked his seatbelt over his belly and cleared his throat. Then they both kept their gaze straight ahead. The inside of the windshield was covered in a sheet of ice crystals.

Franc was clearly not in the mood to talk; he rarely seemed to be. He was the first to arrive in the morning and the last to leave at night. It was only at nine o'clock, when he distributed his sticky notes, and later in the production room before the *Nugget* went to print, that he engaged with his staff. The rest of the day he kept to himself. He even carried his boombox to the bathroom so that when he walked across the sprawling newsroom he didn't have to make small talk with her or Bryce. He held the radio on his shoulder, the volume cranked, his gaze fixed on the bathroom door.

The mornings at the *Nugget* went by in a blur. Every day Millicent thought *We're not going to make deadline, there will be no paper today.* But every day at noon the alarm blared as the *Golden Nugget* spat out of the printing press: a small miracle.

The afternoons were the opposite. After the adrenalin high of the morning, the hours stretched on like a hangover. Franc played solitaire with his door shut. Some days Bryce listened to scratchy Aretha Franklin or Sam Cooke albums. Other days he looked up new recipes. Millicent tried to get a start on the *Meet Your Next Representative* article for the following day, deciding what question to ask and which candidate to call, but lately she had been distracted and she found herself staring out the window, wishing time would move faster so she could be with Pascal.

Now, in Franc's truck, Millicent shifted her feet, crinkling a Subway wrapper on the floor. She kept her fists jammed in her pockets to stay warm and her shoulders hunched up to her ears.

"Radio?" Franc asked. She could see his breath as he spoke.

"Sure."

The vents blew out cold air. Millicent looked at the ice scraper on the cab floor.

"Do you want me to scrape the wind—"

"Nah," Franc interrupted. He pounded his fist on the dashboard, trying to get the heat going. "She'll melt."

Millicent wondered if Bryce had told him about Pascal, that she had spent the night with her interview subject. That sickening thought made the silence feel even thicker.

Franc turned up the radio. Full of static, a classical tune was playing on CBC. Franc took a cigarette from the pack in his jacket pocket and slipped it between his lips. He twisted around to reach into the back seat for a jumbo pack of matches.

It was 9:50. This was getting ridiculous. They only had ten minutes to get to Charlie's smudge for the caribou, then she still had to write the article by deadline. Millicent knew Franc and Charlie were old friends, but she was still surprised that Franc wanted her to come to the ceremony, let alone drive her there in his truck. He never came out to press conferences—never left his office, for that matter—never seemed to care about anything aside from a story's word count. Would it fill the page? Would they need to scramble for more copy? Millicent knew he cared, though. It was there in the way he grumbled at the radio when politics came on the news, the way he stood at his window for long stretches in the afternoon, staring out at the Yukon River and jingling the change in his pockets.

The song on the radio reached its crescendo. Millicent wondered what the smudge would be like, if she would finally get a real interview with Charlie. She had called him a handful of times, but he was never in the office and he never called her back. Compared to Jakowsky's carefully crafted funding announcements and all the pictures of him cutting a ribbon or hugging a child, Charlie's voice was being quietly tuned out. Franc never wanted to print the pictures of Jakowsky, but come deadline there was always a gaping hole to fill on page seven or eight and nothing else to fill it with.

Millicent looked out the window. The broad bellies of mountains slid by. The leaves had turned honey-yellow, softening the land. Franc turned the radio off and cleared his throat. His jawline glistened with sweat. "Old piece of shit," he mumbled, tugging off the sleeve of his jacket. "Either the Arctic in here or fucking Miami. Take the wheel?" he asked.

"Me?"

"No, I was talking to the other reporter," Franc said with a grin, showing his yellow teeth. Millicent leaned over the middle seat and clutched the steering wheel. Franc tossed his jacket in the back seat and took the wheel. He smelled like he hadn't showered.

"Why are you coming out to the smudge?"

Franc kept his eyes on the highway and didn't answer. He must have heard her.

"Franc?"

"The trapline's out in the Vista," he said.

"Right, Bryce told me that you used to go out there every winter with Charlie."

He turned off the highway and onto a steep, narrow dirt road.

"Used to spend months out at the trapline before I got stuck in the office. Martens, rabbits, beavers, weasels, lynx, you name it, we got it. One year I even got a wolverine. I thought I was hallucinating. But there it was, right there in the trap."

"Oh yeah?"

"I slung it over my back, his head right up against my ass. The thing weighed a ton. After a couple steps I thought I felt it moving a bit, breathing or something. Hard to explain, I just felt its spirit."

Millicent had never heard Franc talk this much, especially about something other than work. She knew that if she spoke too soon she would break the spell.

"I remember crunching through that hard snow. When I got closer to the cabin, I could see the lights on, I knew that Charlie was inside and I thought, this is it. Never going to see my best friend again. This motherfucker is going to wake up and kill me right here. Never been so scared in my life."

"So did you make it back to the cabin, was it dead?" Millicent asked.

A dry laugh came out of Franc's mouth. "Yup. But the bush does that to you after so long. Sharpens your senses. Turns you into an animal. It was probably still alive, taking its last breath right there on my back before I got to the cabin. Still haunts me."

The road narrowed. Spruce boughs thwacked against the side windows as the truck bounced over ruts. Millicent clutched the handle above her door.

"Have you seen the caribou migration then?"

Franc swallowed.

"Never there at the right time of year. Gwich'in say we can't understand the land until we understand the caribou. It was Charlie's grandparents' trapline, you know," Franc said, glancing at Millicent then back at the potholed road.

"Still to this day I don't understand why Charlie took me under his wing, some wide-eyed white guy. He taught me everything I know."

Dozens of vehicles were jammed at the lip of the river, bumper to bumper. A trail of smoke arched above the tree-line and hazed into the sky. Franc stopped the truck, pocketed his keys and reached in the back for his jacket. He opened his door an inch but didn't make another move to get out.

"That piece about the filmmaker who lives in a bus," he said.

Millicent's palms immediately became hot.

"You mean Pascal?" she said.

"Yes."

She told herself to breathe. Bryce must have told him. He must have.

"Oh. Well. It's an interesting story, what happened with Pascal. I don't know quite how to explain it ..." Millicent started to say, but Franc interrupted.

"What you do on your time off is none of my business. All I wanted to tell you is it was a good story. You're a good writer."

Millicent swallowed, her cheeks burning. "Thank you."

Franc looked out the windshield.

"With these politicians, even Charlie, you gotta be brave," he said. "Ask the questions you want to ask. They're trying to keep to a script and you're trying to get them off of it. Be bold. Shock them. That's when the truth happens."

DOZENS OF PEOPLE HUDDLED around the fire. Some had wool blankets draped over their shoulders to stay warm. Toddlers straddled their parents' heads. Others stood alone, waiting for Charlie to start speaking. The sun fought through the morning mist, the warmth leaking through the thin clouds, yellow as egg yolk.

Sophie and a group of campaigners were there passing out paper cups, orange campaign T-shirts stretched over their winter jackets. A few of the campaigners were Gwich'in, but most where young white women like Sophie, with trendy bottlecap glasses and long, straight hair coming out of their toques. One of them poured water from a jug into each cup. Sophie had told Millicent about this: first there would be a water ceremony and then a smudge with sage.

Charlie moved into the centre of the group. He wore the same faded jeans and cowboy hat as he had last time Millicent saw him. He began to speak. He talked about life out in the Vista. He'd been born out there, in a tent right on the shore of Duo Lakes. When he was a kid, the water was chock full of grayling. You could catch them with your eyes closed.

Millicent looked at Franc. He stood with hands clasped at the waist, eyes fixed on the fire. The bowl of smoking sage was passed around. When it reached Millicent, she washed herself in the smoke; first her head, then her eyes, ears and mouth, and finally her heart, just like Sophie had taught her. She passed the bowl to Franc, who kept his eyes closed as he swept the smoke around his face, his lips curved in a faint smile.

"The caribou come like a stampede down the valley when they're migrating," Charlie was saying. "Usually early in the morning when the mist is still coming up off the river. At first you can't take your eyes off them. All you can do is open up your tent and watch the caribou run, sometimes right through camp, feeling like a damn lucky fool. They come like a river, swallow you up. Thousands of them at once. You gotta just let yourself get swept up in it, you know? They come through for hours, until the sun is high over the mountains. Eventually you gotta get up and start a fire, and they're still running right by, don't even notice you. Soon you're sitting there with your cup of coffee, watching the land like this is any old morning." Charlie lulled the crowd into a trance with his stories.

AFTER THE SMUDGE, the air hung still and sharp. The heat from the fire licked at the faces of the crowd. The sun burned the morning fog off the water. For the next few minutes, nobody moved from the circle. Some gazed skywards as three ravens played on a thermal above the tree line, wings slicing in thick, clean strokes as if the air were made of construction paper. Others kept their gaze on their feet as if Charlie were still speaking.

Millicent waited until people began to move and the crowd had thinned before she approached Charlie. She slipped her notepad and pen from her pocket.

"Hi Charlie. Got a few minutes to talk? I'd like to ask you some questions for the *Nugget*."

"Every time I open the newspaper some new white kid is writing it," Charlie said with a grin, seemingly amused with himself.

Millicent kicked her boot against the ground. "We met at the newspaper office a few weeks ago. My name is Millicent."

Charlie looked at the sky, watching the ravens play. "Oh yeah, I remember. What can I help you with, Millicent?"

She forced a professional smile. "So the election is just days away. How does it feel knowing you could be Yukon's first Indigenous premier?"

"Don't really care about titles."

"No?"

"I care about integrity. Whether I'm the premier or the man picking up your garbage doesn't really matter, as long as I do what I say and I say what I do. I don't need a university degree for that, wouldn't you agree?"

"Sure," Millicent said, her pen hovering over the blank page. She had 750 words to write by deadline. She could pull some quotes from what he had said in front of the crowd, but what was the story exactly? The Gwich'in want to save the Vista? That was old news. There was more to Charlie than that. She needed depth.

"I want to play devil's advocate here," Millicent said. "Why are you running, if you don't care, as you say, about titles?"

Charlie folded his arms over his chest and looked her in the eye. "I guided in those mountains my entire life.

I could make it through them blindfolded. Can't say the same for Jakowsky. He's never set foot out of his fancy office."

"That's impressive."

"Just living on the land is all it is. We've been doing it for thousands of years."

Millicent knew she had to ask a difficult question. She cleared her throat. "So obviously you're a great advocate for protecting the Vista, but what about your experience in politics?"

Charlie's knees cracked as he squatted to pick a smooth, flat stone from the river's edge. He stood up, and with a flick of the wrist, sent it skipping across the surface of the rushing current.

"How hard can the job be?" he asked, grinning.

Millicent was filled with a sudden rush of confidence. "Tell me then. What do you plan to do about the highways that are being destroyed by melting permafrost? And about the unemployment rate that keeps growing every month. More importantly, what about the homeless population that is literally freezing to death on the streets every winter? If elected, what exactly will you do to address these problems?"

Charlie's expression changed from playful to sombre.

"I care about every single living thing as much as I care about myself. This river. These trees. Those children," he said, pointing at the riverbed, where a Gwich'in boy was giving a girl a piggyback ride. He paused. "Even you, and I don't even know you."

Millicent hurried to capture his words on her notepad.

"Right," she said. "So even though Jakowsky hasn't officially said he's opening the Vista to industrial development,
rumour is he's in bed with GoldPower, and they're going
to build a mine that could employ hundreds of Yukoners,
right in the middle of the caribou's calving grounds."

Charlie looked at his boots.

"Yes."

"What about all those jobs? Don't Yukoners need to work?
This could be the biggest mine Yukon has seen in decades."

He grinned again.

"I don't think Jakowsky's in bed with any Chinese."

"No?"

"I met his wife. She wouldn't have any of that." He
broke into a fit of giggling, then doubled over, trying to
catch his breath. Millicent flipped her notepad shut.

"So really," she said, as Charlie wiped a tear from his
cheek. "What would happen to the caribou if a mine were
built?"

Now he looked as if he had suddenly been transported
somewhere far away. Millicent had to repeat the question.
When she did, he waved a hand dismissively. "How am I
supposed to know? The caribou have been following their
routes forever."

Millicent nodded, repeating his words silently so she
would remember them back at the office.

"Nothing good can come from it," Charlie continued.
"Those caribou are driven mad by mosquitoes. Now
imagine helicopters, drills, cranes—right where calves are
being born!" He kicked at loose pebbles, shaking his head.
"What you don't understand is this: land isn't just rocks and

earth. Everything is connected to the land. Our language, our stories, our sense of space and time." Charlie paused and looked at her intently. "Why am I telling you this?"

Millicent's throat was very dry. "Because I asked you, and it's important for the election that people understand—"

"I don't owe you anything."

"I know that!" she said defensively.

His gaze was hard as stone. "You'll quit next week, and some new white girl will come and ask me the same questions."

Out of the corner of her eye, Millicent saw Sophie watching her from the fire. She took a deep breath and forced herself to press on.

"I just want to give you a fair chance to show your platform, Charlie, like I'm giving all the other candidates."

He held up his hand, as if to stop her. "Ok, I'll tell you everything you want to know. But first, you tell me. Do you know what self-government means?"

"Yes," she said simply, hoping he wouldn't test her.

"Do you?"

"Of course. It's about, well, governing yourselves, like autonomy—"

"All you rich, educated white kids come up to run the territory, but you haven't been educated, have you?"

Charlie raised his eyebrows and waited for Millicent to respond. But she had gone mute. He turned around and strolled back towards the fire.

"Write me up good, will you?" he said, looking back. "Got an election to win."

14

PASCAL WAS TWENTY MINUTES LATE. The quiche that Sophie had baked sat steaming and golden brown on a tea towel. Sophie didn't ask Millicent and Bryce if they wanted more wine; she just leaned over the kitchen table to top up their glasses, her rings clinking against the bottle as she poured.

Bryce was there to ease any tension, although he was unaware of his role, as was Sophie. When Millicent had asked him the day before if he wanted to come to a dinner party, he accepted without hesitation. He arrived at the door the next evening wearing a stiff-looking jacket with big buttons and carrying a wheel of brie. Once inside, he brushed the fresh snow off his jacket and went immediately to the oven to bake the cheese until it was hot and oozing on the inside.

"That much coverage is a big deal, even for the *Nugget*. You killed it yesterday," Bryce said as he spread the soft cheese onto a cracker. Millicent had written a 2,000-word piece about Charlie that appeared in Friday's paper.

She had phoned his cell—Sophie had gifted her the number—the day after the smudge. Charlie picked up on the first ring. He was fixing the fence on his property but said he had time to talk. Millicent asked if there was anything else he wanted to say about his campaign. It was just a warm-up question, but it was all Charlie needed. He opened up as if he had been waiting for her call all day.

First he told her more about the porcupine caribou. How everyone is out on the land when the herd migrates in the spring and the fall. That when a caribou is killed, every part of it is used. The head is used to make soup. The hooves are boiled down for jelly or made into rattles to hang on hunters' belts. Even the bone marrow is cooked and eaten.

Then he told her about his plan for a homeless shelter where people could finish their high school education on-site. How he would reinvigorate the economy through northern-lights tourism.

"Build a handful of huts with glass roofs and you got the Japanese paying 500 dollars a night, easy," he said.

Millicent had taken everything she learned at the smudge, during their phone call, and through her research into his campaign and pieced it together into a feature with the headline "Yukon's Next Leader?" At first, Franc was worried he would be called out for bias for giving Charlie that much real estate, especially because of their history, but Bryce and Millicent reminded him that Jakowsky was getting much more ink altogether with his daily press releases and all the cheesy photos submitted by his campaign team. It was only fair to put the spotlight on Charlie.

MILLICENT TOOK A SIP of wine and swilled it around in her mouth.

"You really did kill it yesterday," Bryce repeated.

She smiled into her glass. "What about your story about the shortage of pork at the grocery stores? You deserve some praise for that too."

Bryce popped a cracker into his mouth and spoke with his mouth full.

"Someone call the Pulitzer committee!" he said.

"What was the headline? 'Nobody's Bringing Home the Bacon'? I mean, it's one of Franc's finest, you have to admit."

Bryce laughed. Sophie rolled her eyes dramatically.

"But really, Franc did like your story," Bryce said. "He always says the problem with reporters is they work so fast they forget they have a soul, and it leaves the writing flat."

"You're saying Franc thinks I have a soul?" Millicent kept her eyes on her wineglass to hide her pride. "I'm so honoured," she said.

"You should be. Franc doesn't give out compliments—"

"Millicent is a brilliant writer. I've always told her so," Sophie interrupted. "But now we know she's a brilliant reporter too. Charlie called her out on some serious colonialist issues that still exist within our community, and she listened, took it in stride and wrote something for the paper that like, actually really matters."

Sophie's lips were already plum coloured from the wine. She seemed pleased the spotlight was on her now. Sensing this, Bryce turned to her and gave her his full attention.

"You're volunteering for Charlie's campaign team. What do you think's going to happen with all of this?"

"What do I think?" Sophie asked, sitting up straighter. "I think if Jakowsky starts fucking with the Vista, the Gwich'in will make his life very, very ugly."

Bryce frowned. "I don't know. If Jakowsky gets re-elected, first thing he does is break ground, and he'll move so fast nobody will have time to stop him. You don't think they've been planning this for years?"

"Maybe," Sophie said. "But if he does go ahead with this beast of a gold mine that no one wants, he's going to get one hell of a fight. Honestly, Bryce? I wouldn't be surprised if the Gwich'in take him to court for lack of consultation."

Bryce shook his head. "Trust me, some people do want this mine. Many people do. We have to get out of our siloed way of thinking."

Millicent, worried about Pascal, was distracted. She gazed out the kitchen window into the night, waiting for the sound of his diesel engine or the sight of the bus's headlights. It had been storming all day and there must have been at least two feet of new snow on the ground. Maybe the bus had got stuck. Millicent checked her phone for new messages, then forced her attention back to the table.

"What if Jakowsky doesn't win?" she asked.

Sophie downed her wine and held her glass up for emphasis. "Exactly!"

The conversation continued with hypotheticals until Pascal finally arrived, bursting into the apartment without knocking. His pants were covered with grease stains and his beard seemed to have greyed overnight. He stomped snow from his boots and placed them neatly on the floor. He came into the room and kissed Millicent on the top of her head.

"Hello, beautiful," he said, as if she was the only person in the room. Her blood ran through her veins like champagne. Millicent was flooded with an unfamiliar possessive feeling, followed by a sensation of pulling in her chest. She was his. He was hers. Then Pascal leaned down and kissed Sophie on both cheeks.

"This is a French custom," he said. "The kissing."

"Oui, je ne suis pas stupide," Sophie answered with a flawless accent. Millicent always forgot that French was actually her first language.

"Tu parle français!" Pascal said with surprise.

"Mais oui. My mother is from northern Ontario."

They spoke together in rapid French as Pascal settled into the empty chair. They sounded serious for a few minutes but then they burst into laughter. Millicent could pick out a few words but couldn't piece together what they were saying. She looked wryly at Bryce. He shrugged, took a gulp of wine and stood up. He wiped his palms on the front of his pants as if they were wet.

"I'm Bryce," he said, stretching his hand out to Pascal. He took it and whistled.

"You are a refrigerator," he said.

"A what, man? A refrigerator?" Bryce said, laughing.

"I think something got lost in translation," Millicent said, giggling.

"No, no. That's what we say in Quebec. A refrigerator."

Pascal sat down in the chair beside Millicent and put his hand on her thigh. He wore an expression she had never seen. "It means the kind of guy who is hard to move, you know? Once he is around your woman."

Sophie put her head on the table and began laughing. It was a silent laugh that seemed almost hysterical. Her shoulders heaved with quick breaths. Millicent wondered if Sophie was really drunk or if she was putting on a show. She watched her roommate lift her head from the table and wipe a tear from her cheek, waiting to hear Bryce's response. But Bryce was silent, his hand around his glass. The clock on the wall was ticking loudly in the quiet room. Millicent wondered what had happened to the music.

"Bryce is my co-worker, you know that, Pascal," she said warily.

"Yes, I know. I'm not worried about you," Pascal said. "But I could smell love all the way from the parking lot! Now I see who it is between, Bryce and Sophie. I'm just saying, he'll be hard to move. A refrigerator."

Bryce choked out a laugh. "That's a bit of a stretch, man." Millicent felt a stab of disappointment that Pascal wasn't jealous.

"Is it?" Pascal asked.

Sophie glanced at Bryce and smirked. "Why do we insist that every male-female relationship has to be sexual?" she asked. "It's a bit juvenile, isn't it? Haven't we evolved past that?" She went to the fridge and took out a salad, which she placed on the table with a pair of serving spoons. Then she took the quiche out of the oven where it was keeping warm and put it on the table as well.

"Pascal, would you like to serve the salad?" she asked.

Pascal leaned forward and dug into the bowl with the wooden spoons.

"I just tell the truth," he said in answer to her question. Then he put salad on everyone's plate, a mixture of spinach, strawberries and roasted pecans.

"So who will you be voting for, Pascal?" Sophie asked.

"This salad is beautiful. Thank you, Sophia."

"It's Sophie, but thank you."

"Sophie," he said, locking eyes with her. "I will remember."

"Can you vote, living as you do?"

"I don't believe in politics," Pascal said.

"No?" Sophie asked, looking mildly shocked.

"I don't believe in the system," he said, glancing at Millicent as if seeking her support. She stared down at her plate. She still hadn't lifted her fork.

"The system?"

"Politicians are corrupt."

"All of them?"

"Of course not all of them," Millicent said.

"I was asking Pascal," Sophie said.

"I would rather spend my time with pure people," Pascal said.

"Is Millicent pure?"

His hand slid up her smooth tights.

"Millie is pure. This is what I love about her."

"Did you know Pascal is a filmmaker?" Millicent said. "He's about to sign a contract for his own TV show." His hand moved higher up her thigh.

"In the show, Pascal travels around in his bus, meeting other Québécois people who do, like, cool things."

With one hand still on her thigh, Pascal dug his fork into the salad and began to eat. Millicent ignored her own dish as she watched his square jaw working as he chewed. She didn't actually understand his TV show, she realized. Pascal smiled at her and squeezed her thigh. She smiled back and gulped down some wine to drown out her racing thoughts. Sophie put down her fork and addressed Pascal again.

"Not to be rude, Pascal, but you not voting *is* a problem."

"Why is that?" he asked.

"Everyone thinks Oh, no big deal, they're just not going to vote, but this kind of fucking apathy is why democracy fails so often," Sophie said.

Bryce gave a forced laugh. "Sophie, give him a break. The man didn't come here to debate the political system."

Sophie leaned forward, waving her fork. "Give him a break? Jakowsky will get elected again and fuck us all over, and then Pascal will be the one asking what happened."

"I'm just saying it's not a crime to choose not to vote," Bryce said.

"Would anyone like more wine?" Pascal offered.

"Please," Millicent and Sophie said in unison. There was a moment of silence while Pascal refilled their glasses.

"What do your parents do for work, Sophie?" he asked.

"My mother is a receptionist at a company that makes orthotics," Sophie said, her voice flat.

"Oh, yes? I will admit I don't know what orthotics is, but it sounds fascinating," Pascal said. Then he switched to French, enclosing himself and Sophie in a private conversation bubble. As they rattled on in their native tongue, Sophie inspected a lipstick stain on the rim of her wineglass. Millicent observed that there was something about Pascal that changed when he spoke in French, as if he had been holding his breath and could finally exhale. Sophie smiled at something he was saying. Millicent knew that her friend would prefer to remain stoic in her argument about democracy and responsibility. But Pascal could get around anyone.

Now he pushed his chair back and stood up.

"I need to turn on the propane in the bus," he said, sounding stilted now that he had reverted to English.

"Right now?" Millicent asked.

"Yes. My herbs will freeze. You know this."

He kissed her head again.

"Give me ten minutes," he said.

Sophie picked up the empty plates, put them in the sink and turned on the faucet.

"If you wash, I'll dry," Bryce offered.

Sophie squeezed detergent into the sink and was soon up to her elbows in soap. Bryce hovered nearby, armed with a towel. Millicent pulled the broom out of the closet. For a few minutes nobody spoke, and the half-drunk silence lay like a wet blanket over the kitchen.

At last Millicent said, "Don't you think you were a little harsh, Soph?"

Sophie twisted her neck to look at her and smiled, her eyes shining.

"No, not really."

Why was she being so playful? Millicent wondered. Was she that drunk?

Millicent swept the floor with quick, hard strokes. Maybe Sophie hadn't evolved since university after all, at least not as much as she claimed she had. Maybe she was the same person she had always been, out for the thrill of it all.

"C'mon," Millicent persisted.

"What?"

"You don't even know him, and you tried to burn him at the stake over the election. There's more to life than politics. Pascal is interested in other things." Millicent paused. "He's an artist."

Sophie scrubbed a pan energetically but said nothing. Bryce wiped down the stove with a wet cloth.

"But you've got to admit the man's got a great beard," he said. Sophie dried her hands on her dress. "Let's all sit down, okay?"

She pulled her chair out and sat, her hands clasped, ready to give her speech. Bryce sat down across from her. Millicent leaned against the stove, broom in her hand.

"Yes, I was riled up about the election. Maybe too riled up," Sophie conceded. "But Millicent, you deserve the best."

Millicent felt her chest tighten. Why did Sophie think she could have her all to herself?

"You were the one who wanted to have this dinner!" she accused her.

Sophie's tone was diplomatic. "I'm glad we had this dinner. I wanted to get to know Pascal."

Millicent ignored the burning lump in her throat. She knew if she allowed herself to let go, she would lose control.

"What do you think of him, really?" she asked.

In the parking lot, the generator sprang into life. They listened to the sound for a moment. Pascal would be back soon.

"Like I said, you deserve the best, Mill."

Pascal returned just as Sophie and Bryce were setting up a game of cribbage in the living room. They asked Millicent if she wanted to join them, but she said she had to go get her laundry.

Millicent asked Pascal to come with her. The laundry room was on the far side of the apartment complex. It was a damp room that reeked of weed. The washer and dryer, which looked like they were from the 1950s, took two quarters each. There was also a rickety table and a broken pinball machine. The bare light bulb that hung from the ceiling had burnt out, so Millicent had asked Pascal to bring a spare bulb. He had also brought his head-lamp, which he aimed at the ceiling while he stood on the table to replace the bulb.

What a relief it was to be alone together. They were at their best when they were alone. No one else could know the inside of a relationship, Millicent reflected, its tender, beautiful parts. She took her clothes out from the ancient dryer and began folding items on the table. Pascal dedicated himself to folding her socks and underwear.

"Spend the night with me," he said.

Millicent searched his eyes. The light was too dim to make out his pupils.

"Don't you think we should go back to the apartment? Sophie wanted us to play crib," Millicent said.

"You know they want to be alone."

"I really don't think so—"

"We want to be alone."

Pascal folded her underwear into perfect little squares, like cocktail napkins. "Are you scared of me?"

Millicent forced a teasing tone into her voice. "Should I be scared?"

He drew her in, kissed her forehead for what seemed like the hundredth time that night. "Of course not. You're my Little Rabbit."

Outside, Bryce's Ford was blanketed in snow. The subtle roar from the highway and the river were snuffed out by the falling snow. Millicent had never heard this kind of quiet; it was both peaceful and unnerving. She thought about taking her laundry back to the apartment, but she fell into step with Pascal as they trudged through the parking lot towards the bus. He carried the laundry basket as she walked with her head down and her bare hands stuffed into her jacket pockets. When they got to the bus, she turned around to look back at the warm glow of light coming from the apartment window. Then they entered the bus and pulled the door shut.

15

MOMENTUM IS DELIRIOUS. Once Millicent started sleeping in the bus she couldn't stop.

She kept a toothbrush in a jar by the kitchen sink and jiggled a window open to spit, the blue hue from the Walmart sign lighting up the parking lot.

"Good night, Little Rabbit," Pascal said before turning to face the wall.

"Why do you call me that?" she asked one night, her lips on his spine.

"I don't know. You are cute. Like a little rabbit," he mumbled before falling asleep.

In the morning, Millicent would drive back to the apartment, shower, shove a piece of toast in her mouth and gulp down a cup of lukewarm coffee from Sophie's Bodum.

Sophie left notes for Millicent on the kitchen table. In her neat cursive writing, they might read *There are leftovers you can eat in the fridge*; or *The hot water has gone bananas, don't even try showering*; or one day, simply *I miss you, Milli Vanilli*. Millicent made sure to scribble something back. *Thank you. I'll see you soon. I can't believe we keep missing each other!*

It wasn't that she timed her arrival for after Sophie had left for work, but it always seemed to end up that way, and when Millicent entered the apartment and Sophie wasn't there, she felt relieved. She wasn't avoiding Sophie. But with the election so close, she was working like crazy, and it was just easier to be in separate orbits. She wasn't even mad about the dinner party, she had decided. Sophie was just being Sophie, and she was entitled to her opinion.

At least, this was what Millicent told herself as she got back onto the Alaska Highway, a piece of toast wrapped in a napkin on her lap. She had to drive 120 all the way in order to make it to the *Nugget* on time. She didn't want Franc phoning to tell her it was 9:05 and he had a paper to fill, and was she planning on coming in to work?

On the morning of the election Millicent didn't bother going back home first. Conversations from the newsroom looped through her head as she pulled tights up over her hips in the bedroom of the bus. Maybe Charlie would actually win. Franc was coming around to the idea since Jakowsky hadn't budged on his secrecy about the Vista.

"Voters will see right through him, won't they?" he said, talking to himself. Although he was staring out at the newsroom, Millicent and Bryce knew he wasn't even aware of them.

Now that election day had finally arrived, Millicent grasped the point whose historic significance she had not fully understood before: by the end of the evening, an Indigenous person might very well be premier—something that hadn't happened anywhere in the country, let alone the Yukon. History was taking place today. And she was part of it.

She applied deodorant to her hot armpits, barely aware of Pascal as he leaned against the door, holding a cup of tea and watching her. Millicent put the bottle back on the shelf where Pascal kept it.

"If Charlie wins, I could be in the newsroom all night," she said. Pascal set his tea down and wrapped his arms around her waist from behind. He held her and whispered something in her ear.

"What did you say?" Millicent asked, smiling.

"Don't get swept up in the game," he said.

She turned around to face him. "What game?"

"You and I are better than this."

"What are you talking about?"

Pascal pressed his finger into the centre of her forehead. "Everything going on in here," he said.

"My brain?" Millicent toyed with a button on his shirt, still smiling, but Pascal looked serious.

"What's important is what's going on in here," he said, pressing his palm against her chest, over her heart. "We are artists."

LATER THAT NIGHT, AFTER the polls had closed and Charlie's gathering had died down, Millicent stood in the parking lot of the hotel looking at the sea of cars, trying to remember where she had parked. In a daze, she walked through the dirty packed snow, clutching her keys tightly in her mitten. She located the Mazda and drove across town to the *Nugget*.

She unlocked the door to the building and climbed the stairs without turning on the lights. Charlie's party lost by one seat. Thirty-six votes. How could the fate of the territory be determined by thirty-six votes? She typed quickly, bathed in the blue light of her monitor, trying not to think about Charlie's team gathering, the bannock and the rosehip jelly that had melted in her mouth, the Elders jigging on the dance floor to live fiddle music, Charlie's beaded buckskin vest. And how, after the results came in, she found him slouched over in a plastic folding chair, holding a Styrofoam cup full of coffee.

"Are you okay?" she asked him. "How are you feeling?"

They were stupid words, but it was all she could think of.

He looked at the floor. "Like I got shot in the heart."

She used the quote. She had to.

WHEN MILLICENT FINISHED THE story, she turned off her computer and sat in the dark, listening to the sound of her heartbeat. She couldn't believe how close Charlie had come to winning, and how it didn't matter. It was of no consequence that Charlie's party had lost by only thirty-six votes; it might as well have been a thousand. With Jakowsky securing his second term, he would finally make the announcement about his partnership with GoldPower. She wouldn't be surprised if

GoldPower began breaking ground in the Vista as soon as the earth thawed in spring, maybe even sooner. Staring out the window at the flickering, fluorescent *Liquor 4 Less* sign across Fourth Avenue, Millicent wondered if Sophie was right, if the Gwich'in would take the government to court. But on what grounds? Lack of consultation? She doubted Jakowsky's government would be so sloppy as to not carry out thorough consultations. They would have predicted potential court cases and done everything in their power to avoid them.

Her phone beeped, shattering her daze. The message was from Bryce, who had been covering Jakowsky's shindig at the conference centre on the other side of town. *We're at the Mad Hatter*, Bryce wrote. *Come.*

IT WAS WEDNESDAY, KARAOKE NIGHT. The stage was empty. A DJ with grey hair and purple jeans who called himself the Northern Fox was coaxing a table of young girls to get on stage.

"C'mon ladies," he purred into the microphone. "Who wants to sing some Mariah Carey for this old fox?"

They shrieked and shook their heads.

Millicent ordered an IPA at the bar, then found the booth where Bryce and Franc were sitting. Franc was signalling that he wanted another drink. He kept looking around in a goofy way as if he was on the verge of telling a joke. Millicent took a sip of beer and it went straight to her head. She realized that she hadn't eaten anything since morning, and the excitement of the day had numbed her hunger. Now it was all over. *Like I got shot in the heart.*

"Well, I guess that's over and done with," Millicent said.

Bryce was flipping through the photos on his SLR, frowning. "You should have seen Jakowsky when they made the announcement. He dipped his wife and kissed her like they were on their honeymoon."

Millicent craned her neck to see Bryce's screen. "The man knows how to pose for the camera, I'll give him that."

"I refused to capture it," he said. "It's theatrics. I want real politics, sweat and anger. This is not a family-portrait session."

The server placed a boilermaker in front of Franc. He downed the shot of whiskey, took a chug of his pint and wiped the foam from his lip with the heel of his hand.

Bryce looked up from his camera. "You okay, man?"

"Better than ever, my dear Bryce!" Franc said, putting on a Scottish accent. He slapped Bryce on the shoulder hard and plucked a chicken wing from the basket in the middle of the table. Hot sauce bled down his hand. He must have sensed that Millicent was watching him because he pushed the basket over, urging her, "Eat, eat." Millicent washed a wing down with a gulp of beer and reached for another.

"You wanna know why Jakowsky won?" Franc said.

Millicent licked her fingers, "Why's that, Franc?"

"Fear. That's how guys like Jakowsky get into office. And no, I'm not allowed to say these things because I'm the editor of a very, very prestigious publication." He slung his arm over Bryce, whose body tensed visibly.

"Have you heard of it? It's called the *Golden Nugget*. Has a nice ring to it, doesn't it? The *Golden Nugget*. You can bet it's not the type of paper that's about to drown in its own debt, because a newspaper—who reads those things anyway?"

Bryce shrugged Franc's arm off gently but firmly. "Should I grab you a glass of water, Franc?"

Millicent lifted her glass and stared in disbelief when she saw it was empty. How had she drunk a whole beer so quickly? She wondered what time it was, if she should go back to the bus. She'd told Pascal she might be at the office till late, but what if he went to find her and she wasn't there? She pushed the thought out of her mind. She had said she might be gone all night. There was nothing for him to worry about.

Franc whistled at the server.

"Are you sure you need another one, man?" Bryce said loudly, but Franc had already launched into a slurred monologue.

"Right-wing tyrants get into power because we're all scared of losing our security, our jobs and houses, our children and wives and husbands. We work hard to convince ourselves we are comfortable, that everything is fine and will remain fine as long as we hold on to a semblance of control. All a politician has to do is tell you his opponent wants to change that. What we don't realize, kiddos, is that we never had it to begin with!"

Bryce was pretending to watch the karaoke. Warming to his subject, Franc focused his attention on Millicent.

"Had what, Franc?" she asked.

Bryce tapped his fingers on the table and inhaled loudly.

"Security! It's a fallacy! Your house could burn to the ground, *whoosh*. The job you go to every morning, that could disappear any day." Franc was speaking now with surprising eloquence. "In fact, you can count on it at the *Nugget*. You better believe we're going to be kicked to the curb once these octogenarians all die and there's nobody left to buy newspapers."

His monologue finished, Franc sat staring into his drink. On stage, a man dressed in a white suit with rhinestones cooed into the microphone. He was singing "Don't Be Cruel" with his eyes closed, his fist wrapped around the mic, transported elsewhere. With his sideburns and sunglasses, he looked unnervingly like the real celebrity.

The door to the kitchen swung open and a server yelled out that it was last call. Bryce sat motionless. Franc had heaved himself out of the booth. Now he was swaying between the tables towards the bar.

"Oh fuck," Bryce whispered.

When the bell rang, Elvis stopped singing. A group of construction workers cheered and pounded their fists on the table. Franc kept ringing the bell, hard, until the man behind the bar grabbed his wrist gently, with sympathy, as if this was not the first time Franc had drunk their whiskey or rung their bell. When Bryce put a hand on his back and led him to the door, he didn't resist. Bryce helped him put on his jacket. Someone yelled out, "Coward," but Millicent could tell that he didn't hear it.

She snaked her scarf around her neck and zipped her

jacket over her chin as she waited for Bryce to return so she could say goodbye and leave to join Pascal on the bus. She was overheated in her winter gear, exhausted and half-drunk off a single pint. Millicent leaned her head back against the back of the booth and closed her eyes. She thought about Franc, how bottled-up he was at work. His emotions had to come out somehow. She wondered if, other than Charlie, he had any friends; what it was like at home every night; how lonely he was.

She wondered if she was sober enough to drive.

When Bryce returned, he signalled for another beer. When the server nodded, Millicent looked at Bryce and frowned, confused.

"Last call is just a legal formality," he said, using air quotes. "This bar will take any money they can get."

"Where did you put our boss?" Millicent asked.

"In a taxi. Stay for another with me?"

They had never been alone like this, without work to fall back on. Millicent didn't know if she should stay, but her hands automatically started to uncoil her scarf.

"Do you think he's okay?"

"He'll be back in the office bright-eyed and bushy tailed tomorrow morning."

"But is he okay?"

Bryce looked down at his beer and seemed to think about this. He dipped his finger into the foam and put it in his mouth. When he realized what he was doing, he wedged his hands under his thighs.

"Here's the story," he said.

"What story?" Millicent asked.

"Franc's. You deserve to know."

Taxi lights shone through the bar windows and the cabs honked loudly. Bryce and Millicent instinctively leaned closer together.

"The trapline that Franc used to go to belonged to Charlie's grandparents. Once they died, it was Charlie who took it on. But he never had a family of his own, and it was too much work for just one person." Bryce was choosing his words carefully, as if he was afraid of saying too much. "Now, what you need to know about Franc," he continued, "is he was one of those twenty-five-year-olds who arrived in the Yukon all keen and excited, thirsty to trap and fish and live off the land. He probably read Thoreau."

Millicent could hear him more clearly now that the bar was emptying, but neither of them moved out from their huddle.

"Like you?" she said, teasing.

Bryce blushed. "Sure." After thinking for a moment, he added, "Well, I've never actually read *Walden*."

"But you moved here for the promise of a simpler life."

"Yes," Bryce agreed. "Although, no matter how many birds I can hear singing from my cabin in the morning, covering daily news at the *Nugget* doesn't really allow for a simple life. The world is too fucked for that."

"Agreed," Millicent said.

"Anyway, believe it or not, Franc met Charlie right here at the Mad Hatter one night. It was just a few days after Charlie's grandfather had died. They started talking and they got along like long-lost brothers. That's what Franc always said. I don't know what it was, exactly. They both had a similar dry personality and they appreciated each other, you know? Anyway, Charlie took Franc out to the trapline and taught him everything."

"Like what?" Millicent asked.

"Where to find the secret berry spots, how to kill and dress a caribou, how to eddy out in a canoe, everything," Bryce repeated.

They were the only ones left in the bar. Now that Bryce had started talking about Franc, he couldn't stop.

"Listen to this. It's nuts. In the seventies, Franc was out in the Vista for two years straight. I don't even think Charlie was there, just Franc and all this land. Didn't see another soul for two years. And when he finally came back into town?"

Bryce took a long gulp of beer.

"What?"

"Walked straight into the door at the grocery store, like a bird, and shattered the glass. The whole town was talking about it. They called him Bushed Franc."

Millicent smiled and dipped her finger absentmindedly into the hot pool of melted candle wax, trying to imagine a younger Franc, fresh from years in the bush. What would he have looked like?

"Did you think he was going to win?" she asked. "Charlie?"

Staring at the exit sign over the front door, Bryce looked lost in thought.

"Bryce?"

"You don't know how many years it took Franc to convince Charlie to run," he said.

"Why didn't Franc just run himself?"

"It's a good question. I bet a younger Franc would have. But now? I don't know. Feels like the older we get, the less brave we become."

Suddenly, Bryce's gaze shot to the entrance of the bar. He shoved his arm through the sleeve of his parka before Millicent understood what was happening.

Pascal had come in. Down jacket, pajama bottoms, work boots. He didn't move towards their table, just stood there in the entranceway with the door wide open, letting the cold air sweep into the bar. The bus could be heard idling in the street.

The throaty engine. Her body reacted on instinct. Mumbling goodbye to Bryce, she slid out of the booth, her scarf still clutched in her hand, and ran over to the entrance. Pascal held the door open for her, then followed her out into the night.

THE MOON HUNG BLOATED in the sky. Pascal's bed lay parallel to the window like a train berth. Millicent watched Second Avenue slide by, the yellow arches of McDonald's, the dark snake of the river, an empty parking lot. She wished the Walmart parking lot were farther away, that Pascal would drive through the night and she could remain still like this, cocooned underneath the blanket, numbing out the evening.

She rolled onto her side and wiped the fogged-up window with her palm. The light from the moon painted the bedroom a milky hue. Millicent burrowed deeper into the flannel sheets, pulling the comforter over her head to trap the heat. Pascal had been keeping the propane heat on low to save money.

Why had she just left the bar like that? She didn't even say goodbye to Bryce, just got up from the booth and followed Pascal onto the bus, driven by an urgency in her body she did not understand and could not control.

The bus lurched to a stop. Millicent listened to Pascal's footsteps, the buzz of his electric toothbrush, the clank of clothes hangers. The excitement of the election had deadened inside of her. It was as if the whole night had never even happened, as if she hadn't left the bus that morning.

"Rabbit?"

She lay completely still. Her breath expanded her lungs, waiting to be released.

"Where's my Rabbit?" Pacal said, lying down over top of her.

The smell of him was diesel and Old Spice. He didn't put his entire weight on her. She could feel that he was on his forearms, that he didn't want to hurt her. He peeled the comforter from her face. Millicent blinked. A familiar yellow hue poured through the bedroom window. The streetlight buzzed. They were in the regular spot, next to the growing mountain of dirty snow that plows added to every morning.

He kissed her on the forehead.

"Are you going to sleep like this? Wearing your jacket?" He tugged at her scarf, grinning, trying to tease her open.

She rose, stripped to her underwear and brushed her teeth while he waited for her in bed, reading the first page of *One Hundred Years of Solitude*. She had never seen him touch any of the books on the shelf before. Why was he doing it now? Was this some sort of gesture? Millicent jiggled the window open and spat the toothpaste onto the snowbank. When she climbed back under the comforter, he slipped a bookmark between the pages of the novel and closed it. Then he turned off the light and spooned her. His breath was steady in her ear. Pascal combed his fingers through her hair, working out the tangled bits.

"Why didn't you call?" he asked.

Millicent tensed. She tried to wiggle away from him but he had his arm tight around her like a seatbelt. She spoke to the wall.

"I told you I was going to work late."

"You need to call me."

"I was working, Pascal. You know it was election night."

"You need to call me so I know you are safe. It is so simple. We are partners."

She felt as if a wasp was stinging deep in her throat. Maybe he was right, she thought, allowing herself to relax into his body, to forgive. She should have called. It would have been easy. He was her boyfriend, after all. What was she running away from? Millicent turned over to face him, her lips a breath away from his.

Her words came out wooden. "I'm sorry."

With that, Pascal tugged off her underwear, climbed on top and filled her. He kissed each eyelid, then pushed himself deeper until the entire night was erased. It was pleasure, pleasure on the border of pain.

"I'm the wolf," he whispered hotly in her ear. "I'm the wolf. You're the rabbit."

16

DECEMBER 1, MIDAFTERNOON, HER BIRTHDAY. With no clouds as insulation, the air outside had the cold precision of a blade slicing through skin during the half-second before blood pools to the surface of the cut. The thermometer read −30. With a wind chill it was likely closer to −40. The living room window rattled every time the wind roared through the valley. Outside, the land had vanished, swallowed by the black whale of night.

Millicent was not allowed to help in the kitchen because it was her birthday; Sophie had decreed it and she had not resisted. Lying on the couch, her head propped up on two cushions, Millicent took a sip of Moët & Chandon Grand Vintage Rosé, savouring the sweetness. As soon as the alcohol entered her bloodstream, a wave of exhaustion hit her. When was the last time she had sat down and done … nothing? She realized she hadn't felt the sun on her skin in weeks. She couldn't even remember the last time she slept in this apartment.

Millicent balanced the champagne glass on her chest with her hand, staring at the steady stream of rising bubbles and listening to the clatter of Sophie and Bryce baking a chocolate clementine cake in the kitchen. It was a relief to be back home, to be off the bus, where heat existed only in small pockets, where Pascal insisted every single item had its place, like a museum. *Cleanliness is godliness*, he kept saying like a child who just learned a new phrase. Now that she was back in the comfortable mess of the apartment, Millicent realized how careful she had to be on the bus. She had the sense that if she accidently bumped into the kitchen table or his work desk it would ruin the entire feng shui that Pascal had worked so hard to create.

One evening after post-dinner sex, Millicent rolled over and tried to jiggle one of the windows open a crack. A tiny piece of the latch snapped off in her hand.

"Whoops," Millicent said. "It appears that latch was made of LEGO."

Pascal looked over and grimaced.

"Sorry," she said, placing the piece of plastic on Pascal's bare chest.

"It's okay."

"Is it?"

"These little pieces of hardware are actually very expensive."

"Oh, I didn't know."

When Pascal didn't reply, she said, "I can pay for it."

Pascal sat up, opened the cupboard door and took out his fleece jacket. He unzipped one of the pockets and put the piece of plastic inside for safekeeping.

"It's not the money I am worried about," he said as he lay back down. "It's the time to fix it. My time is very important. But this is a sacrifice I must make for having a Little Rabbit around the bus," he said, smiling. "A clumsy Little Rabbit."

MILLICENT TOOK ANOTHER SIP of champagne, feeling each individual bubble fizzle on her tongue. Bryce had brought the bottle as a gift. He arrived early to help Sophie bake the cake. They boiled whole clementines in water, melted baker's chocolate with butter and beat the thick batter with a wooden spoon. The secret, Bryce explained, was pure vanilla. He'd bought it in Mexico City. Vanilla you buy at the Superstore, he said, is not real vanilla. It's all in the origin of the beans.

When Millicent uncorked the champagne, the froth volcanoed over the lip. Sophie and Bryce gathered in close and chanted "Drink, drink, drink, it's your birthday!" After Millicent had the first swallow she felt a warmth spread from the centre of her chest up to her throat. Sophie slung her arm around Millicent's shoulder, then leaned in to kiss her on the cheek.

Throwing a birthday party seemed to give Sophie a sense of purpose. She had been in a slump ever since Charlie lost the election. Whenever Millicent dropped by the apartment for clean clothes or to get her vegetables from the fridge before they spoiled, Sophie was soaking in a lukewarm bath. When she heard Millicent come in the door, she would yell "Come see me!" Millicent would push open the bathroom door and there she was, listening to a podcast with her arms draped over the edge of the clawfoot tub, her eyelids closed, her breasts like low-lying islands in the water. Millicent would sit cross-legged on the tile floor for a few minutes, taking deep breaths of the warm, humid air, and learn about the plight of the bumblebees, or how to rewire your brain for optimal happiness, until she knew Pascal would be worrying about her.

The truth was, Millicent realized this evening as she lay back in her black-and-white polka-dot dress: it wasn't just that Sophie needed her. She needed Sophie too. The days were stretching out in a dark, disorienting way that made Millicent feel lonely; even at night on the bus, after sex and before falling asleep, when her cheek was pressed so firmly against Pascal's chest that she could hardly breathe—there it was.

Looking out the living room window now, Millicent watched as Pascal doused wooden pallets with a jerry can of gasoline. He was the only one brave enough to be outside. He had assigned himself the task of building a bonfire out back. She had not asked him to do this. He had come over early too, and there was nothing he could help with so he'd driven into town to find old packing pallets.

Millicent pressed her hand against the icy glass and watched him place the gas can a safe distance from the pallets. He moved in the dark like a fox, barely visible. Pascal lit a match and jumped back. For the flash of a moment there was a *whoosh* of orange that lit up the entire property.

The smell of warm chocolate and orange spilled from the oven and seeped through the apartment. Suddenly, Millicent missed her mother deeply, missed the way she used to bake a giant blueberry muffin in a cereal bowl on her birthday. She would bring it to Millicent in bed with a single candle. It was the only day of the year when her mother mustered enough energy to behave like she was healthy. She even took off her nightgown and washed her hair. Then Millicent saw how beautiful her mother was. It wasn't just her body, scrubbed clean of weeks of feverish sweat, but the way she sang so slowly and peacefully, as if she were the last person left on earth who remembered: There is no rush. There is never any rush.

The last phone conversation Millicent had with her mother had lasted ten minutes. She had told her nothing about Pascal. All she wanted to do was hang up and join him in bed. She felt that if she waited one more second she might explode. That had been weeks ago now. Millicent had been avoiding her mother's calls since then, deleting her voice mails without listening to them, promising herself she would call her back the following night, and then the next, until the guilt hardened into a pit inside her stomach.

Millicent downed the rest of her champagne and went to the kitchen to refill her glass. Sophie was wearing a gold sequined dress that hugged her small frame.

"Birthday girl! Your glass cannot be empty. That's the only rule."

"Hey, it's *my* birthday," Millicent said.

Sophie smiled. Her lips tonight were a fire-engine red that Millicent hadn't seen her wear since university.

"That does not mean you get to make the rules," Sophie said.

She filled Millicent's glass a millimetre from over-flowing, then opened the oven door a crack to check on the cake, the heat fogging up her glasses. Sophie rummaged blindly in the cutlery drawer to find a wooden chopstick, then crouched in front of the oven and wrestled the metal rack towards her, her short dress rising up the back of her thighs.

"Fuck," she muttered.

"Here." Bryce slipped the glasses off her nose as she pricked the cake with the chopstick. He rubbed the lenses with his sweater, then lifted them to eye level to inspect his work. He handed the glasses back and admired the cake.

"It's beautiful," he said.

Sophie looked up at him, beaming.

"Help me blow up the balloons?" she asked, leading him to her bedroom before he had a chance to answer.

Pascal came in, bringing a billow of cold air. He still wore his headlamp, and the beam was shining directly in Millicent's eyes.

"Babe," she said, holding her hand up to her eyes. She had started calling him *babe* as a joke, but it had turned into a serious pet name without her noticing.

"What?"

"The light!"

Pascal clicked off his headlamp. His eyelashes were

frozen white. He looked out at the bonfire with his hands on his hips, satisfied.

"That will keep us warm all night." With his jacket and work gloves still on, he poured himself the last of the champagne and raised his flute to Millicent.

"Chin-chin," he said, looking at his glass, and then at the door. "I guess the bus will be staying here tonight."

A burst of laughter erupted from Sophie's room. Pascal raised his eyebrows suggestively and motioned for Millicent to sit with him on the couch. She leaned in to kiss his cold stubble.

Pascal took off his gloves and set them neatly on the couch beside him.

"I have a present for you."

"You didn't have to."

"Of course I did." Pascal's eyes were sharp. The gift was simple, he explained.

"You will be part of my TV show. I've already written you into the proposal and the budget and given you a wage. You will come to meetings, be part of pre- and post-production, the filming, everything!"

Pascal was vibrating with excitement. She had never seen him this happy.

"Wow," Millicent said.

"And you know what this means? You can quit your job, stop paying all of this rent. You can move onto the bus and do what you actually wanted to do, write poems." Golden balloons drifted along the floor towards his feet as if drawn to his energy. "We will be travelling and filming too, of course. We'll have a film crew with us at all times."

"That's insane!" Millicent was laughing now. She couldn't help herself. This was an absurd birthday present and yet, coming from Pascal, it wasn't surprising at all.

"I actually like my job," she said. "I like going to work. And now you want me to drop everything, move into the bus and just ..." Millicent paused, searching for the right words. "... and just write poems?"

"Rabbit, what I'm saying is, you no longer have to go to work with all those small people with small dreams. I'm handing you an opportunity. Take it."

Millicent tried to soften the look on her face. She knew how serious Pascal was, but how did he expect her to pack her bags, move out of her apartment and star in some fledgling reality TV show on a French network she had never heard of, without even considering all that she would have to give up in the process? Millicent drew her legs up on the couch and looked towards the kitchen. Sophie was carefully releasing the cake from the Bundt pan with a knife. Bryce was standing on the kitchen table in his socks, hanging a bundle of golden balloons from the ceiling fan.

"The producer loved the idea, you know," Pascal said.

"So you spoke with him about me, specifically?" she asked.

"Once the contract is signed, we will get money to film a pilot. This is how the film industry works. The show is going to be big. I can feel it." Pascal paused, then he added, "Things are really starting to roll. Please don't get left behind in this place."

Millicent looked at him steadily and tried to speak in her most diplomatic tone.

"Pascal, does the producer know about this plan?"

"Of course, I emailed him all about it. I sent him your picture too."

"And did he reply?"

Pascal stuffed his fists in his jacket pockets and leaned back deeper into the couch. He looked at her with a mix of love and frustration.

"Yes, he did reply, Millicent. And do you know what he said? That you have the exact right look. That you would be beautiful on camera."

She glanced at her reflection in the window.

"I honestly have no idea what to say about all of this."

Pascal spoke in a soft, shy voice that Millicent had never heard before. "I know, I know," he said. "It is big. I have never asked a girlfriend to do something like this with me."

WHO WERE THESE PEOPLE? Sophie's friends from Charlie's campaign team, and a couple from the coffee shop where she worked. A few women from the advertising department at the *Nugget* who Bryce had invited because he knew the party needed more bodies. She had only herself to blame for this party full of strangers. Did they even know it was her birthday? She had racked her brain for people to invite, but the only one she came up with was Franc, who had grunted something about "popping by," but of course he wouldn't.

Alone in the kitchen, Millicent licked the batter from the wooden mixing spoon. She squinted at the handful of strangers who stood in bean-shape formation in the living room, holding cake on paper napkins and struggling with small talk.

Pascal's idea was insane, Millicent said to herself again, standing to the side of the refrigerator where she could remain unseen but still watch the party. It was not a birthday present, asking her to leave everything she knew to follow *his* dreams. Had he shown her a single email from this producer? And was this producer really interested enough to hand over a wad of cash to Pascal? It all seemed a bit absurd.

Yet the more she drank and the longer she watched the party, the more the idea settled inside her. Wu-wei, she thought, feeling strangely at peace with the idea of leaving this life. Would these people care if she slipped away? Why did she always force her life to stay so small? Two of Sophie's co-workers sat facing each other on the chaise longue, their faces glowing in the warm light of the lamp. Sophie threaded her way through the crowd in her sequined dress. Millicent watched the way she touched guests on the shoulder as she passed by, the way she threw her head back to laugh at a joke. This wasn't even her life, Millicent realized. It was Sophie's life.

BY MIDNIGHT EVERYONE HAD left the party, except for Sophie, Bryce and Pascal.

"I have to go add another pallet to the fire," Pascal announced, unwilling, it seemed, to accept the party was over. He had been in and out of the apartment all evening, deeply committed to his self-appointed job of fire-tender, even though nobody had gathered around it.

"Oh!" Sophie said, leaping up from her seat. "I want to pour the gas! Can I?"

Pascal was already at the door in his winter gear. He waited while Sophie stuffed her stockinged feet into her boots, holding on to the wall for support.

"Well, it does not need any gas at this point, Sophie," he said, pointing out the window at the soaring flames. "Obviously."

Sophie, still struggling with her boots, made a face at Pascal.

"C'mon Pascal, lemme pour just a bit. It'll be cathartic."

"What does that mean?"

Sophie tossed her head and said something in fast French that made Pascal laugh. She joined him and they went out, slamming the door shut. Sophie hadn't even bothered with a jacket.

Millicent and Bryce sat on the living room floor. Bryce was going on again about Franc and Millicent was only half-listening; she was more interested in what was happening outside. It was too dark for her to tell exactly what Sophie and Pascal were doing, but from their shadows it looked like they were chasing each other around the fire. Yes, she realized, they were playing like children.

Bryce continued, the back of his head resting against the couch, his eyes on the stucco ceiling. "He's a fucking vault of knowledge about everything up here. Politics, the land, sports, you name it. And he's just got no one anymore."

Sophie must have doused the fire with gasoline, because Millicent could see the flames grow high from the living room and hear a whoop of delight. Sophie's face, her dress, gleamed in the heat of the fire. She looked maniacal, gleeful, and for a moment, devilish.

"He's just lonely as hell, you know?" Bryce went on. "His wife died years ago. His only real friend is Charlie, and Charlie lives out of town and never comes in unless he has to."

Sophie and Pascal were waving their arms now. She wondered how drunk Sophie was. She must be pretty hammered; it was cold enough to snap the door handle off a car yet she seemed perfectly comfortable with bare arms. And then, as if he had been reading her thoughts, Pascal removed his jacket and draped it over Sophie's shoulders. Millicent couldn't believe how well they were getting along. It was a relief, but more than that, it was bizarre.

"Loneliness is a slow killer, but it's a real killer," Bryce was saying, playing with a pink hair elastic he had found on the floor. He stretched it against his thumb, pulled it back and aimed it like a bow and arrow. Millicent realized that she had tuned out most of what he was saying. The elastic flew across the room and landed in an abandoned Mason jar full of beer.

"Bull's eye!" Bryce yelled, raising his arms as if crossing a finish line.

Millicent felt her head was too heavy to hold up. She let it fall back against the couch and closed her eyes, trying to ignore the scene outside. She was drunker than she'd realized. The smell of Bryce's shirt—champagne mixed with floral laundry detergent—lulled her into something between a daydream and sleep.

"Do you think ..." she said slowly, a thought pushing through to the front of her mind, "... that the reason you still work at the *Nugget* ... is that you don't want to abandon Franc?"

"Of course not," Bryce said, shaking his head.

"I saw the way you took care of him at the Mad Hatter. I see how you protect him at work. You're all he has."

Bryce finished his beer and winced. It was probably warm, Millicent thought without surprise. "All I'm saying is ... you're too good ... for the *Nugget*."

He set the bottle on the floor and glared at her. "Why are you trying to get rid of me?"

"I'm not trying to get rid of you!"

"No?"

"All I'm saying, Bryce, is you've got big dreams," she mumbled indistinctly.

"Do I really?"

He heaved himself up to standing. "Is this what Pascal is telling you, that anyone who has a nine-to-five job isn't living up to their potential?"

Millicent didn't answer. Bryce went to the kitchen, poured himself a big glass of water and drank it in one go. She looked out the window again and could no longer see Sophie and Pascal. She waited for the door to open as they came back in. She wanted Pascal to sit next to her on the floor. She needed to feel his warmth and smell the smoke on his clothes.

Bryce came back into the room. "Maybe you didn't realize it yet, Millicent, but what we are doing at the *Nugget* is not only good work, it's integral to a functioning, healthy society." He started to pace the living room, waving his arms for emphasis. "Forget that the *Nugget* is dying because nobody reads the newspaper anymore and forget that our daily deadlines make it nearly impossible to write with nuance and thoughtfulness, which really is the key to good reportage. Journalism is journalism, whether it's the *New York Times* or the *Golden Nugget*: keeping the people with the most power accountable." He paused, waiting for Millicent to respond. She was sitting on the floor, staring at the label on her beer bottle as if it had the answers.

"Do you understand that?" Bryce asked.

"Yes, I get it," she said. "It's quite the speech." She agreed with every word he said. Still, as she watched him pace back and forth, lost in his anger, she couldn't stop thinking about Pascal's words: small people with small dreams. She would never say so to Bryce, but she couldn't help wondering if Pascal was right. Maybe she was supposed to be out in the world, making art. Real art. Not worrying about bills and rent and getting to work at exactly nine o'clock. She should be focusing on her poetry. During her final year at Horizon, Tim had urged her to keep writing. On the last poem she handed in before graduation, he wrote: *You have a voice. I urge you to use it*. She shouldn't forget that.

"Why don't you like him?" Millicent said at last.

Bryce stopped pacing and sat on the arm of the couch.

She could see the outline of his wallet in his back pocket. He closed his eyes and massaged his temples. Then he looked back at Millicent and smiled in the sad way people do when they give up. He spoke softly. "If you like him, I like him."

A draft of icy air invaded the apartment. Sophie came in, tracking snow with her boots. She hovered over Millicent, shivering, as if deciding whether to sit on the floor with her. Her bangs were pushed to one side of her forehead. The swooping neck of her sequined dress revealed her collarbone. She looked like she was literally starving. Snow from her boots melted into a puddle on the floor.

"Soph?" Millicent reached out and touched her arm.

"Are you okay?" Bryce asked.

Sophie looked at them with a hollow gaze. "Yes, I'm fine. Why do you ask?"

"Where's Pascal?"

"He's just gone to brush his teeth." Sophie went back to the door and kicked off her boots, then placed them neatly side by side. "That's what he told me," she added. "One last drink?"

"I'm on the water train," Bryce said, lifting his empty glass.

"I could have one more," Millicent said.

Sophie reached into the fridge and grabbed two bottles of beer. Her hand shook as she popped the caps off. She handed Millicent a bottle, then perched bird-like on the edge of the couch. Millicent stood up and moved to the far end of the couch. She realized she was afraid to be too close to Sophie.

Sophie drank a slow glug of beer as she stared out the living room window. The bonfire was dead now, the night black. Millicent took a few sips of beer. She had been drinking the same kind of beer all night, but now it tasted disgusting, flat and cheap, and she couldn't stomach it. She set it on the floor and waited for one of them to say something. After a while, she spoke.

"Where is Pascal? What's taking him so long?"

Bryce was scrolling through his phone. "He's probably watering his *'erbs*," he said.

Sophie smiled and sat down on the couch. There were tears in the corners of her eyes and her silver hoop earrings shook. Her lipstick was worn off; all that was left was a pink rash around her lips.

"Gosh," she said, struggling to get any sound out of her throat. "Happy birthday, Millicent."

Millicent felt completely sober. "Sophie," she said. "Are you okay?"

"Of course!" she said, regaining her composure. "Just had one too many drinks."

"Do you want some toast?" Millicent asked.

Sophie spoke into her beer bottle, refusing to meet Millicent's eyes. "No, no, it's your birthday. You don't have to make me toast."

"I really don't mind."

Sophie was quiet. She clutched her beer as if someone was threatening to take it from her.

Pascal entered the apartment, humming to himself. He took his time removing his jacket, hat, boots and gloves.

"You're still up!" Pascal said as he moved through

the apartment, flashing Millicent a thumbs-up. Then he disappeared into the bathroom to brush his teeth.

Sophie rose from the couch. "I have to go to bed. I love you, Millicent."

She went into her bedroom and closed the door.

MILLICENT PUT THE REST of the cake in the fridge. She collected beer bottles and shoved them into a black garbage bag. Her mind was frantic, tripping over itself with images of the night. Sophie and Pascal playing around the campfire like children. Pascal draping his jacket over her shoulders. Sophie perched on the edge of the couch, the colour drained from her face, the pink rash of lipstick around her lips.

Millicent handed Bryce a pillow and mumbled *good night*. In the bathroom, she brushed her teeth slowly, trying to focus on the feeling of the soft bristles on her gums. She rinsed her mouth and leaned her head under the faucet to drink water. Then she wiped her mouth with a towel and stared at her reflection in the mirror, unable, it seemed, to leave the bathroom. Just move, she told herself. Sophie was drunk. *She* was drunk. Things would look different in the morning.

Her bedroom was dark. At first she couldn't even make out the shape of Pascal in the bed. Millicent stripped off her dress and climbed under the cold sheets in her underwear. *Go to sleep*, she told herself. *Just go to sleep.* They could all have breakfast together. She wasn't seeing things clearly now.

Pascal lay a foot away facing the wall, his feet sticking out from the end of the comforter. His breath was steady. She listened for movement in Sophie's room, but the only sound she could hear was Bryce shifting on the couch, followed by his footsteps across the room and the sound of the toilet flushing. Millicent lay on her back, stiff as a soldier, staring into the darkness.

The highway was dead at this time of night. The silence rang. She could tell from the sound of his breathing on the other side of the wall that Bryce had fallen asleep. Everyone was asleep except for her. It couldn't be true. Nothing could have happened between Pascal and Sophie. Sophie was attracted to men who read Dostoevsky and smoked cigarettes after sex and talked about the problems with the first-past-the-post voting system. Pascal didn't even vote. It was almost laughable how her mind played tricks on her.

"Pascal," she whispered. He remained still.

"Pascal," she said again, rolling onto her side and placing a hand on his chest. She hated herself for this ability to be tender.

"Rabbit," he mumbled.

"Are you awake?" she asked.

"No."

"That was a weird night."

"Was it?" he mumbled again.

Millicent blinked in the darkness.

"Well, you left with Sophie and when she came back, she was … all weird."

"How so?"

Millicent's words were suddenly filled with acid. *"Are you saying you didn't notice?"*

Now Pascal opened his eyes.

"Why are you upset, Rabbit?"

"Because, because ..." Millicent replied, stumbling over what to say next. "When she was on the couch just now, she was crying. Before you came in."

Pascal was fully awake now.

"Sophie is just dramatic," he said.

The champagne and the cake churned in her stomach. There was something underneath his matter-of-fact tone. Millicent imagined Sophie in her bed on the other side of the wall and with that image, heat rose in her throat. She felt she was going to vomit. When she finally spoke again, her voice was strangled. The sound didn't originate in her own body. It was not her.

"Did something happen?" she asked.

"Of course not."

"Okay," she whispered.

She thought back to that first night on the bus by the river. *Chin-chin*, he had said, clinking her glass. Winking. *To a beautiful night with a beautiful woman.* He had just drawn her in, like it was the most instinctual thing to do.

"Are you sure, Pascal?"

He was so quiet, like he wasn't even breathing, that she swore she could hear the river now, the faint hush of the water slipping under the ice.

"Answer me."

He didn't say a word.

"Pascal," she insisted.

"What do you mean by all this with Sophie?" he said.

"Did you just, just …" Millicent couldn't get the words out. She swallowed painfully, then took a slow breath in and let it out. "Did you just sleep with her?"

Pascal rolled onto his back so that they were lying side by side, like children gazing at the stars. Millicent struggled to find a way to press him when he denied it all; of course he didn't sleep with her, they probably just drunkenly kissed or something stupid like that. But he just grabbed her hand and let out a long breath.

"She asked for a tour of the bus."

"And?"

"And I was showing her the herbs and she just came on to me."

A strange sound came from Millicent's throat. Was she laughing? She imagined Sophie leaning into Pascal, her sparkly dress, his hands on her tiny waist. Millicent went numb. She no longer had the ability to move her legs. Her body was made of lead, not flesh.

"It didn't mean anything," Pascal said.

"But you just let it happen," she croaked.

"Any other women, they are nothing compared to you. You are magnificent," Pascal whispered. "You know this, right?"

Millicent split herself into two women. One woman rose out of bed, got dressed and told Pascal to *get the fuck out*. To never return and never contact her again. That woman watched Pascal scurry to gather his clothes. Without saying a word, without even moving a muscle on her face, she listened to him beg for forgiveness. She watched the bus pull out of the parking lot, then she drew a hot bubble bath and scrubbed herself until she was cleansed of him.

She just needed to take control of her body, rise out of bed and begin. Once she started, momentum would take over. It would be easy.

"I'm sorry," Pascal whispered. He raked his fingers through her hair. If she could only find a way to emit sound. If she could only remember how to speak.

"I love *you*," he said. "Did you know this?"

The other woman lay paralyzed. She begged herself to work up the courage to move, even just an inch, to prove to herself that she could. They were still holding hands. Unthread your fingers, Millicent instructed herself. Take your hand back. Take your hand back and roll over to the edge of the bed and pretend to sleep. This is the least you can do. Take your hand back. Do it.

17

MILLICENT WOKE ON THE edge of the mattress. She had one minute of dazed bliss. Then, as she remembered where she was, the memories of the night before returned. How had she slept so deeply? Like a newborn. Pascal moaned in his sleep. His eyelids fluttered but he didn't wake. He reached blindly for a pillow and cocooned his head underneath it. She knew this move. He wouldn't wake up for hours.

Millicent tiptoed to the front door, stepping over paper plates smeared with chocolate icing, careful not to wake Bryce on the couch. The apartment smelled like warm beer and sweat. She held her breath as she shoved her arms into the sleeves of her down jacket and wrapped her scarf over her mouth and nose, bracing herself for the cold. Millicent glanced at the door to Sophie's room, half-expecting it to open and for her roommate to emerge in her pajamas and tell her none of it was real. It was all a practical joke they'd decided to play on her because it was her birthday.

Pascal? She would say. *Come on, Millicent.*

The moon still blazed over the horizon. She had no idea what time it was, but the highway droned with the odd passing car, so it had to be morning. She looked at the thermometer hanging beside the door: –35.

In her car, she jammed the keys in the ignition. The engine screamed, sputtered and died.

"Fuck it," she said, forcing herself not to cry. Millicent opened the glove box, relieved that the emergency flashlight was still there. The only thing she was sure of right now was that she needed to follow her instincts and keep moving.

The wind slapped at her face. Millicent followed the bouncing beam of yellow across the parking lot and towards the steep bank that led to the frozen river. The hair in her nostrils stiffened. Her muscles burned from trudging through the snow. As she scrambled down the bank, the small flashlight clamped in her mouth as she clutched flimsy branches of rose bushes to slow herself down, she thought about the last words Pascal had said to her the night before: *I love you.* Millicent allowed herself to separate what had happened the night before from the words. I love you.

Images spilled back: the ghost of Sophie perched on the couch; the way Pascal had said "Rabbit." He hadn't even tried to lie, hadn't even braced himself for the repercussions of the truth. This was the part she didn't understand. As the bank became steeper, Millicent stopped trying to slow down. She slid down the bank, arms outstretched in case she fell, trusting that the weight of the snow around her thighs would keep her from losing all control.

The sky broke open once as she stumbled to the river's edge, pink and yellow and streaked with heavy clouds. The river was a fresh, white canvas lending her a moment of clarity.

It didn't matter how long Sophie forced herself to stay single, her self-worth was still driven by the attention of men. She had pranced through the party in her gold sequined dress, the drunkest person there. Laughing loudly, begging to be seen, to be heard. And then, because it was easy or because it was fun, or because she was lonely— Millicent didn't know which—she had fucked her boyfriend.

Sophie would never change.

Pascal. She couldn't even think about Pascal.

Snow particles sparkled under the heavy blanket of yellow light. The current ran under the ice with a faint hush that Millicent could hear only if she stood completely still, ignoring the sound of her own heartbeat.

She couldn't go back to the apartment. She couldn't go back to Pascal and the bus. She needed to be alone to sort out her thoughts. Whitehorse was only five kilometres away by river—that's what Sophie had told her when she moved in. It would be much faster than walking along the highway, and besides, she had no choice; with the shock of the night before sinking deeper into her body, staying still would kill her. She needed to keep moving.

Millicent was certain the ice was thick enough. Up in Dawson City you could drive a semi-truck over the river at this time of year. The only place she could think to go was the newspaper office. Yes, she would hide in the basement with the printing press. It was always warm in there, and it was Sunday so no one would find her. She would call her mother and tell her everything. Her mother would help her figure out what to do next.

Millicent closed her eyes and lifted her face to the sun, warming her skin. How long since she had felt the sun? Godly. It was nothing short of godly. Wisps of fog swirled a foot above the ice.

Pascal's voice cut through the forest, causing a tiny explosion of fireworks in her chest.

"Rabbit!" he yelled again. "Where are you?"

Millicent clamped her mitt over her mouth, suffocating herself, so that her body would not follow the instinct to answer him. It didn't matter. The crackle of bushes grew louder and then he was standing there, arms wrapped around her waist. Of course. He had followed her wide trail through the snow.

"I'm sorry," he whispered. She could tell he had been crying. Millicent unlatched herself from his grip.

"That was so stupid what I did."

"Stupid?!" Millicent said.

They fought until her voice became so raw that it grew soft. Millicent called him a pig and a liar and a piece of shit, words she thought belonged to other people in other, dire situations. The words flew out of her mouth, angry and full of spit.

"How the fuck could you do this to me, on my own birthday, and with my own roommate? Are you a complete narcissist? Do you have no conscience? Do you realize you haven't just ruined our relationship, but my relationship with Sophie? And probably Bryce too? Do you realize you've ruined my entire foundation? I have nothing, Pascal. What am I supposed to do now? Where am I supposed to go?"

Millicent didn't know she was capable of such anger. As she yelled, she left her body and floated above it, watching her face as it contorted into ugly shapes, tears and mucus running into her mouth. A flock of waxwings arced and swooped across the sky to the rhythm of her screaming, as if she was their conductor.

Pascal absorbed the words, shifting from foot to foot. Ice clung to his beard and his eyelashes.

"What about you and Bryce?" he said finally. "I see how you look at each other."

Millicent glared at him as a new feeling of relief came over her.

"Bryce? Come on. You're grasping at straws."

She felt hollowed out. Excavated. There was nothing left. The whole situation seemed suddenly deeply funny. The way Pascal was standing, hangdog, his chin tucked into his parka, obviously freezing but unable to complain. He was afraid of her, and this felt wonderful. Maybe it was the lack of oxygen to her brain; she had to stop herself from laughing. Laughing would ruin everything. Millicent forced herself to focus on something else. Her fingers. Her fingers were aching. She could barely wiggle them. She dropped her mittens onto the snow and tried to cup her palms at her mouth, but her fingers wouldn't bend.

"Fuck. I hate the north," she said.

Pascal took a tentative step towards her and unzipped his jacket.

"Put them in here."

"No."

"You will lose a finger out here, crazy Rabbit," he said, smiling. He winced as her numb fingers found his hot stomach. Her cheek pressed against his parka. The scratchy fabric still smelled like gasoline.

"I can't stand the idea of going back to that apartment," Millicent whispered. Pascal swallowed loudly.

"Sophie is not good for you."

"Jesus."

"She is lacking love," he said. "She can't help it. She's a leech. She has been leeching off your positive energy this whole time." He drew her in closer and wrapped his parka around her so that Millicent was cocooned inside, her cheek against his wool sweater.

"I'm sorry, Rabbit, I am." Pascal fiddled with the parka zipper. "It was crazy how she came on to me." When he pulled the zipper up behind her back, blocking the wind and the air, Millicent understood just how cold she was.

"I love you," he said.

They breathed together like one lung: expanding, contracting, expanding, contracting.

"Don't say that."

"Move onto the bus." His words were muffled but she was certain she had heard him right.

"No," she said.

"Yes. Right now. You can quit your job on Monday, and we can start our new life together. The film crew will be here within the month. This I am sure of."

Millicent squeezed her eyes shut and breathed hot moisture into his sweater.

"You are not grounded in reality, Pascal," she said.

He pulled her even closer so that when he spoke she could feel the vibrations in his chest.

"No, you are just scared of what your reality could be. You are keeping yourself small."

THE SUN HOVERED JUST above the skyline as Millicent and Pascal trudged up the steep bank, following Millicent's trail through the snow. She was unsure if the sun was rising or setting, or how much time had passed. She thought about the day Sophie had taken her blueberry picking, how they squatted on the top of the mountain and picked those tiny sour berries until their fingers and lips were stained blue. The warmth. The sun. How long ago that seemed now.

Bryce's car was gone from the parking lot.

"I'll wait on the bus," Pascal said. "Take as long as you need."

"I'm just coming for a night until I figure out where to go," Millicent said.

Pascal nodded solemnly, then kissed her on the forehead.

"We are over," she added.

"Yes, I know," Pascal said. "But no matter what, you always have a home on the bus."

The apartment was tropical. Bryce had rolled up the sleeping bag and stacked it on the pillow at the end of the couch. Sophie's door was shut, but there were signs that she and Bryce had eaten breakfast: an empty coffee Bodum in the sink, the smell of bacon and fried eggs. Millicent wondered what they had talked about, if Sophie had told him the truth.

Millicent held her fingers under hot running water. She forced herself not to make a sound, even though the pain was excruciating.

In her bedroom, she yanked random items of clothing from hangers and stuffed them into her duffel bag. On the other side of the wall, Sophie's bed creaked. Millicent zipped up the bag, then went to the bathroom and grabbed her toothbrush. At the door, she fumbled back into her boots.

From behind her came Sophie's voice, fragile as a robin's egg.

"Wait, Milli," she said.

Millicent looked out through the peephole. She could hear the bus engine turning over and over.

"Please," Sophie added.

"Why the fuck should I wait," Millicent said. It wasn't a question.

"Last night was such a mess."

Sophie stood in the doorway to her bedroom in bare feet. There was still a trace of makeup on her face. Millicent resisted the urge to go to her, to coax her back into her room, put her to bed and tell her everything would be okay.

"Did he hurt you?" Millicent said in a whisper.

Tears slipped down Sophie's cheeks. Finally, the bus engine roared into life.

"Jesus Sophie, did he or didn't he?"

"That's not really the right question, Mill," she said, her voice hoarse now.

"Isn't it?"

"I can't remember what happened, exactly."

Millicent laughed. "So, basically you guys just fucked each other. Cool."

She felt energized by her anger.

"Last night was so messed up, I was out of control. There's nothing I can say to take it back. I know that. I know I have a lot of work to do on myself. And you can be mad at me for as long as you like."

"Wow, thanks!" Millicent said.

"Mill, please don't go back to the bus."

Millicent thought about this, thought about staying. She imagined taking off her jacket and sleeping in the boozy stale-smelling apartment all day. No. She needed to get out. She would come back in a few days once her thoughts were sorted.

"Please," Sophie begged.

"I can't," Millicent said.

With that, she opened the door and took a gulp of air, the frozen particles sliding down her throat like sewing needles.

SHE SAT AT THE kitchen table, far enough away that Pascal couldn't hear if she spoke softly. He pulled the bus onto the Alaska Highway, taking the corner so aggressively a plastic pot of thyme tipped over, spilling soil on his pants.

"Ay yay ay," he said, twisting his head back and flashing her a wide grin. Acid heat rose up into her throat. She closed her eyes, forcing herself to breathe in and out to hold down the vomit. Massive Attack seeped out of the speakers. Pascal turned up the volume.

"Our song!" he yelled. "Remember?"

Pascal settled deeper into the seat. His fingers tapped the steering wheel. The frozen landscape rolled by. In her pocket, Millicent's hand closed around her cellphone. She needed to talk to her mother right now. She couldn't wait a second longer.

Her mother picked up on the first ring.

"Mill! Happy birthday." The relief in her mother's voice was audible. "Are you okay? You haven't called in weeks."

"Yes, everything is fine," Millicent heard herself saying. Her own voice sounded far-off, like she was underwater.

"Millicent, be honest," her mother said more quietly. "What's going on?"

"Everything is fine!" she repeated.

"Whatever happened to the man on the school bus?"

"I don't know," Millicent said, staring at the back of Pascal's head.

"What do you mean, you don't know?" her mother asked. It was possible, Millicent realized, that the words would simply refuse to come out. She breathed into the phone, begging herself to say something, anything, but it was too late. The road dipped into the valley and she lost reception.

18

AFTER MILLICENT'S THIRD NIGHT in the Walmart parking lot, when it became clear they were not breaking up, Pascal emptied his drawer of dead batteries so she had somewhere to put her panties. She folded each pair in half, smoothed the cotton with her fingers. She kept her things neat.

December passed. Then January. Two months blurred by in the dark. Winter wouldn't give up. It wasn't just the temperature that made it painful to go outside; it was the wind. The whole shopping complex that Millicent now called home—Walmart, Canadian Tire, Starbucks—had been built on a wetland, Pascal told her, and when the area was paved over, a natural wind barrier between the river and clay cliffs was destroyed. Every time a gust of wind tore through the parking lot, the bus rattled.

Millicent and Pascal never talked about the birthday party. She couldn't. When she tried to bring it up, to ask him why he didn't stop—stop Sophie, stop himself—the clamp around her throat grew tighter until there was no space for oxygen to travel into her lungs.

Their daily routine quickly cemented. They lived together on the bus as if they had done so for years. At 8:00 a.m., after cowboy coffee and oats with pitted prunes, Millicent brushed her greasy hair into a ponytail and added a stroke of Sun-Kissed Peach blush to each cheekbone while Pascal hunched over the kitchen table with his massive headphones, working on local commercials. His latest was for Dirty Bird Hot Chicken, which was, ironically, a block away from Walmart and the other chain stores. The fast-food joint released wafts of deep-fried meat that drifted into the bus when the door opened.

Pascal didn't remove his headphones to say goodbye when Millicent left for work; he pulled her over and kissed her hard.

On the dark morning walk to the *Nugget* (she still hadn't gone back to the apartment to get her car), Millicent tried not to let her thoughts wander to Sophie, but it was impossible. The steady chew of her boots on the dry snow was the only distraction. When Millicent first left the apartment, Sophie reached out to her daily. Her messages were apologetic yet buoyant. *Mill, I'm so sorry. Come home!* As time went by, however, the texts became words of deep concern. *Mill, please just tell me you're ok? This is very unlike you. I'm worried.*

After a few weeks, Sophie stopped calling and texting. Millicent didn't blame her. She never picked up the phone calls; her reply to the texts was always a curt *I'm fine.* She just wanted some space. Didn't she deserve that? Pascal would say she was defining her boundaries. She had outgrown Sophie, and this was perfectly natural.

Once Millicent drafted a long text reply. *Hi Sophie. I really am happy living on the bus. This is the right decision for me, and I hope you understand my choice, even if you don't agree with it. I will return the apartment key soon and pay whatever rent is fair.* But she couldn't bring herself to send it. It felt too final, too frightening.

When she started obsessing about Sophie and the birthday party, Millicent tried to steer her mind towards the simplicity of her new life: the bus, Pascal, work. How she would start writing poetry again soon. She had even bought a ruled Moleskine notebook and written her name and phone number on the inside cover. It was tucked into her purse, next to her recorder and the Tupperware full of leftovers that Pascal packed for her.

At the office, Franc had been spending more time in the newsroom. Millicent had the sense that he wanted to talk to her in particular. She felt it in the way he stood by her desk after delivering an assignment. She knew he was lonely and needed to talk, but instead of engaging with him, Millicent acknowledged the assignment and immediately began typing, sometimes just random lines so he would go away. It wasn't that she didn't want to talk to him. But what if he asked her about Pascal, right there in the newsroom? Just thinking about it made her feet feel on fire. It was safer to just turn away.

She was certain that by now Bryce had told Franc she was living on the bus. She and Bryce had never discussed it; they didn't talk about life outside of work anymore.

They were nothing more than co-workers, and they communicated only when necessary. Had she proofed page 2? Did he have a cutline for the front-page photo?

But Millicent knew Bryce was hanging out with Sophie. She detected a whiff of lavender and Nag Champa on him one day when they were checking proofs in the production room. He had probably lost respect for her because she stayed with Pascal after what he did. She imagined he wanted nothing to do with her. Millicent reminded herself that no one could see inside a relationship. Nobody knew what she and Pascal had.

When she returned from the *Nugget* at 5:30, Pascal cooked the nearly spoiled vegetables he found on sale, alongside rice or beans or lentils. After dinner, Millicent boiled a pot of water and washed the dishes. She checked the herb garden on the dash. If the soil was dry, she gave the herbs small sips of water; if it was still damp from the night before, she simply leaned over the oregano, thyme and mint, closed her eyes and inhaled, transporting herself somewhere far away. It didn't matter that the sun only shone through the windshield for two hours in the middle of the day, or that at night the temperature inside dropped to freezing. The herbs grew thick and pungent as if they were soaking up nutrients from memories of endless summer days.

Before going to bed, Millicent brought soap and a towel and washed herself in the bathroom at Starbucks, the cleanest bathroom in the shopping complex. She splashed hot water on her face, her armpits and her crotch. She avoided looking in the mirror. When she did look up by chance, she saw that her skin had lost its pigment. She was almost translucent.

They went to bed between 9:45 and 10:00. Pascal said they had to be mindful of their sex life now that they were living together. They couldn't let it "slip away." He kissed her nipple and she grew wet. She slid her hand inside his boxers and his breath sharpened. When his cock slipped inside her, she imagined his eyes looking down at Sophie. A fistful of Sophie's thick hair. The smell of lavender on her neck. Millicent wanted to scream, to push him off her. Instead, she shut her eyes, whispering "That's good," until her back was slick with sweat and the image of Sophie led her to orgasm with an explosion of tiny carbonated stars.

She felt closest to Pascal when his muscles softened into her, like butter left out on the counter. She would pull the blanket over their hot skin and settle onto his chest. No matter how tightly she nuzzled in, she couldn't get close enough to him. She wanted to be inside him, like a Russian nesting doll. She wondered if this was love.

"I love you," she said one night, trying it out. It was easy.

"I know, Rabbit."

"How?"

"The way you look at me."

"How do I look at you?" Millicent asked.

"Like you never want to look away," Pascal said, tightening his arms around her. Millicent squeezed her eyes closed, wondering whether if she stayed like that for long enough, she would disappear.

Every night, at 3:00 a.m. on the dot, Millicent woke with a bursting bladder. Pascal slept like a restless infant beside her, taking small sips of breath as if the oxygen might run out. This was new. She wondered if it was anxiety over the TV show. He hadn't talked about it very much. There had been no mention lately of the film crew flying up to Whitehorse or of Millicent joining in at their meetings. He had been so sure about all this on her birthday.

In fact, one day when she happened to glance at Pascal's computer screen, she saw the subject line of an email to the producer: *dernier email?!* She knew enough French to understand the desperation in those words. It seemed the producer had stopped writing Pascal back. Millicent didn't have the heart to ask what was really going on.

She tried to recall an expression as she gazed out the window at the flickering streetlight illuminating the dirty mountain of snow. *Let sleeping dogs lie.* Maybe Pascal would move on from this obsession.

When the tension in her bladder became too painful, Millicent scrambled to the front of the bus in her underwear and T-shirt. She shoved on her boots, wrenched the lever that opened the door and squatted on the snowbank.

The freezing air knifed her skin until her whole body began to shake. Millicent looked at the clay cliffs, imagining that the black outline of trees at the top was a hysterical line measuring her heart rate on an electrocardiogram. It was there, with the steam from her piss warming her ankles, that the fogginess that had blurred her mind lifted and she finally saw things clearly, if only for a moment.

How could she let him touch her?

Her breath was loud and ragged as she pulled her underpants up her thighs and tried to stop shaking. Every night she had the urge to run. Run down Second Avenue, past the *Nugget* and towards the Alaska Highway. It would take just one move to begin. She could do it right now.

BACK ON THE BUS, thawing next to Pascal's hot body, the urgency to flee disintegrated. Unable to fall back asleep, Millicent allowed her mind to wander freely back to her old life. She thought about Sophie and Pascal speaking French the night he came over for dinner, the way Sophie had smiled at him behind her wineglass. Millicent should have known what was happening when she saw her signature coy smile. Why did she assume Sophie had changed? That smile defined her—who she was at school, who she was now and who she would always be.

When Millicent couldn't bear to think about Sophie anymore, she spooned Pascal harder, pressing her breasts into his back. She wanted to inhale his heat, to seep into his unconsciousness and float into sleep with him.

Some nights she drifted into memories of her mother, how she used to braid Millicent's hair for school picture day before she was old enough to do it herself. When her mother finished, Millicent would run to the bathroom, look at her reflection and hold back tears. There were always bumps in the braids. How could she ask her mother to start over when the first attempt had already drained her energy? "Do you like it?" her mother would ask, already back on the couch with her eyes closed. Millicent would choke out, "Yes."

She thought about calling her mother and telling her everything.

She wished she could call Sophie, just to hear her voice for a second on the other end.

19

IT WAS A THURSDAY at the end of February, the lazy hour of the afternoon just before the office closed. Millicent was trying to finish a story about the top five dog names registered at city hall the year before—Diesel, Max, Jackson, Blue and Rex—but all she could do was stare numbly at the 150 words she had written.

Bryce was tossing a hacky sack in the air, waiting for a source to call him back. Millicent swivelled her chair around. She watched the crocheted ball soar towards the ceiling, pause for a millisecond at its peak, then descend back into Bryce's open palm.

She didn't know what had brought on this sudden need for finality, to gather the rest of her belongings from the apartment, to see Sophie, for real, in the flesh, and hear her out. All she knew was that she couldn't sit at her desk for one second longer. She needed to go.

Millicent saved her article, powered down her

computer and wrapped her scarf around her neck. The problem, she realized as she dug through her purse for her mittens, was that she didn't have a car. She had actually forgotten about her car. It had been easy to do because, other than the twenty-minute walk between the *Nugget* and the parking lot, she didn't have anywhere to go. She had forgotten that her car was still parked at the Pit with a dead battery.

Millicent knocked on Franc's door and nudged it open. He was eating a KitKat at his desk.

"Franc," she started.

"Yes?"

"Can I borrow your truck? Just for an hour?"

Without a single question, Franc threw her the keys. "The left turn signal doesn't work. Neither do the head-lights, so make sure you're back before dark."

"How do you get home after dark?"

Franc tossed the chocolate wrapper in the garbage can beside his desk.

"I know these roads," he said.

In the newsroom, Bryce took his headphones off and hung them around his neck as he watched Millicent get ready to leave. She gave a weak smile.

"Long day," she said lamely.

Bryce looked at her blankly. "Tell me about it."

Millicent had no idea how to read Bryce anymore. The day before, he had caught her coming out of the bath-room after washing her hair in the sink. He said nothing, just gave a sad smile as he brushed past her.

"Where are you going?" he asked.

"For a drive."

"Oh," he said. "Right."

Millicent pushed her chair flush with her desk and spoke facing the window.

"Just need to clear my head, you know?"

"Where are you driving to?"

"Nowhere in particular."

She turned around and sat on the edge of his desk like she used to do. Bryce shuffled papers over to give her more room.

"Like I said, I just need to clear my head."

Bryce nodded. He tapped his pencil against the edge of the desk. "Hey, do you want to go for a beer instead?"

Millicent squeezed Franc's keys in her hand. "I can't right now."

"Okay," he said slowly, "but Millicent?"

"Yeah?"

"How are you?"

She forced a bright smile. "I'm fine."

"Sophie and I, we're worried about you."

She laughed and it came out like an awful squeak. "Worried, why?"

"You know ..." Bryce said, trailing off into silence.

"I don't."

"You just don't seem like yourself ever since you left with Pascal."

Millicent forced another smile. Tears sprang into her eyes. "I'm totally fine, Bryce," she said. "You really don't have to worry about me."

She took the stairs slowly, not knowing why she was

lingering, but by the time she hit the landing, she had the answer: part of her was hoping Bryce would follow. If he asked just one more time, *How are you?* she would break open. She knew she would.

Millicent traced her fingers over the railing. Bryce had said *Sophie and I.* Maybe Pascal had been right and they were together, a couple. Now that Millicent had left, Sophie needed somebody to cling to. She wondered what they said about her when they were together, whether they called her *sad*, or worse, *crazy*. She paused on the bottom step and gazed out the windows at the liquor store across Second Avenue, forcing back her tears. If Bryce would just come to the top of the stairwell and call her name …

Finally, Millicent opened the door and stepped out onto the snow-packed sidewalk. One block away, the Northern Tax Solutions mascot was back doing the Macarena. She inhaled the mint-fresh winter air, then let out a strange sound, a mix of a laugh and a sob that thankfully, nobody heard.

SUBWAY WRAPPERS AND EMPTY cigarette cartons littered the floor of Franc's truck. Millicent bobbed her head to the radio and banged the heel of her hand against the steering wheel. Now that she was out on the open road, she was sure of herself and her decision. She would knock on the door, hear Sophie out and give her back the key. Then she would return Franc's truck and walk home to the bus.

Home, Millicent thought, savouring the sweetness of the word.

She turned off the highway and onto the dirt road that led to the Pit. The late-afternoon light had swept through the forest, giving the land a sharp yellow tinge. The tires bounced along icy ruts on the road. What a relief to finally be making a break, cutting off her old life and making room for the new. Change. Growth. You can't stop it, Millicent thought.

Sophie's truck was in the parking lot right outside the apartment. With her heart pounding inside her head, Millicent cranked the wheel and pulled a U-turn. She drove past Dave's mechanic shop, the dogs yipping behind the fence. Then, much to her own surprise, she pulled another U-turn and returned to the parking lot.

She idled, staring at her Mazda next to Sophie's truck. It was exactly where she had left it in December, except now a front tire was flat. Pascal was going to teach her how to drive the bus. She could leave the car here to rot.

With the engine still running, Millicent got out and walked towards the red door. The cautious chords of "Zombie" could be heard through the door. Was Sophie singing? Millicent stood with her arms limp by her side, staring at the peephole. She didn't have to do this. She didn't have to ever see Sophie again. She knocked three times softly, her body braver than her head.

Sophie answered the door wearing her overalls and a spaghetti-strap tank top. A wave of heat from inside rolled over Millicent and out the front door. Now she saw that

Sophie had cut her hair an inch long. It was thick and ragged and yet somehow, elegant.

"Your hair," Millicent said. "What happened?

Sophie looked self-conscious. She ran her hand over the tips of her hair. Millicent had forgotten how beautiful she was. How real.

"Come in?" Sophie asked. She closed the door behind her and their bodies melted into a hug. When they let go, Millicent ran her hand over her own stringy hair, realizing how dirty she was, how she must look to Sophie.

"How's it going?" she asked. But Sophie wasn't interested in small talk.

"Mill. I am so sorry. I can't explain how sorry I am." She spoke slowly and carefully, as if she had planned for this moment. "I wish I could go back to that night and just take it all back."

Sophie was clasping her hands together and rocking from her heels to her toes like a child. Millicent didn't know what to say or where to look. She gazed past Sophie into the kitchen. The spider plant on the windowsill was dying; limp yellow strands collapsed over the clay pot. A ketchup bottle filled with water sat next to the faucet. How long had it been there? She herself had finished the ketchup and filled the bottle with hot soapy water to let it soak. That was the morning of her birthday party. Two months ago. It was disgusting. Nothing had changed. Nothing would change.

"I really am sorry," Sophie repeated. "Do you want to take your jacket off, stay for a cup of coffee?

She didn't want to hear Sophie's side of the story anymore. She just wanted to go home to Pascal.

"I don't know, Soph," Millicent said quietly.

"I'm not going to look for a new roommate," Sophie said. "This is your apartment. You know that, right?"

Millicent stared down at her boots, imagining what Pascal would say if he were with her.

"I'm moving forward in life, not backwards," she said. "I'm just here to grab the rest of my stuff."

Sophie sounded choked up. "It's like Pascal has brainwashed you," she said.

Millicent looked at her. "Brainwashed?"

"I'm serious."

They could hear footsteps upstairs. Millicent's eyes were on her boots again.

"Pascal and I are happy together," she said. When she looked at Sophie, there were tears in her friend's eyes.

"You need to snap out of this," Sophie urged.

Millicent let out a pained laugh. "Let me be happy, Soph."

"Mill."

"Do you even know me? Why can't you accept that I might actually be happy?"

Sophie looked at the ceiling. She tightened her lips and shook her head.

"Are you fucking serious?"

"Dead serious."

Sophie lost all composure.

"Do you know *yourself*? Can you see what's happening? You've completely avoided me for two whole months! And for what? To live on a school bus with a homeless, middle-aged man who is so delusional and self-centred he thinks a film crew is going to follow him around? Living in a fucking parking lot like a fucking rat! Soon you'll be pregnant with a litter of rat babies."

Millicent brushed past Sophie, tracking snow across the floor. In the tight space of the furnace room she found a box half-full of recycling and dumped its contents—empty beer cans and old toilet paper rolls—onto the floor. In her bedroom, she ripped her bath towel curtains from the window and shoved them into the box. As Sophie knocked around in the kitchen, Millicent grabbed the rest of her belongings: the sheets from her bed, the few books left on her windowsill and her bedside light.

In a few minutes Millicent smelled coffee. As she reached into the cupboard to retrieve some sweaters, she could sense Sophie standing in the doorway. Millicent placed the sweaters in the box on top of the rest of her belongings and turned to face her, hands on her hips.

"Rat babies. Really?"

Sophie slid down the wall until she was sitting on the floor. "What I'm trying to say is you're just throwing your sanity away. He's got to your head, Mill. I can't watch it anymore."

"He's not who you think he is," Millicent said.

"I don't care about Pascal," she said. "I'm only concerned about your wellbeing."

"Don't give me that. If my wellbeing were your concern, you wouldn't have …" Millicent trailed off. She looked out the window, then bent over and picked up the box.

"What?"

"If my wellbeing were really your concern," she repeated, "you wouldn't have fucked him."

Sophie dropped her head into her hands.

"Stay for coffee," she said to the floor. "Please."

"*Why did you do it?*" Millicent demanded, her voice full of anger and frustration.

Sophie looked up at her, her eyes wild. Millicent's arms burned from the weight of the box as she waited for Sophie to answer. When she didn't, Millicent transferred the box to her hip, took the key to the apartment from her pocket and placed it on the windowsill.

"Maybe I'm just fucked up and starved for attention and will do anything to feel needed!" Sophie cried out, scrambling to stand up. She followed Millicent as she made her way to the door. "Is that what you want to hear?"

Millicent set the box down to open the door, indifferent to the wave of frozen air particles. It was almost dark now.

"Yes, maybe you are just fucked up," she said to the parking lot.

Sophie was standing so close she could feel her breath on her neck.

"You've turned into someone I don't know," she said with a whimper.

Millicent hoisted the box back into her arms and crunched through the snow, past her dead car towards the idling truck. She drove to the bus with no headlights and arrived back at the newspaper office just as Whitehorse was absorbed by night.

For the next few days, Sophie's words stung. Soon,

however, when Millicent replayed the scene in her mind, the feelings faded.

And then one night at three in the morning, her urine burning a hole in the snowbank as the stars burned billions of holes in the sky, the words brought her a sense of peace. *You've turned into someone I don't know.* The past must dissolve. Humans transform. There is no stopping it.

20

THURSDAY AFTERNOON AND THE *Golden Nugget* was a submarine deep in the ocean. Franc had just left for the day with his plastic bag of lunch remains clutched in his hand. Millicent was alone in the building. With her winter boots tucked underneath the desk, she sat cross-legged in her chair in thick wool socks—the pair she wore every day to keep her feet from freezing on the bus—staring at her computer, which she had already shut down. She didn't feel like going back to the bus, but she had nowhere else to go.

Night pressed heavily against the windows. There was only the dull orange glow of streetlights. How long had it been since she had felt daylight? Sure, the sun shone brightly for a few hours midday, but that was right before the *Nugget* went to print and Millicent hardly had time to even look out the window. The rest of the day was defined by a dusky twilight, a deep blue light that bathed the town in a melancholic haze.

When she heard Franc's truck leaving the parking lot, Millicent let herself be led down the stairs. Leaving all the lights off, she continued down the final set of stairs into the windowless basement. Millicent closed her eyes and inhaled the warm air that still smelled like ink. Breathing in the familiar scent, the muscles in her shoulders began to soften. How long had they been clenched like that?

Instinctively, like she had done all those months ago when she first started at the *Nugget*, Millicent picked a newspaper from the shelves at random, peeled off her sweater and stretched out on the ratty couch in her tank top. The issue she picked was dated May 19, 2002. The headline: "The Rally for Archer's Wetlands."

Before she could read further, her phone buzzed. Pascal. He would just be starting to make dinner. *Are you coming home, Rabbit?* he wrote.

This wasn't the first time Pascal had hounded her at the end of the workday. Earlier that week he had walked into the newsroom just before five.

"Pascal," Millicent said, her hands frozen on the keyboard.

"Rabbit." Pascal leaned over her chair and kissed the back of her neck.

"You shouldn't be in here," she said.

"Why not? I wanted to see my Rabbit."

Millicent's face flared with heat.

"It's just a rule, man. Nothing personal," Bryce said without looking up from his screen.

Then Franc was out of his office and walking towards Pascal. He offered a handshake, which Pascal returned vigorously, and said that Bryce was correct.

"Only editorial staff are allowed in the newsroom. Can't have irate locals and politicians just barging in whenever they don't like a story."

"Don't worry. I am not an angry politician. I just came to tell Millicent I made homemade perogies for dinner, and they are ready." Smiling, Pascal sat down on the edge of Millicent's desk and squinted at her screen. "What are you writing, babe?"

Millicent's hand was sweaty on her mouse. As her private life suddenly became public, the walls of the newsroom seemed to be closing in on her. "Pascal, you should go," she said weakly. "I'll be down soon."

"I'll wait for you here," he said.

"Pascal," Millicent pleaded.

Franc took another step towards Pascal and folded his arms over his fleece vest.

"I have to ask you to leave, Pascal," he said.

Next to Franc, who was built like a stack of bricks, Pascal seemed birdlike, fragile. Millicent wondered again how much Bryce had told Franc. What did he know about her and Pascal? Plenty of other people had come into the office—even local candidates before the election—and Franc hadn't made this big of a deal out of it.

"Now, please," Franc said.

Pascal raised his eyebrows at Millicent and mouthed "Wow" before leaning in for another kiss. He smiled at Bryce before heading towards the stairs.

"Goodbye, refrigerator."

IN THE BASEMENT, MILLICENT typed *I'll be home soon*, and then, as if another being had taken control of her reflexes, she deleted the words and turned off her phone. The silver printing press made a sighing sound as it slipped into a deeper sleep, and with that, the basement became as quiet as if it were underwater.

With the newspaper tented over her head and the springs of the couch digging into her back, Millicent began to read. The entire page two was a story about the new commercial complex being built on the fragile ecosystem of Archer's Wetlands. She stared at the black and white aerial photo, wondering why the topography looked so familiar. Her eyes kept returning to the clay cliffs that bordered the dense wooded area. She saw those cliffs every morning from the bus windows. Archer's Wetlands was the Walmart parking lot. Her home.

As Millicent checked more of the back issues, it became clear that there had been a public outcry for years over construction in the wetlands. There were rallies, protests and letters to the editors. It wasn't the simple narrative of an evil corporation against a humble small town. The issue went deeper than that; the marsh on the west side of the contested land was a resting and feeding ground for endangered tundra swans that migrated from the southern states to breed in Alaska every spring.

For the next few days after work, Millicent waited until the sound of Franc's engine disappeared, then made her way down to the basement. She made up a reasonable story to tell Pascal—she needed to work later now that she was no longer a newbie and Franc was giving her more responsibility. She thought he would be upset by the news, or at least warn her that she needed to get her priorities straight, to think about what she was giving up for her art, but he simply nodded. However, he made it his duty to pick her up at 6:00 on the dot, even on days when she told him she wanted to walk home.

Millicent must have read a dozen issues from 2002 about Archer's Wetlands. During those evenings, she didn't notice the hour go by or feel herself growing hungry. It reminded her of those Friday nights in the library at university, how she forgot she had a body entirely. It was only when her back began to ache from the couch springs and she was forced to roll onto her side that she remembered where she was.

The real issue with Archer's Wetlands, Millicent soon understood, was that if the tundra swans couldn't rest in their usual spot in Whitehorse, they would likely be too weak and exhausted to breed once they arrived in Alaska. Nobody was certain why swans chose the particular routes they did. Some scientists claimed it was an instinctive decision; they stopped when they were tired. Others said their flight paths were connected to the stars, or perhaps to the earth's magnetic field. Either way, local ornithologists feared that disturbing a centuries-old migration pattern could be disastrous for the species. *We can't just play God with nature and think there will be no consequences*, one ornithologist wrote in an opinion piece; *there is always, always a consequence.*

The *Nugget*, of course, covered both sides of the controversy. *We suffer enough through these dark frigid winters, why do we have to suffer by depriving ourselves of the luxuries of down south? Welcome to the 21st century, people. Buy yourself an Xbox and shut up.* Millicent laughed out loud at that quote. The sound echoed off the cement walls.

The more Millicent read, the more baffled she became at how much of the *Nugget*'s real estate this one subject took up. She wondered if, on some days, Franc had simply needed to fill the blank pages. The town had clearly been divided on the issue. After a few months of coverage and nothing significantly new to report, it seemed that Franc was just pouring acid on an open wound. But if the *Nugget* hadn't covered this story, Millicent realized, no one would, and the fate of an entire species could have been completely overlooked.

One night, with the newspaper draped over her stomach like a blanket and the back of her head cradled in her hands, Millicent gazed at the ceiling, wondering what had happened to the tundra swans after Walmart, and eventually the rest of the shopping complex, was built. Did they find another place to rest? She hadn't seen a single swan in the time she had lived here, at least not that she could remember. But then how could she know? She rarely paused just to look up at the sky.

Millicent's legs twitched as she woke up. Outside, a horn was honking. She looked at her phone. She had missed three calls from Pascal. It was ten after six. She left the newspaper splayed open on the couch and took the stairs two at a time.

21

WHAT MILLICENT DIDN'T KNOW by spending those early evenings at the *Nugget* was that Sophie had dropped by the bus to check on her twice. She wanted to apologize for her comment about rat babies—that was cruel—but more than that, she wanted to make sure Millicent was okay. Bryce had told her that Millicent moved through the newsroom lately as if there were a rain cloud above her head, barely even making eye contact with him.

The first time Sophie went to check on her friend, she sat in her car a few parking spots away, hoping to see Millicent in the window before she knocked on the door. When she caught a glimpse of only one silhouette moving through the bus, she lost her nerve and left, promising herself she'd try again soon.

The next day Sophie drove to Walmart after work. She parked flush with the bus and, without hesitating, knocked hard on the glass as the red generator hummed noisily by her feet.

Pascal opened the door. He was sitting on the driver's seat in a down jacket with duct tape on the arm.

"Sophie! Your hair, where did it go?"

"Where's Milli?" Sophie demanded.

If Pascal felt any anxiety about seeing Sophie, he didn't show it. He smiled and looked directly into her eyes, unfazed.

"Come into the bus," he said. "It's too cold outside. I have some wine. It's from a box, but I think it is still decent. A Cabernet Sauvignon. French wine, it's the best, isn't it?"

"I'm here for Millicent. Where is she?"

"She's not here."

"When will she be back?"

Pascal laughed. "Why are you coming around looking to make trouble, Sophie?"

Sophie looked towards the Walmart entrance at the evening shoppers pushing carts into the store. She shook her head in disbelief. "*I'm* making trouble? C'mon, Pascal. You're lucky I'm even talking to you."

Pascal stood up and came down the steps until he was standing just inches from Sophie. With his arms crossed over his chest, he leaned against the folded bus door as he towered above her.

"Why, you think what happened at the birthday party is my fault? You know you are responsible for this too, Sophie."

Sophie's eyes filled with tears and she drew in a long breath. "I know," she said quietly.

"Millicent, she is happy, finally," Pascal said.

"I don't believe that."

"You should."

"Why should I, Pascal?"

"Come inside and see for yourself."

The sweet, tangy scent of whatever Pascal was cooking for dinner drifted out into the parking lot. Sophie looked at her truck, then past Pascal and into the dimly lit bus.

"Fine," she said. "Just for one minute."

She followed Pascal onto the bus, past the herbs on the dash releasing their fresh earthy scent. A giant pot simmered on the stove. Pascal stirred it, brought the wooden spoon to his lips and tasted a bite.

"It's moose," he said with his mouth full. "I shot it last fall, my first one. Try some," he insisted.

"No, thank you." Sophie stood awkwardly in the kitchen. It was cold enough inside the bus to keep her jacket on. Pascal kept his on, but he rolled up the sleeves as he shook a generous amount of salt into the pot.

"What exactly did you want to show me?" she asked.

Pascal pointed to Millicent's red Moleskine notebook on the kitchen table, open to a page of scribbles. "She's writing poetry again."

Sophie leaned over the table and saw that it was true: stanzas of Millicent's almost illegible writing filled the page. Sophie flipped back several pages to find more scribbled lines. She had filled half the notebook already. Sophie closed the Moleskine and moved past the kitchen towards the entrance to the bedroom. She looked at Millicent's slippers placed tidily on the floor. Her pajamas hung on a hook by the bed.

"You have to leave her alone, Sophie. She doesn't want to see you. It's no offence to you," Pascal said.

Sophie fought back the tears that welled in her eyes again. "That *is* offensive, Pascal," she snapped.

"It's not. She is finally living how she wants to live. She is just ..." he trailed off, searching for the right words. "She's vibrating differently now."

Sophie stared at the flannel pajama set hanging so neatly on the hook, as if placed there for a photo shoot.

"Like I said, she's focused on our new life together and making her art, not distractions."

Sophie held his gaze for a long moment, then nodded and moved to the front of the bus.

"Will you tell her I stopped by, at least?" she asked from the top of the stairs.

"Of course," Pascal said.

22

AT NIGHT, PASCAL WAITED for Millicent in bed while she wrote at the kitchen table. Her poems weren't anything special, just random lines that came into her head about the northern landscape, or melancholy thoughts or sometimes, her mother. She had decided to just let it flow and see what happened. It was all about getting words on the page, then you could shape them. That's what Tim always said.

"Come to bed," Pascal pleaded one night. "I need my Rabbit."

Millicent finished her thought and closed her notebook.

"I thought the whole point of this was so I could write?" she said, stripping off her clothes. She pulled her pajamas from the hook and put them on, knowing Pascal would just take them off again. The propane heater was still broken and even with the space heater at the foot of the bed, it was far too cold for bare skin.

Pascal was in his boxer shorts, tucked neatly under the comforter like a small child. Millicent crawled in beside him and traced her finger along the thin line of hair that ran down from his bellybutton.

"Pascal? Isn't the whole point of me living here that we can become artists?"

"You are already an incredible artist. We both are," he said.

Her hand rose and fell on his stomach in rhythm with his breath. Pascal lifted her pajama top and began playing with her breast.

"You can't just forget about our quality time together," he continued with a small frown. "We are a team, now. You understand this, right?"

An acid taste seeped into her throat. When was the last time he had even mentioned the TV show? What about all the filmmakers who would be coming out to document their lives together? It had been weeks. Months, maybe. Could they really call themselves artists? She wrote down random thoughts in her journal for half an hour before bed, and he—well, he was still making commercials for fried chicken.

"I guess," she said.

Pascal twisted her nipple, hard, and a shock like electricity rippled through her body.

"Fuck!" Millicent gasped.

Pascal laughed. "That was not so bad, Rabbit, I'm just playing," he said. He kissed her nipple, gently, before grabbing the waistband of her pajamas and pulling them down her thighs.

MILLICENT BEGAN TAKING HER birdie baths at Starbucks every morning to wash off the traces of sex. She draped her jacket, shirt and bra over the coat hook on the door and pulled her pants and underwear down to her ankles. After splashing face, armpits and crotch with hot water and hospital-scented foam soap, she stood naked next to the hand dryer, letting the downward blast of hot air blow over her thighs. Millicent ignored the sound of the jiggling deadlock or the occasional hard knock. The other customers always gave up after a minute.

She found this part of her morning routine soothing. The loud hum and the heat of the dryer loosened her tightly wound thoughts, diminished their urgency and miraculously dissolved them. So what if, no matter how hard she tried, she couldn't see a way out? Even with her eyes closed, she was unable to visualize walking down the steps of the bus and simply leaving. Her mind put a stop to the scene before she could begin packing her bags.

The word *leaving* seemed to have lost its forward momentum, its very purpose. *Staying.* She saw the word in an imaginary dictionary. Dealing with the cards you have been dealt. Learning to see your life from a new perspective. Loving what you already have. Once Millicent concluded that she had no choice but to stick to her current life with Pascal, she put herself back together, squirming into her bra, brushing the knots out of her hair and highlighting her cheeks with blush. Sophie had always said that Sun-Kissed Peach brought out her eyes.

She was okay, Millicent told herself, staring at the reflection of her hard blue eyes above the bathroom sink.

She was more than okay. She might even be happy.

Out in the café, Millicent sat by the window in a purple velvet chair, gazing at the parking lot as it filled with cars, waiting for her order. *Rabbit*. Once she started using the word, she couldn't stop. At first, the baristas looked at her in alarm, as if she had ordered a cup of motor oil, but after a while they stopped asking her name and wrote a simple *R* on her cup. The staff knew she lived on the bus in the parking lot. With him. They were scared of her; she could tell by the way they avoided eye contact when they handed her a venti caramel macchiato and a cinnamon bun inside a butter-soaked bag.

She would let her boots sit in a small puddle on the tile floor, put her feet on a chair and think about Sophie and Bryce. Of course they were together, a couple, and of course she had lost them both, for good. That was why Bryce was so awkward with her in the newsroom. He and Sophie must have fallen together after the "trauma" of her birthday party.

Trauma, Millicent repeated. Sophie, as usual, wanted all the spotlight. That's why she had cut her hair. Now the whole world could see just how much pain she was in. Millicent imagined Sophie and Bryce curled up on the couch, talking about her, shaking their heads in disgust or pity or whatever it was they felt. *What happened to her?*

Millicent tore off a hunk of cinnamon bun and folded it into her mouth. Wu-wei, she thought, things were as they were. She couldn't change them.

She saved the gooey core of the bun for last, then licked each finger clean of sticky sugar so Pascal wouldn't know about her morning routine. He would say it was a waste of money. He would never understand that the sickening sweetness satisfied an urgent need. Without the macchiato and the cinnamon bun, the rest of the day would feel frantic, like a continuous attempt to grasp something physically impossible—a beam of sunlight, the smell of the river. The sugar and warm bread sedated her.

Some days, her ear sweaty against the phone, she worked up the courage to listen to her mother's voice mails. She always pressed delete before her mother finished talking. She had to. She couldn't call her back; her mother could read the slightest variation in the tone of her voice. Millicent would crack. Instead, she sent a text every few days to her mother's cellphone. *Work is busy. I'll call you in a few days. I'm doing good.*

One morning, after her birdie bath but still heavy with filth, unable to shake the feeling that she was rotting from the inside out, Millicent called home and let her parents' phone ring and ring. She knew that her mother would be in her deepest sleep this early in the morning and her father would already be at work. When Millicent heard his voice, the familiar *Hello, we're not home, but we'll get back you as soon as we can*, she gave a small gasp, as if finally coming up for air after a deep dive in the lake.

23

PASCAL WAS WORKING ON another commercial for Dirty Bird Hot Chicken.

Millicent knew that his TV show would never happen, she knew it in her very core. It hit her on a random Tuesday. She had just got home from work after writing a story about the rising cost of electricity. She was emptying her pockets—wallet, lip balm and a crumpled Starbucks receipt—into the drawer Pascal had designated for her "knick-knacks." She was careful to do this every day, knowing he would get quietly frustrated if she left anything out on the counter.

Millicent didn't know exactly what tipped her off. Maybe it was the way he sat stiffly at the computer, pencil behind his ear, headphones blaring the same cheesy theme song on repeat. Maybe it was his beard, now mostly grey, as if he had been waiting for Millicent to settle into his life before he could allow himself to let go, to age.

Pascal had blown his relationship with the producer entirely out of proportion. This was perfectly clear to her now. Millicent searched herself for anger, for flares of heat in her chest and throat, but found she was calm inside. Sophie had known. Bryce had known. God, Franc probably knew it as soon as he read her gushy article all those months ago. "Local Filmmaker Finds Freedom Living without Permanent Address." No wonder he didn't like him.

Millicent thought back to the many times Pascal had spoken about this *producer from Montreal* as if he were a god who would grant his every wish; his repeated promises that their life would be much better once they were out on the open road. She wondered if the producer had even read Pascal's emails, if he even knew Pascal existed.

Millicent shut the knick-knack drawer with her hip, softly, so he wouldn't look up from his work.

The truth was, she had known all along too. She had just chosen not to listen to herself.

She watched Pascal as he paused a scene and leaned closer to the screen. The frame was a steaming bucket of chicken with the words *hot* and *tender* in cursive overtop. He slipped the pencil from his ear and bit down on the end. It hung from his mouth like a cigarette. *Real artists*, Millicent reflected. It was something to believe in. She wondered if Pascal had admitted it to himself yet—that the commercials, the generator chugging outside on the snow, the Walmart parking lot—this was his life. There was no taking it to another level. There was no escape.

LATER THAT EVENING, PASCAL wiped down the counters with hot water and vinegar. Millicent was surprised that he was up and cleaning at this time of night. He was usually in bed by now, waiting for her. He wore his blue bandana to keep the hair off his face and yellow rubber gloves that reached his elbows. As he cleaned, he kept muttering "the number one rule for living on a bus," although Millicent wasn't sure if he was talking to himself or her. It didn't matter. She knew the number one rule: cleanliness is next to godliness. This seemed to be especially true when he was working on a commercial for Dirty Bird Hot Chicken.

Millicent sat five feet away at the kitchen table with a mug of tea and her Moleskine notebook. It was the farthest she could get from his frenetic energy without moving to the bed.

She liked to flip through her poetry at night to see if there was anything worth keeping. *The baritone groans of ice.* Millicent wrapped her hands around the hot mug and stared at the words. She had started coming up with these lines in her head on her walk to work. The deep freeze was finally over and by the time she stepped off the bus it was already light out, a small indication of the change of season that felt like a miracle.

Millicent would let the words surface as she crunched through the boggy mess of the thawing Millennium Trail. She didn't know what it was, maybe the constant rhythm of her footsteps, maybe the vitamins her body was soaking up from the sunlight, but during the walks to work a dormant part of her brain seemed to come alive.

The whole west side of the river was washed in cold sunlight at that time of day. Fragile birdsong rang intermittently through the perfectly blue sky. The river was waking up now too. The ice emitted deep, unnerving groans that moved Millicent in a way she could not explain. She had never heard anything like it.

With only a few minutes left before she had to be at her desk, Millicent perched on the edge of the bench outside the *Nugget* and burned the lines into her memory. *The baritone groans of ice.* Then, with her head tilted towards the sun and her eyes closed, she wallowed in the morning light, forgetting where she was.

AT THE KITCHEN TABLE, Millicent's pen hovered above the line *The baritone groans of ice.* She could do better. She crossed out the line, closed her notebook and secured the elastic over the front cover. Then, with a racing heart, she let the words fall out of her.

"Is this even a thing anymore, the TV show?" she asked.

Pascal was on his hands and knees, scrubbing a stain on the floor.

"Of course," he said, keeping his focus on the task.

He unfolded himself from the floor and began spritzing the stovetop. The sharp smell of vinegar drifted through the bus. She couldn't stop now.

"Why do you never talk about it?"

"I live in the moment, Rabbit," he said.

"But nothing has changed. There are no film crews.

You still live in this parking lot." Millicent paused, fiddling with the elastic on her notebook. "And you're working on a commercial for fried chicken," she said quietly.

Pascal scrubbed the stovetop even harder, the veins in his neck bulging.

"Pascal?"

"Patience is everything," he said.

Eventually he removed the rubber gloves and hung them inside out on the handle of the oven. He sat down next to her at the table and slid his hand underneath the back of her sweater, tracing his fingers up and down her spine.

"We're just waiting for the phone call," he said. "Then the world is ours."

24

BY THE THIRD WEEK of March, daylight finally stretched past dinnertime, hovering above the mountains and blanketing the town in a light that felt godly. Godly because it was absent all winter and now that it was back, it shook the town awake. Godly in the way it felt on the body, as if the light originated underneath the skin and shone outwards.

Then the river broke into a jumble of car-sized chunks of ice and green soupy water. What had been silent for months was now loud and raging, full of desperation, a snake trying to shed its skin. The morning the ice chunks jammed underneath the bridge, piling up so high that city crews closed it for fear its structural integrity was in jeopardy, the premier finally made the big announcement.

The press conference was exactly as Franc had predicted. Jakowsky stood at the podium with his freshly shaven goatee. He announced that, after years of consultation with all stakeholders, 95 percent of the Vista would be open to industrial development. GoldPower would begin construction within months. His hand strangled the throat of the microphone as he said the word "months." That's when the group of Gwich'in at the back of the room began yelling. Millicent had interviewed most of them at protests over the last few months. Their message was clear: they demanded 100-percent protection of their traditional territory.

"We are the caribou people!"

"This is not politics! It's genocide!"

Jakowsky pretended not to hear them. He continued speaking about the number of new jobs that would be created, the long-term security and the necessary balance between the economy and the environment.

"You can't please everyone," he said, "but you can do your best to listen to all the voices and make sound decisions from a place of integrity."

As he stepped away from the podium, Millicent forced her way into the scrum and thrust her recorder towards him. "Exactly what sorts of consultation," she asked, "has your government undertaken? If you have, in fact, had 'meaningful consultation' as outlined in the land claim agreements, why are you so secretive about them?"

Jakowsky gave a prepared answer. "We've done our work, now it's time to move on, in everyone's interest," he said, and then on cue he was ushered away.

While Bryce followed Jakowsky with his camera, Millicent found a quiet corner of the legislative building and called Charlie. Her hands were trembling. She was surprised when he picked up. Charlie's voice was emotionless.

"I'm quitting," he said.

"Politics?"

"Why did I ever put any trust in the white man's system? No such thing as reconciliation. Just a nice word white people use to feel better about the horror they cause."

"I'm so sorry Charlie," Millicent said.

The line fell silent.

"Can you tell me about the consultations? What were they like?"

There was rustling on the other end.

"For the story," she continued.

Charlie muttered to himself, words she couldn't make out.

"I'm not just trying to get you to open up for me, Charlie."

He laughed sourly.

"No? Seems like it."

"You're right about what you said at the smudge. Maybe I don't deserve to know. But right now, more than ever, your words deserve to be in this story. Lots of people voted for you. Lots of people want to hear what you have to say." Millicent forced herself to slow down, to breathe, to speak firmly. "What I'm trying to say is your story needs to be in print today."

Charlie's voice cracked with anger. "They signed land-claim agreements in good faith and now this? Consultation? Is that what Jakowsky calls the government flying into Old Crow, holding a half-hour meeting to announce their plans? Bringing a box of Timbits to make us feel better? Is that a fucking consultation?"

He inhaled, trying to control his voice.

"If the caribou population isn't healthy, we won't have enough to eat. If we don't have enough to eat, our people will get sick and die. That's all there is to it."

The line fell silent again.

"I'm so sorry about this, Charlie."

He laughed again.

"Don't be sorry for me. I feel sorry for you."

"What do you mean?"

"You gotta stay here with all this bullshit. I'm going back out to the land, where things make sense."

"Out to the trapline?" Millicent asked.

"A fishing camp. Right where the premier's gonna build his mine. Not just me, my uncles and cousins too. He's gonna have to kill us first before he starts blasting the earth open."

WHEN SHE RETURNED FROM the press conference, Millicent found Franc lying on his back on the newsroom floor. His glasses lay on top of his belly, rising and falling with his breath.

She thought he was sleeping, but when she came closer she saw that his eyes were open, his pupils tracking the spinning fan. Was he drunk? It was ten in the morning. Franc wouldn't drink in the morning when the paper had to go out. He had too much pride.

"Franc?"

"Millicent," Franc said to the ceiling.

"You heard the news?"

"Ninety-five percent. I mean, fuck, why not just round it up to one hundred percent? A nice whole number."

"Do you want to talk about it?" she asked.

"No."

Millicent sucked in a long breath of air and stared at her boss on the floor. She couldn't stop shaking. She knew the only way to calm down was to get the contents of her mind onto the page. When it became clear that Franc wasn't going to move, she stepped over his legs, tossed her notepad on her desk and booted up her computer.

"How many words do you want?" she asked.

"Whatever," Franc said. "Half a page, a page, write the whole newspaper. I don't care."

IT WAS FORTY-FIVE MINUTES until deadline and Millicent couldn't get the lede right. She gnawed at her thumbnail, watching the cursor blink methodically on her screen. She wiped the film of sweat from her palms on her jeans, rearranged the words in the first sentence, then quickly arranged them back to their original order. At last, she rested her head on her desk and closed her eyes, at peace with the fact that they wouldn't put out a paper today, thus missing out on the biggest news in years.

"Feels good to give up," Franc said from the floor behind her. He seemed to feel unashamed to spend the entire morning there.

Millicent swivelled around in her chair.

"Charlie said he's going out to a fishing camp in the Vista. His cousins and aunts and uncles too, they'll be dozens of them. GoldPower can't build a mine right on top of them. It's not over, Franc."

Franc spoke, barely moving his lips, "Can you really call it a protest if it's on their own land?"

Millicent suddenly felt dizzy, as if she was falling. "I don't know," she said.

Franc struggled to his feet, wiped his glasses on his sleeve and adjusted them on his nose. He looked at Millicent as if he was only now remembering who she was.

"Fuck," he said, glancing at the clock, and walked stiffly to his office. Millicent followed him, stepping over the stacks of newspapers.

Franc leaned his forehead against his window and jiggled the keys in his pocket. Millicent stood next to him, mimicking his body language. She gazed out the glass past Riverbend Estate. The condo building was free of scaffolding and at the main entrance was a sign that said *Rent Me!* From here, the river appeared to be quietly shimmering, but she had walked by that morning and seen the chunks of ice being swept down current. It sounded like crystal chandeliers crashing to the floor, as if the river was furious when it realized it had been asleep all those months.

"Pretend for a second that this isn't a story you're writing for the newspaper," Franc said, still staring out the window. "Imagine I announced one day that I'm going to take your house away just like that. I mean, it's not that bad, right? I give you a couple of months' notice."

He turned to face her. He looked absolutely exhausted,

as if one more day, one more hour at the newspaper would break him. But when he spoke, his voice had a steely edge.

"But it's not just your house, no. I'm also going to demolish your grocery store, your bank and whatever other services you depend on to survive. And I'm going to turn all the taps off, so no one will have access to clean water."

Millicent stared at the hair on the back of his hands.

"I will take away everything you need to survive."

"It's horrible," she said.

Franc closed his eyes and rubbed his temples, making slow circles with two fingers.

"It's really horrible," she continued. "I can't believe our government is so short-sighted and—"

"I wasn't asking for your opinion, Millicent," Franc said, cutting her off. He motioned for her to sit on the chair facing his desk. "I was asking you to imagine what it would be like to have that all taken away from you."

Millicent crossed her legs, remembering her first day of work, sitting in this very chair knowing nothing about the Vista or Jakowsky or Pascal. The way Franc was look-ing at her now made her feel just as young and raw as she had that day.

Her voice sounded fragile. "It's hard to imagine that."

"Exactly," Franc said, sitting down across from her. "But do we even try?"

"I guess not," Millicent said.

"We'll always have problems, Millicent. You, for some reason I will never understand, have given your heart to a middle-aged loser with a terrible reputation after I let you interview him as a fluff piece to get you going. I mean, I thought you could handle it, Millicent. I really did."

She opened her mouth to speak but no sound emerged, only hot breath.

"And now you spend your time after work in the basement to get away from him. You think I don't know? You think I'm not worried, that Bryce isn't worried? He doesn't even know what to say to you anymore. I come back at night sometimes too, Millicent. Sit in my office. Listen to the radio. You're not the only one who wants to escape."

So Franc had been upstairs in his office when she was in the basement. He'd heard Pascal honking the horn. She wasn't living a secret life. She wasn't invisible. Millicent gripped the arms of the chair, wanting to exit her own body. Her vision grew blurry. Franc had never even acknowledged her relationship with Pascal, but the truth was that he and Bryce had been watching her the whole time. She saw herself as Franc must see her: her pale face covered in blush, her hair heavy with grease, the wool socks she wore day in and day out. With nausea swelling in her stomach, she heard the honking of the bus in his ears on all those nights at exactly six o'clock.

Franc reached up to scratch the scruff of the bear's neck.

"We're too lost in our own human problems to understand what's happening to the world," he said gently. "That's why nobody reads the newspaper—they can't handle more bad news. It's not just you, it's everyone. It's me. We're obsessed with our own pain."

Then he laughed, and Millicent realized she was

laughing along with him, wanting to feel anything but the fear and shame she was trapped inside.

She stared at the plastic bag that held his lunch hanging on the back of the door.

"We have to try to see past our own goddamn problems, Millicent. We have to. Because one day the premier makes an announcement that will change the balance of the planet. And locals yell and scream and kick, and we print the story and make room for a follow-up story the next day. But then the next day, well, something more sexy will happen, won't it? Maybe a cabinet minister will be charged with sexual harassment or we'll get a new fast-food chain, and this issue will fade into the background. But it's not just an *issue*," he said, using air quotes. "It's not an environmental issue. It's not even a political issue." Franc paused to catch his breath, and when he continued it was with such seething anger that Millicent finally understood him.

"The plan the premier has approved will likely kill entire species. What he is condoning will poison water that has been running clear for thousands of fucking years."

Millicent nodded rapidly. She couldn't believe she had actually considered leaving this job—a job that suddenly felt like the most urgent thing in the world—to follow Pascal's delusions.

The only words she could muster were "Politics are evil."

Franc slammed his fist against his desk. "It's not fucking *politics*. That's the whole fucking problem! It's humanity. It's real lives that are being destroyed." He inhaled deeply, bit his lip and looked out the window, trying to keep his emotions in check.

Millicent's blood coursed calmly through her body now. She felt calmer than she had in months. She thought about what a Gwich'in Elder had told her: that when the Gwich'in come back from the hunt, a certain peace is restored within the community. Going out on the land had been in their blood for thousands of years. She said there were no words in English to explain the feeling; the clearest words she could use were that everything was connected to the earth, the animals and the water.

We are the land, she had said.

"So, do you want me to write the story or not?" Millicent asked.

Franc swept the cursor over his computer screen. He looked at the clock in the newsroom.

"You have fifteen minutes. All the time in the world."

As she made her way to her desk, the first paragraph came to her perfectly formed: Yukon Premier Conrad Jakowsky has announced that 95 percent of the Vista, a 60,000-square-kilometre stretch of wilderness in northern Yukon, will be open to industrial development. Approximately three quarters of the Vista lies within the traditional territory of the Gwich'in, who have lived, hunted and trapped on the land for millennia. The Gwich'in have not been consulted regarding the plan, as required in land claims agreements signed less than two decades ago. During the election campaign last fall, Jakowsky ignored dozens of requests from the *Nugget* to answer the simple question *What are your plans for the Vista?*

25

THE FIRST DAY OF APRIL. The river swelled, running like cold coffee through town, carrying with it logs, a grocery cart, the body of a man who had gone for a drunk swim the night before and never returned to shore.

Pascal put his turn signal on, craned his neck to make sure the lane was clear and merged onto Two-Mile Hill. He weaved through traffic. He passed a school bus full of children who slammed their palms against the windows when they saw him. Pascal honked his horn three times and the children exploded, hopping in their seats like kernels of popcorn. He hummed along to the electronic remix of Bob Marley's "Sun Is Shining." The bass rattled the Mason jars, the cast iron pan hanging above the stove and the dirty dishes in the Tupperware bin underneath the kitchen table.

Millicent covered the phone speaker with her hand.

"Can you turn it down?" she yelled.

"Anything for my Rabbit!"

Pascal was happy, happier than he had been in months. The producer was going to call today—he had promised. When Pascal announced it earlier that morning, it was with such genuine confidence that Millicent began to doubt herself again. She didn't know how to process this news. They hadn't talked about the producer for weeks. After seeing that email header on his screen a while back, she had come to terms with the fact that there was no producer anymore, and that it was Pascal's ego that stopped him from telling her the truth.

Millicent almost brought it up one night as they lay in bed, a fistful of her hair in his hand—a recent habit he had developed that helped him fall asleep. She wanted to finally be rid of the story, but when she rehearsed the lines in her head, a cold knife of fear pierced her chest, leaving her mute. She really had no idea how Pascal would react to such an accusation.

From the top of the hill, Whitehorse looked like the perfect little town. Ten in the morning and the day was bright as a nickel. Millicent watched Pascal as he sang along to Bob Marley.

"Are you sure you don't want me to cover the drowning?" Millicent asked Franc on the phone.

"I've got it. Can't do much until the autopsy. Just go to Dawson. Stay out of trouble," Franc said.

It was Thaw-Di-Gras weekend in Dawson City, a celebration to mark the yearly thaw of the Yukon River. Franc had assigned both her and Bryce to take photos, since there wasn't much they couldn't cover in cutlines. He handed Millicent a crumpled hundred-dollar bill, telling her it was a per diem. The words sounded awkwardly formal coming from Franc's mouth; there was no way the *Nugget* could afford a per diem.

She tried to give it back—it was obviously his own money—but he just shook his head and told her she deserved it.

Millicent knew it wasn't really a per diem; it was Franc's way of congratulating her on her article about the Vista. The national wire had picked it up. Her byline was printed in over a dozen newspapers across the country. She couldn't believe it. Neither could Franc. She had watched him through the newsroom window that afternoon. He swung open his office door at 3:00 and returned fifteen minutes later with a bag from the bookstore full of newspapers: the *Globe and Mail*, the *National Post*, the *Vancouver Sun*. He unfolded the newspapers on his desk and just stared at them, hands on his hips.

The next day the Gwich'in Nation announced they were suing the Yukon government for failure to consult. Franc had said it could go all the way to the Supreme Court. It could set a precedent. This was the biggest news the territory had seen in many years.

PASCAL ACCELERATED ONTO THE Alaska Highway.

"What should I take pictures of?" Millicent said into the phone.

"The cat in costume, the arm wrestling, the strippers. Bryce'll do the same."

"The strippers?"

"You going with Bryce?" Franc asked.

"No."

"Riding solo?"

"No."

The line went silent.

"Pascal, then." Franc breathed into the phone.

She forged ahead, anything to shift the conversation. "Are you sure you want to print photos of strippers? Seems a bit unethical."

"*Before* they take their clothes off, obviously, Millicent. It is technically news. Bylaw says we can't have strippers in Dawson, but every year the government flies a plane full of 'em up from Edmonton for Thaw-Di-Gras."

"You're kidding," Millicent said.

"I wish. It's a ludicrous use of the government coffer. I've tried to call them out on it before in an editorial. Someone egged the *Nugget* after that was printed. God forbid our strippers are taken away."

"Right," she said.

Millicent watched Pascal drive. He had rolled the sleeves of his flannel shirt above his elbows. Every time he moved the steering wheel he seemed to do so with intention. It was all about control. She could see this now.

"And Millicent?" Franc said. "Be careful. Everyone is manic from all the daylight this time of year."

"I'll be fine, Franc."

Millicent hung up. *You are now leaving city limits.* Soon the traffic thinned to nothing. The windshield was streaked in dirt, spattered with dead bugs. Outside the windows it was one quarter land, three quarters sky, matchstick trees for as far as she could see. Around every few corners was a perfect emerald lake.

Millicent allowed her body to be carried along through the landscape. She tried to focus on the pure elation of seeing her byline in the *Globe and Mail*, but the feeling was distant now, out of her grasp. When she told Pascal the news, he was at his desk with his headphones on, editing. Millicent replayed the scene in her mind. For a few minutes he didn't turn around. He didn't even stop working. She could see his mood in the stiffness of his neck.

"Pascal? Did you hear me?"

He spun around with a tense smile. "That's great."

"You don't sound excited."

Pascal got out of his chair and stood an inch away from Millicent. He didn't seem to know what to do with his hands. He kept balling them up, stretching them out and then balling them up again.

"You know what I think?"

"What do you think?"

"I've told you this a million times. You are an artist. We are artists. All this other stuff is just a distraction from making art."

"That is ridiculous," she said.

"Is it?" Pascal hooked two fingers through one of her belt loops. Millicent scanned his face—his hooked nose, his thick, caterpillar eyebrows, his eyes that seemed to have lost all their shine.

"This has nothing to do with being an artist, you can't just use that line to justify everything." She inhaled sharply, waiting for his response. He blinked and gazed right back at her. Millicent couldn't tell if he was being playful or serious. She smiled and he didn't smile back. Then, before she could say anything else, he put his arms around her and kissed her so hard and for so long she had to wriggle out of his grasp to catch her breath.

THE BUS ASCENDED a steep hill. The smell of diesel and the chili Pascal had cooked the night before hung in the air. She missed Sophie. The memories came on hard and fast. The smell of lavender on her neck. The easy silence that had fallen between them when they picked blue-berries in the fall. Her first days at Horizon—Millicent so shy she could barely look at the other students—Sophie inviting her next door, where they would drink negronis and talk for hours about everything and noth-ing, Millicent in awe of Sophie's bohemian style, discov-ering a new part of herself, an easier part, a part of herself she liked.

There was no stopping these memories. They rose to the surface like bloated fish. Millicent had the urge to bury her head in her arms to block them out, although she knew this was no use. She even missed Sophie as she had been at their dinner party, the night of the first snowfall, when she kept smiling in her drunken, coy way, luring the conversation back to her.

Millicent opened her eyes and watched the land pass-ing by, allowing the greens and blues to swim into each other. She had been trying to suppress these memories all winter, but what was the point? The harder she pushed them down, the more forcefully they came back up.

IN THE TINY TOWN of Carmacks, halfway between Whitehorse and Dawson, Pascal stopped to buy over-priced gas. He went into the store to pay and emerged with two sticks of red licorice.

They lost cell service soon afterwards. The empty high-way stretched in front of them like a serpent's tongue. Millicent sat next to Pascal on the hump between the driver's seat and the door, her hand manoeuvring the stick shift—their highway game. The stale licorice hung from her lips. Pascal kept his stick in the pocket of his shirt, like a pen. He reached for his sunglasses on the dash. He seemed to calm down now that he was unable to obsessively check his phone.

Millicent thought back to the first time they met, at Bear Lake. How they sat with their feet dangling off the back of the bus, listening to a woodpecker up in the trees, and Pascal had opened up to her so effortlessly, like they were the last two people on the entire planet.

Millicent chewed the last of her licorice and swallowed. "Are you still lonely?"

Pascal stretched his leg out to push down the clutch. "Shift."

Millicent pushed the stick from fifth to fourth, then down to third as the road dipped sharply and the earth caved in on itself due to the melting permafrost.

"How could I be lonely? I have you," he said. "Shift, please."

Millicent yanked the stick back to fifth. The odometer read 125 kph, cruising speed.

"So?"

"And you are magnificent."

She inspected him again. His salt-and-pepper moustache was growing over his lip. He hadn't trimmed it in weeks. Why hadn't she allowed herself to see him like this, falling apart?

"I miss Sophie."

She hadn't spoken Sophie's name out loud since the birthday party almost six months ago. Just saying it made her feel instantly lighter, like she wanted to laugh.

"And Bryce," she added with finality.

Pascal kept his focus on the road. "Why do you need these people?"

"*These people?*"

Pascal's jaw tightened. "They are toxic. I've told you this. Little people with little dreams, trying to pull you down with them because they can't stand to see you happy."

He took his attention off the road to look at her. She wouldn't meet his eyes.

"You don't need these people in your life to be happy, Rabbit. They are just distractions."

"Distraction from what, Pascal? Why do you keep talking about distractions?"

"Distractions from us!"

They crossed a wooden, single-lane bridge over the

Yukon River. Millicent looked down through the bus door. The water slipped through the land silently. Millicent thought she would never do it, never get the words past the tightening in her throat but there they were, crowning towards daylight.

"Why did you do it?"

"Do what?"

"Sophie."

Pascal jerked the wheel to the right. He pulled over on the side of the road and cut the engine. He undid his seatbelt.

"I told you all of this. When will we move on? We can do great things. Do you understand this?"

He stood up and pulled her towards him, brought her face to his and put his mouth against hers. His tongue searched her mouth. She could feel him getting hard. Every cell in her body revolted. It was automatic, the way she shoved him off. Her muscles moved before her brain had a chance to process the situation. Pascal sat down and slumped over, his forehead on the steering wheel.

Millicent sat on the top step, looking out at the ditch through the folding door. There wasn't another car as far as she could see.

"There is no producer anymore, is there?" she said quietly.

"What are you talking about?"

"The producer? The phone call you're waiting for? It's not going to happen, is it? You're either a liar or you're delusional. The frightening thing is I don't know which one it is."

Pascal pulled on the lever and a rush of sharp air entered the bus.

"Get out," he spat. "Now."

He had never spoken to her with such violence. "At the side of the highway in the middle of nowhere?" she asked.

Pascal said nothing. She could gauge his anger by how hard he looked at her. Millicent let her eyes become unfocused until all she saw was an endless green blur. The wind picked up, carrying the sweet, fertile scent of new life blooming from the forest floor.

"I really did let myself love you," she said.

The anger inside him changed to relief, she could tell by the way he sighed. Now he sat down directly behind her and extended his legs out long and wide, straddling her torso so she was tucked safely inside. He wrapped his arms around her waist. His beard rubbed against her neck. How badly he needed her. She wondered if she would ever be needed like this again.

26

BY THE TIME THEY rolled into town, Pascal was rattling off the handful of facts he knew about the gold rush and playing with the soft curls at the base of Millicent's neck with his right hand.

The sound of the diesel engine. The feeling of his fingers on her neck. The smell of him, sweat and stale chili and clothes that hadn't been washed. Millicent told herself to inhale and then exhale. If she focused entirely on the task of breathing, she would be okay.

Pascal parked under the wooden sign for the Dawson City Hotel and turned off the ignition.

"You booked a room here?" Millicent asked. They were the first words she had spoken in ages, although Pascal hadn't seemed to notice her silence.

He stuffed the keys in his pocket. "No. Tomorrow we will shower in this hotel."

Millicent let out a loud sigh. "How?"

"The rooms need to be cleaned anyway. We will ask if we can shower in one of them first. Why would they say no?"

Millicent stared out the window, fighting the impulse to smash her fist through the glass. She wanted to feel the glass pierce through her skin. She wanted to see the blood. Instead, she swallowed her hot saliva and pulled out the hundred-dollar bill Franc had given her as a per diem.

"I'll pay for a room," she said.

Pascal had his phone to his ear and he looked distracted. "Rabbit, it's a waste of your money." He was checking his voice mails again. "We have to think outside of the box, remember?" he said, more gently.

You have no new messages.

Millicent went to the bedroom for her warmer clothing to go out into the street. Pascal rose from the driver's seat and paced around the bus, shaking his head and muttering to himself. After a few minutes of this, he announced he was going to bed.

"Jesus Christ," Millicent said as she looped her scarf around her neck.

"What?" Pascal asked.

"Give up the act already."

"What act? I just can't believe he still has not called me. This is ridiculous." He grabbed his jacket from the hook, stabbed an arm through each sleeve and followed her outside.

Across the street, the windows of the Grits Diner were fogged up. The smell of bacon and coffee wafted onto the street even though it was past seven at night. Pascal followed her, silent, his hands stuffed into his pockets. The town looked like it hadn't changed in a hundred years. A sign in peeling paint on a pink clapboard building boasted ten-cent haircuts. Millicent and Pascal weaved through loiterers in the middle of the street. Men in flannel shirts and women in chiffon dresses over long johns smoked cigars. A Rottweiler dog chased its own tail. Millicent felt as if she was seeing, really seeing, the Yukon for the first time.

The Boiler Room boasted that it was the only bar in Dawson, and it felt as if everyone in Yukon and Alaska was packed inside. The room was hot as a sauna and shoes stuck to the floor. The smell of hops and piss and sweat filled Millicent's nostrils.

She lost Pascal immediately. One minute his fingers were hooked to the belt loop of her jeans, the next he was gone. Millicent shoved her way to the back of the bar, took off her jacket and scarf and hung the camera around her neck. Putting aside the blistering anger that flickered inside her chest, the feeling that she was on the verge of crawling out of her own skin, she lost herself in work.

An elderly woman with a mass of white hair stood rigidly by the bathroom door, cradling a Siamese cat in her arms. Woman and cat were wearing matching top hats and bow ties. Click. Click. Click.

On the stage, a stripper in a pink sequined dress wrapped her thigh around a pole and leaned so far back her breasts spilled out towards her face, eliciting whoops and screams. A cannon on the side of the stage released a blast of sparkles over the stripper and into the crowd. Millicent got the shot.

A group of volunteers in high-visibility vests cleared the stage for the Calmest Cat competition. A man dressed as Big Bird came out and explained to the crowd that cats would be judged on their stoicism. Cat owners would place their pet on stage and the last one to run away was declared the winner.

Millicent bought a shot of tequila—salted rim, wedge of lime—and found an empty stool. The liquid scorched her throat. The warmth travelled all the way through her veins and to her fingertips and she felt freer than she had in months, as if she kept tossing the liquid down her throat she would eventually sink into the floor and disappear entirely.

She snagged an empty bar stool, leaned back and watched the room, which had become a thick soup of drunk bodies. On stage, the Siamese cat curled its tail into a question mark and watched, perfectly still, as the other cats hissed and ran offstage. The cat's owner stood nearby, her hands cupped over her mouth, her eyes wide as moons.

After the last cat was rounded up, a shotgun blast out in the street announced the start of the tricycle race. Lines of duct tape on the bar floor marked the route, looping through the tables and the dance floor. The crowd made room for the contestants. From behind the lens, Millicent watched the tricyclists wobble through the course, all knees and hunched backs.

At the far end of the bar near the finish line, she spotted Bryce, his blond hair sticking up messily without his baseball cap. He leaned against the bar, talking to a slight woman with short ginger hair. Millicent couldn't see her face, but she could tell from the sharp shoulder blades half-covered by a silky scarf. Sophie.

Millicent put the camera on her lap. The room swam, hot and beery, around her. She bit down hard on her bottom lip to keep her composure. Breathe in. Breathe out. Breathe in. Breathe out. Had Sophie seen her? Was she pretending she hadn't and ignoring her? She needed to do something with her hands. Millicent leaned forward and tried to make eye contact with the bartender.

"Another shot, please," she said, but it was just her lips moving. The drunken pitch of the bar completely drowned out her voice. Millicent watched more people shove their way to the bar, stumbling and snorting like barnyard animals just freed from their pens. As she picked up the camera again, an elbow dug into her rib cage, making her scream. The bar carried on in its mayhem without a single glance in her direction. Had she even made a sound?

Millicent twisted the lens to zoom in closer on Bryce and Sophie. Bryce had a camera around his neck too, although he didn't look concerned about taking any pictures. He ran a hand through his hair self-consciously.

Sophie turned around and handed Bryce a fresh pint. As he leaned down to suck off the foam, Sophie whispered something in his ear. Millicent felt her stomach cave in on itself when Bryce tossed his head, laughing with his whole body. She used to laugh like that. She remembered the feeling of laughter, real laughter. Another gun discharged on the street. The techno music pumped louder, *What is love? Baby don't hurt me, don't hurt me, no more.* The beat exploded in her eardrums and the air was too thick to breathe. She was suffocating, but she didn't know what she needed: air, water, Pascal?

Bryce had turned his back to her and was gesticulating to the bartender. Now Sophie was waving. Sophie was waving at her, smiling. A small smile. An invitation. Millicent did not wave back but pushed through the mess of bodies towards her old friend.

"Mill!" Sophie said. "I thought I might see you here."

"Hi!" Millicent croaked. "I guess you did."

"Are you getting some good shots?"

Millicent looked down at the camera.

"Mill, are you okay?" Sophie asked.

No words came to her.

"You don't seem okay," Sophie said more softly.

Millicent wanted to crumple into Sophie's arms like a small child, but instead she forced an awful smile and said in a shaky voice, "I'll be right back."

Millicent found herself slumped on the cold floor of the bathroom, her back to the wall. The toilet in the stall closest to her flushed and a woman dressed as Batgirl stumbled out. The stripper in the sequined dress was at the sink, her face an inch away from the mirror.

"Hon?" she asked Millicent. Batgirl swung the door open and left.

It was simple. Just take a breath in. Then let it out.

"Guess not," the stripper said, checking her black eyeliner in the mirror.

She would go back to Pascal that night, like she always

did. She would sleep between his arms. And in the morning, she would think about how simple it would be to pack her bags and get off the bus, yet she would choose to stay again and again. Of course she would. Pascal was all she knew now. They had created a whole universe together.

The stripper swiftly applied juicy purple colour to her lips and zipped her purse closed, barely glancing in the mirror. She left, banging through the swinging door. Out in the bar, the announcer's voice boomed: *And here she is, ladies and gentlemen, back for round two to soothe your dark and desperate souls, the one and only Big Rock Candy Mountain!*

Millicent forced herself to stand up. Looking down at the sink, she clutched the edge, trying to regain composure. She turned the faucet on and splashed her face. The water felt as if it was being pumped straight from the thawing river.

It wasn't until she looked in the mirror—pale-faced, hair greasy and tangled—that Millicent realized why Big Rock Candy Mountain had been in such a hurry.

She had made her nervous.

She emerged from the bathroom more certain than ever that she was living inside a lucid dream: her body was commanded purely by willpower rather than physics. Millicent was scanning the room for Sophie, but a man in a high-vis vest and a clipboard intercepted her.

"Need more girls for arm wrestling. You in?"

"Okay," she said, numbly.

"Fantastic. What's your name?"

She scanned the other names scribbled on the page. Amanda, Katie, Sarah, Pattie and Siobhan. *Rabbit.*

"Millicent," she said.

The arm-wrestling table was made of two-by-fours nailed together and covered with orange carpeting. The announcer called for Millicent and Amanda. Amanda, in a tutu and a blond wig, giggled as if saying *how silly it is for women to arm wrestle!* Millicent forced her arm to the table within seconds. Despite the cheering crowd, she didn't laugh or even smile. She wanted to feel joy, but her body wasn't willing to pretend. She beat the other three contestants easily. The crowd drew in closer and became hushed.

"You're a monster!" someone yelled from the crowd.

Millicent knew this. She had seen it in the bathroom mirror. She had known it on those nights she woke up to pee in the parking lot, when the cold burned her lungs. She was a monster.

Her final opponent was Siobhan. She wore a hoodie and her hair in a ponytail, and she was a foot taller than Millicent. Siobhan did not make eye contact. Millicent leaned her weight into the table. The whistle blew and they pushed into a deadlock. The bar chanted *Millicent, Millicent, Millicent*, and she wanted to look up and see Pascal, or Bryce or Sophie. Instead, she focused on curling her wrist towards Siobhan to gain leverage.

At first Siobhan wouldn't budge, but little by little she saw her opponent's face go from stern concentration, to pain, to defeat. Millicent knew she had passed the sacred point of no return. She pinned Siobhan's arm to the table.

The announcer was exuberant; he took Millicent's hand and pulled it into the air.

The gold medal was heavy. The crowd buzzed around her. She could see Pascal elbowing his way towards her, a look of hunger on his face. She grabbed her jacket and her camera and ran towards the door.

She veered down the main street and away from the crowds. Once she hit the path that ran along the river, Millicent slowed down to a walk. The moon hung full and bloated, as if it might fall from the sky and splinter across the land. She kept expecting the sound of his footsteps, expecting him to call her name from behind—*Rabbit, Rabbit, Rabbit*—but the only sound was the crashing of chunks of ice as they floated with the current.

27

THE HANDLE ON THE hotel door wouldn't budge. She knocked three times with her fist, waited, then knocked again, this time harder. *We're closed!* a voice yelled from inside.

Millicent slid her back down the door and sat there, listening to the distant hollering from outside the bar and staring at the dark school bus a few feet away. This was the only hotel in Dawson City that was open in off season. Unless she wanted to sleep outside, which would be dangerous as the night temperature dipped far below zero, she would have to go back to the bus. Every part of her screamed against going back there.

She toyed with the medal around her neck as the familiar hollow feeling crept into her chest. She had nowhere else to go. Nowhere to be.

When the cold had crept into her core and her hands began to shake, she walked slowly up the steps of the bus and locked the door behind her. She knew it wouldn't do any good, but just being alone on the bus with the door locked gave her a marble-sized sense of peace. She forced herself to focus on this.

When Pascal arrived and found the door locked, he didn't even bother to take his keychain from his pocket. He opened the door by kicking the toe of his boot against the corner and pushing his weight against the glass, not too hard, not too soft. This was a trick only he knew how to perform.

"My champion!" he exclaimed.

Millicent hovered over the kitchen sink, brushing her teeth. She could see his expression even with her eyes closed.

"Where did you go? Why didn't you tell me?"

She kept her eyes squeezed shut. Pascal's voice grew louder as he moved towards her.

"You are incredible. I had no idea you had this in you, Rabbit," he said.

He kept talking. Millicent focused on the hypnotic rhythm of the bristles against her teeth. Then she silently recited the contents of the Mason jars above the sink. She had them memorized in order: lentils, black-eyed peas, dried cranberries, one-minute oats. Pascal spoke rapidly and broke into French every few sentences. He would take her around the world to arm-wrestling competitions. They could make a lot of money. She repeated the list in her mind like a children's song: *lentils, black-eyed peas, dried cranberries, one-minute oats.*

Pascal had become quiet.

"Rabbit, what's the matter? Why won't you look at me?" He sounded desperate now.

"Is something wrong? Did I do something wrong?"

Lentils, black-eyed peas, dried cranberries and one-minute oats. Millicent spat, gargled and headed to the bedroom. She climbed between the cold sheets with her clothes on.

"Rabbit?"

If he touched her, she would kill him.

"Rabbit?"

She stopped breathing.

"Are you alive?"

Someone banged on the side of the bus. *Fucking hippies, get a room!*

When Millicent rolled over, she saw that Pascal was sitting on the edge of the mattress. She turned on the lamp beside the bed. He considered this small movement an invitation and rested his weight on his elbow. He reached for her medal, turned it over, read the inscription and whistled, cheeks hollow in the weak yellow light.

"Will you sleep with your medal?"

His mouth tasted like the bar. She wanted him inside of her. It was not desire. She wanted to feel the pain and disgust, anything but this numbness. He kissed her hungrily and yanked at her bra so hard the gauzy fabric ripped. His mouth was on her nipple, her collarbone, her ear. Her hand clutched the flesh of his back. She couldn't get hold of him. She couldn't get tight enough. His eyes glazed over when he entered her; *Rabbit*, he said. No.

"Stop, Pascal."

She tried to shrug him off, but he pressed his weight into her. His eyes lost their loving look.

"I am the wolf. You are the rabbit."

He kept repeating these words, looking right through her. A tear dropped into her mouth. At first she thought it was her own, but it tasted foreign, salty, and when she looked up she saw that his face was twisted in grief and anger. Millicent arched her back and yelled "Get off!" Her body writhed with animal strength, but it was no use. His arms were steel pipes. She was drowning in the sweat-soaked sheets.

"Do you understand this?" he demanded, pushing himself so deep inside her the pain became sharp. "Do you understand that I am the wolf?"

As suddenly as it began, it was over. Pascal collapsed next to her on the mattress. Returning to his body, he stroked her hair away from her forehead.

Pascal spoke between sobs as Millicent rose from the bed, her thoughts, finally, in perfect alignment. "I am sorry. I would never hurt you. You are incredible."

He kept speaking like this until his sobs drowned out the words. Millicent groped through her drawer until she found a clean pair of underwear. The cold floor stung her bare feet. She bent one knee and threaded a leg through her underwear. Then the other. The smell of diesel choked out the air on the bus.

Pascal stopped crying and caught his breath, and his words spilled out like they were poison, as if he could not hold them in for one moment longer.

"Look at me. I am forty-three years old, living in a school bus and making commercials for fried chicken. I was supposed to be big. I was born to be big! This is why I was put here on earth. I have known since I was a child, did you know this?" His next words were choked, high pitched. "What is the point if the world is always against me?"

Millicent slipped one arm through her sweater, then the other arm and then her head. Dressed and warm, she began sliding her clothes from their hangers and packing them into her duffel bag. She knew there was nowhere to go until morning, but the act of packing was keeping her alive.

"I should just take a machete and cut my head off," Pascal said, wringing the twisted sheet in his hand. "I should really do this." His knuckles were white. "I love you, Rabbit."

Millicent gazed down at him in the bed.

"That doesn't matter," she said.

"Don't you think I should just kill myself?" he asked, staring up at her. "Rabbit?"

THE HERBS ON THE DASH released a fertile, sweet musk. Millicent sat stiffly in the driver's seat, watching the black of night dissolve into dawn. The sky was growing lighter but she did not trust that time was passing.

When she worked up enough will to move, she reached under the seat for the keychain and inserted the square silver key into the ignition. Millicent turned the radio dial, listening for a frequency. *I'm the Queen of Dawson*, a deep, raspy voice cooed, *and for those of you who are still up, I thought you might like one last song. A little John Prine before laying your pretty little head on your pillow. This one's called "In Spite of Ourselves."*

Her eyes stung as if she had a fever. Sleep wouldn't come, but she couldn't lift her eyelids. An image of her mother: green nightgown, brown eyes, the skin on her face as thin as tissue paper. When Millicent was a child and she had the flu, she would wake up at night and call for her mother, forgetting in her feverish state how hard it was for her mother to get out of bed and come to her.

But her mother would arrive in the doorway, and she seemed, in that hazy dreamscape, just like any other mother. Millicent slept on her belly, and her mother would lie on her side on the twin bed beside her and place one cool palm between her shoulder blades, its weight like a sedative. When Millicent woke the next morning and rolled over, there she was, hair fanned out on the pillow: her mother.

The John Prine song had ended. The radio fizzed static. Millicent was sure she hadn't drifted off to sleep but when she opened her eyes, daylight was creeping over the town. She slipped the square key out of the ignition, wrestled it off the keychain and clenched it in her palm. The dome, the rounded mountain that hovered over Dawson, was the first to be licked orange by the sun. Next was the church tower. She clenched the key so tightly she wondered if she had punctured her skin, if she was bleeding. The light crept up the street steadily, setting the pink and blue and yellow clapboard buildings on fire, until it finally touched the nose of the bus and soaked through the windshield.

28

IN THE MORNING PASCAL hovered behind the driver's seat and asked Millicent if she wanted to go to Grits Diner, his treat. She heard her own voice say, "I am hungry."

Her throat was so dry, it hurt to talk.

He needed to touch her. She understood this when she saw the exhaustion in his eyes. She slipped the key in her pocket and unfolded herself from the seat. He stroked her arm as she walked past him.

"Last night ..." he started to say.

"I'll eat and then I'll shower."

Pascal fastened his pants and shrugged on his flannel shirt, rolling the sleeves up to his elbows.

"Yes, Rabbit. Of course."

ANOTHER BLOWN-OUT, CLOUDLESS SPRING day, the sky a saturated blue. The street buzzed with locals preparing for the parade. A young boy with a bowl haircut and a red tracksuit sat on the sidewalk, blowing furiously into a saxophone half the size of his body.

Millicent kept her head down and walked two steps ahead of Pascal, touching the key in her pocket to make sure it was still there. She would wait until after breakfast, when they went to the hotel to shower.

She imagined his face when he came out and saw the bus was gone. She wanted him to feel the panic, the embarrassment, the anger—everything she had felt all winter.

The lineup for the diner wound out of the restaurant and into the street. Pascal craned his neck to look inside the restaurant and fished for her hand. Millicent's arms hung limp by her side. She was thinking about the bus, how until last night she had never even sat in the driver's seat, let alone driven it. Once she left town, where would she go? North, maybe, up the Dempster Highway and towards the Arctic Circle, where the light shone even more fiercely. It would be quiet up that dirt highway. She could spend a few days alone, untangling.

They finally nudged their way inside the diner to the smell of bacon and the loud hum of chatter. It didn't matter where she went, Millicent realized. She just needed to go. Put the key in the ignition and drive out of town. She needed to. The idea of running was the only thing that kept her breathing.

The booths were upholstered in red vinyl. Sophie and Bryce sat by the fogged window. Millicent watched Bryce pour a creamer into his coffee.

When Sophie saw Millicent, she waved at her with the same small smile as the night before. Millicent waved back. The relief of this simple motion sparked laughter that rose up like an air bubble in her throat. Was this all she had needed to do the whole time? Lift her arm, wave? All those nights freezing outside the bus at three in the morning. All those nights returning to bed, to Pascal, wishing she could be inside him like a Russian nesting doll. Had Sophie been there the whole time?

Pascal read the specials on the chalkboard, pretending not to see Sophie and Bryce. A waitress in a tight yellow dress with a frilled collar pushed two menus at his chest.

"I'll put you with your friends," she said, motioning for them to follow her. Pascal clamped the menus under his armpit and leaned against the *Please wait to be seated* sign.

"What's your name?" he asked the waitress.

"Deedra."

"What a pretty name," Pascal said. "Deedra. I have never heard this."

Deedra started across the packed restaurant.

"Are you coming or not?"

"Deedra, can you do us a favour? We'd really like our own—"

"I've got a restaurant packed with a bunch of hungover brats. Nobody's gonna budge for the next hour. Either you sit with them or you starve."

"That's fine," Millicent said, moving towards her.

Pascal followed, his eyes on the floor. He sat in the booth next to Bryce. Millicent sat beside Sophie. The morning light washed through the windows.

"Salut," Pascal said to no one in particular.

Bryce placed a chunk of butter on his waffle. "How goes life on the bus?" he asked.

"You know, living the dream," Pascal said.

Bryce held his knife and fork with his fists. He dipped a bite of the golden waffle in a pool of syrup. His jaw clicked as he chewed. Sophie used the sleeve of her shirt to wipe condensation from the window. A man with a long beard and a sash that read *Mayor* walked a pot-bellied pig on a leash; the parade was in full swing now. How real Sophie was. Alive. Right there. Millicent could smell the lavender on her, and she knew that she could tell her what she was about to do, and that Sophie would understand.

Deedra came back with coffee. Pascal added two creamers and two packets of sugar. His spoon clanked against his mug.

"Big win last night, Mill," Bryce said.

Millicent took a sip of coffee. It was hot and dirt-weak. All she had to do, she told herself, was play a character. Get through breakfast.

"It sure was a surprise," she said.

"She was amazing. I didn't know she had this in her," Pascal said. He stacked four full cream containers into a tower. The creases ran deep across his forehead. His hair, weighed down with oil and sweat, was more grey than brown. Millicent took steady sips of coffee, nursing it between her hands. Sophie did not look away from the window. Millicent could tell she was trying not to smile.

Pascal's tower of creamers collapsed. He took a deep breath, as if preparing to make an announcement.

"I am going to use the bathroom," he said.

When he was out of sight, Sophie looked away from the window.

She wound a strand of hair around her finger and stared at Millicent with her calm demeanour.

"I warned you about the isolation," she said.

"What do you mean?" Millicent asked, although she knew what Sophie meant.

"You look like you've been run over by a bus."

"Soph!" Bryce said, his mouth full of waffle. He shot her a look of disapproval, and Millicent knew for certain they were not a couple and never had been. She had made it all up. She wondered what other stories she had made up, late at night on the bus, when she couldn't sleep.

"Figuratively, you mean?" Millicent said, forcing herself to keep a lighthearted tone.

"Yes, of course." Sophie let the strand of hair fall over her cheek and raised her eyebrows. "Figuratively."

Millicent took the key to the bus out of her pocket and laid it on the table. When she had rehearsed this speech in her head, she spoke with a bold confidence that neither Bryce nor Sophie could argue with. But now that she was actually saying the words, her tone was strained and her voice weak.

"I'm going to leave. Take the bus when he's in the shower. Just … get out of here."

Sophie's eyes widened.

"What happened last night?"

Millicent looked past Sophie and out the window, trying to stop herself from trembling.

"Please Milli, just come home with us," Sophie pleaded, her voice cracking.

No. She needed to get the clawing, desperate animal out of her.

"I can't."

Bryce finished his waffle, pushed his plate away and cleared his throat. He threw his crumpled napkin on top of his syrup-stained plate.

"You've completely lost it, Mill," he said, his eyes flitting up as he saw Pascal heading back towards the booth. "You need to trust us, okay?"

Millicent sat upright, grabbed the key from the table and shoved it deep in her pocket.

Pascal wove his way through the tables, speaking into his cellphone in rapid French, unaware that he was bumping into chairs. The volume of his speech made her courage dissolve. Her plan was foolish. She wouldn't be able to pull it off—manoeuvre the 40-foot school bus out of town before he noticed it was gone. As he reached the booth, she saw that his face was glowing with excitement. *The producer*, he mouthed, then motioned that he was going outside.

The producer. There was a producer. None of it mattered.

"I have to go," Millicent said as Pascal went out the door.

Sophie grabbed her wrist, her delicate fingers pressing hard into Millicent's bones. "This is insane!" she said.

The skin on Bryce's neck had turned a blotchy red. "Millicent," he pleaded. "Please. You don't have to keep doing this."

Millicent pulled away from Sophie and stood up. Her voice was finally clear. "I know what I'm doing."

Outside the window, Pascal paced back and forth on the sidewalk, the phone pressed to his ear. The high-school band marched past in their red tracksuits. The boy with the bowl cut was at the very back, cheeks blown-out, saxophone gleaming.

29

MILLICENT BLENDED INTO THE crowd on the sidewalk, ignoring the parade. She wove through children shrieking for candy and seniors settled in lawn chairs. She walked as fast as she could without breaking into a run. Running would draw attention.

On the bus, sunlight streamed through the windows, illuminating dust particles that floated over the kitchen sink. Millicent stripped off her jacket, threw it on the table and sat, paralyzed, on the edge of the driver's seat. She allowed herself one breath with her eyes closed: bacon, coffee, Old Spice, and beneath it all the faint whiff of vinyl seating. The familiar smells made her nauseous. The bus was the last place on earth she should be. But how else could she get to him? This was all he had. To erase the bus from his life would ruin him. She had to do it.

Millicent swallowed, drew the seatbelt across her chest and blinked hard to clear her vision. The steering wheel.

The stick. The flat windshield spattered with bugs. How many times had she watched him shift into first, ease off the clutch and pull onto the highway?

The key was stuck. It wouldn't turn in the ignition. Millicent twisted it so hard she was afraid it would snap, but it finally engaged. As her hand searched for the lever to slide the seat closer to the steering wheel, she realized how much she was shaking. Her foot pressed down harder on the clutch until it met the steel floor. The engine gave a guttural cough. With her gaze flitting between the rear-view mirror and the side mirror, the clutch slipping between first and reverse, she tried to ease the bus out from its spot between two trucks. The bus rocked, inching forward, backward, forward.

Someone was banging on the door. Millicent cut the engine and lowered her forehead to the steering wheel. She exhaled a balloon of hot breath—of course he had followed her back to the bus! What had she expected? The knocking continued. Why didn't he just kick the door open like he did last night? She imagined him climbing the stairs and hovering above her, asking *What's wrong, Rabbit, what's wrong?* She imagined him undoing her jeans, his hands like cold, writhing, slippery fish, exploring her body.

There was no way out.

When Millicent finally lifted her head, she saw that it wasn't Pascal on the other side of the door. It was Sophie. She was leaning against the door trying to see inside, her hands forming a visor above her eyebrows.

Millicent pulled the lever. The doors folded open. Sophie was panting.

"Can I come in?"

Millicent scanned the street behind her, looking past the seniors folding up their lawn chairs and the couples ambling down the street, hand-in-hand. He would be here at any moment.

"Don't worry, Bryce is keeping him company," Sophie said, climbing the steps. Millicent closed the doors after her.

"What do you mean, keeping him company?" she asked.

Sophie looked at her without answering.

"Tell me," Millicent demanded.

"When he came back into the diner, he looked like his mother had just died."

Millicent kept her hands on the wheel at ten and two.

"I asked him what had happened, but he just sat down and stared out the window as if we weren't there."

Sophie paused, unsure if she should go on. Millicent motioned for Sophie to continue.

"When he finally spoke, he was trying hard not to break down." Sophie sat on the hump beside the stick shift. "He said a producer told him that he wasn't cut out for the screen. That he had to stop contacting him. That he would have to take action if he didn't stop."

Millicent's hands grew clammy on the wheel. She swallowed the hard lump of shame. She thought about her birthday party, when Pascal said the producer thought Millicent would be beautiful on camera. She thought he had simply blown the story about this producer out of proportion. Had it been complete lies?

"Honestly, Mill. He looked like he was about to off

himself. We couldn't just leave him there, so Bryce, being Bryce, offered to take him for a beer—"

"What are you doing here?" Millicent interrupted.

She needed to turn on the ignition, hear the diesel engine, press her foot down hard on the gas.

Sophie scanned her friend's face, searching for a clue that would salvage the conversation. Millicent wondered what she saw when she looked at her. She could feel the trembling coming on again.

"What are *you* doing here, Millicent?" Sophie asked.

"I need to get out of here."

Sophie spoke slowly. "Right. I can understand that."

"I'll head up the Dempster Highway. Be alone for a few days."

"And then what?"

"I don't know," Millicent said quietly. She hadn't thought that far ahead. She hadn't even managed to move the bus from its parking spot, yet she was planning to drive it hundreds of kilometres up an unpaved road? Sophie was right, and then what? Her plan seemed to make sense when she was in a state of shock, but now that she had said it out loud, it seemed absurd.

"Can I come?" Sophie asked.

Millicent laughed. She laughed without moving her lips, or any of the muscles in her face, and without any joy. She laid her head back down on the steering wheel and addressed her feet.

"I hate this bus. I want to drive it off a cliff."

"We could," Sophie said. "We just have to figure out a way to do it without dying in the burning crash."

Millicent imagined launching the thousands of pounds of steel into oblivion and everything inside burning to ashes: his recording equipment, his bed, his hula hoops, his herbs, the dirty dishes underneath the table. His five books—*The 7 Habits of Highly Effective People*; the *Kama Sutra*; *Tintin au Tibet*; *One Hundred Years of Solitude*; and *Filmmaking for Dummies*. How many times had she stared at the spines of those books from the bed, convincing herself that this was enough?

Millicent squeezed her eyes shut to block out the other voice, the louder voice. He was on top of her, trapping her, whispering in her ear. *I am the wolf. You are the rabbit.* His tongue was in her mouth. His sweat was in her mouth. She couldn't breathe.

She lifted her head from the steering wheel and looked at Sophie.

"I came to see you, you know?" Sophie said.

"You did?"

"Of course. Pascal didn't tell you. Yes. I came to check on you. I just needed to make sure you were, you know, alive."

"I thought you were done with me."

"Mill. C'mon."

"I thought everyone was done with me. I thought the only person I had left was Pascal."

Sophie stared hard at her. "That's exactly why I came to see you."

Millicent was overtaken by a wave of exhaustion. "It wouldn't have mattered," she said. "You couldn't have changed anything."

"Because you were mad at me?"

"Because I was…" Millicent paused, holding back tears. "I was just, gone, you know?"

Sophie nodded, then continued. "I always thought: humans improve. With like, hard work, you know? I thought my past was behind me and I was working towards a more desirable version of myself. That was the thought that kept me going every day. That I was better than my past. That I wasn't a slave to the evil inside me."

Millicent fidgeted with the gold medal underneath her shirt.

"But suddenly I'm on the bus with your boyfriend, in your bed, and all of that is falling away," Sophie said, her face crumpling. "Who was that person. Was it me? How could I do something like that? To my *friend*, on her birthday!"

When Millicent answered, it was as if a hundred dead flies were trapped in her throat. "I can't."

"You can't what?" Sophie said.

Millicent gazed out the windshield at the Dawson City Hotel.

"I can't be here anymore."

Sophie nodded as if she had been waiting for her to say those exact five words all along.

30

IN THE PARKING LOT of the Dawson City Hotel the annual spaghetti and meatball cook-off had drawn a crowd. Locals and tourists mingled, carrying Dixie cups of hot pasta from different competitors, tasked with deciding who would take home the top prize: a hunting rifle and $500 cash, plus their recipe engraved on a giant trophy.

The smell of sizzling beef and tomato sauce wafted across the street, where Sophie paced outside the bus, on the lookout for any sign of Pascal. Bryce had promised to distract him with a pint at the Boiler Room, but that was over an hour ago and he could be coming back at any moment.

"C'mon Millicent," Sophie muttered under her breath.

Millicent knew that Pascal would be back soon, but now that she finally understood what she had to do, a calm had settled over her. She felt no rush as she zipped up her duffel bag and slung the handle over her shoulder.

At the front of the bus, she took off her medal and hung it over the rear-view mirror, where it spun slowly, catching the sunlight.

Rabbit, she said out loud, savouring the ugliness of the word.

As she went down the steps, the feeling returned. How many times had it crept over her that winter, the terrible freefall? She stood on the ground and leaned against the bus door to steady her weak legs. With her eyes closed, she let the feeling wash over her: aside from the bus, with Pascal, she had nowhere to go. Nowhere to be. This was her home.

She let herself fall and fall until the moment passed and she could feel the strength slowly returning to her legs.

"Where to, captain?" Sophie asked, snapping her out of her daze. How long had she been standing there? Millicent studied Sophie. Her hair had grown out into waves, framing her face. Her perfect skin glowed under the midday sun. Sophie was trying to appear relaxed, but Millicent could read anxiety in her eyes as they darted from one side of the street to the other.

"The river," Millicent said. "Follow me."

After throwing her duffel bag in the trunk of Bryce's Ford, Millicent and Sophie walked swiftly down the wooden boardwalk towards the edge of town. At the riverbank, they climbed onto some large flat rocks and stared silently at the water, catching their breath. The edges of the river were still frozen, but the middle ran fast and silty. Upstream a few hundred metres, the old ferry that carried cars over to West Dawson looked as if it were about to be swept away in the current. Millicent watched as it powered against the fast-moving water, docking effortlessly on the far bank.

"Want to go for a swim?" she asked, remembering the day she met Pascal at the highway pullout, how she had jumped in that freezing water after him. Anything to feel the cold, raw thrill of it.

Sophie looked at Millicent to see if she was kidding. "No thanks," she said. "I don't have a death wish."

"Me neither."

"But really, what are we doing here?"

Millicent dug the key for the bus out of her pocket. With the weight of it in her open palm, she thought back to the word *Asshole*, written in neat cursive on the side of the bus. How clear it was now: the woman hula-hooping in the photo had spray-painted it. The woman before her. Millicent could have just read that one word and walked away. How simple that would have been. Painless. Yet, much as she didn't want to admit it to herself, somewhere deep inside she knew that she had to move through the pain herself.

Millicent opened her palm and tossed the key into the water. The river swallowed it with a tidy *plunk*. The key was gone.

"It was his only one."

"You are amazing," Sophie said.

Millicent sat down on the cold rock and hugged her knees into her chest. She kept her eyes locked on the spot where the key had disappeared, as if it might float to the surface, as if her courage had been all for nothing.

"What happened last night, Mill?" Sophie asked.

Millicent tried to come up with words, but there were none. Her throat was so tight it burned. She thought she might cry but the tears wouldn't come. She took a big gulp of air and shook her head in disbelief. Sophie sat down beside her and placed her hand on Millicent's thigh.

She spoke so quietly it was almost a whisper. "Do you want to go the police?"

"No."

Sophie nodded, looking out at the ferry returning from the far side of the river. Her red and yellow feather earrings swirled in the wind like bait luring a fish. They sat like this, silent, for what must have been ten minutes, watching chunks of winter ice ride the current and disappear around the bend.

"Do you want me to kill him?" Sophie asked.

Millicent let out a strangled laugh that was closer to a sob.

"You know I will," Sophie said.

"No." Millicent stood up and began walking back towards town. "I just want to go home."

31

MILLICENT STARTED WALKING a fast lap around the Millennium Trail on her lunch break. When the siren rang for the paper to go to print, she stopped her walking and hurried down the flight of stairs before Bryce had the chance to ask her how she was doing and if she wanted company. He was being extra kind to her now, offering to get her coffee from the bakery across the street or take on her assignments if Franc gave her too many, but he never mentioned Pascal's name—not even in the seven-hour drive from Dawson in his Ford, where he and Sophie played Aretha Franklin on the tape deck in the front and Millicent lay in the back without a seatbelt, watching the clouds slide through the moving sky and brushing the tears that welled up whenever she remembered her reality: it was over. It was really over.

It was as if Bryce thought she could just flip the page and move on. Or maybe he just couldn't stand to hear

Pascal's name out loud. Either way, it didn't matter. She needed to be alone.

For the first few minutes, as she walked past the bakery and the canoe-rental shop, where the teenage staff were hosing off the boats in preparation for summer, her legs felt like they might collapse, as if she had just come back from months at sea.

After she got to the trail and felt the cool river air hit her face, she found her rhythm. She walked in a light spring jacket, taking in the scene: the river, running high and blue, slipping through town like a jolt of electricity; the crocuses that had opened, explosions of purple wedged between grey rocks.

She wasn't sure if the walking was a distraction from her pain or a meditation on it. In the newsroom, before deadline, she could immerse herself in work and forget about her reality entirely. It wasn't until she finished the story and yelled the headline at Franc that the memories returned. Watching Pascal drive with one hand on the wheel. The first morning she woke up on the bus and he placed a mug of cowboy coffee on her bare belly. The way he hooked his fingers through her belt loops. How her cheek melted into his chest. How all she wanted was to be deeper inside of him, to be tucked away safely in the heat of his body.

When she was out walking and the memories pressed so heavily on her chest that she felt she could no longer get enough oxygen to her lungs, she stopped and turned her attention to the river, to the way the water was slipping downstream, curving around large, smooth rocks in the middle of the current. She knew her mind was only returning to the good memories, the early ones. It was as if the burning, painful memories were playing hide and seek. When they did surface—the glazed look that came over his eyes, the sweat-soaked sheets—every cell in her body froze.

Maybe it was for the best, Millicent thought, closing her eyes and combing her fingers through her hair, letting the sound of the river, the hundreds of thousands of gallons of water, wash through her. Maybe it was for her own survival. Maybe those memories hid themselves so she could move through her days without collapsing. And with that thought, she told herself to keep walking, to focus on where to go from here.

She had moved back in with Sophie until she could find her own place. Sophie had told her she could stay as long as she liked, but when Millicent dropped her duffel bag on the chaise longue, she smelled the whiskey and the jasmine, saw that the spider plant on the windowsill was dead, and knew she could only stay here temporarily, that this was Sophie's life.

The first thing she did in the apartment was draw a bath in the clawfoot tub. She wasn't paying attention as she turned on the faucet and peeled off her clothes. The water was so hot she had to sit naked on the toilet seat, her head resting on her hands, her elbows pressed into her white thighs, waiting for it to cool down.

Once she finally climbed into the tub, her body exhaled. She was overcome by a lightness that she could only describe as grace. She scrubbed herself with the fresh bar of lemongrass soap that Sophie had left out for her, and then lay there for what must have been over an hour, staring at the ceiling. Maybe her body knew exactly when to leave, just like a flower knows exactly when to seed. Just like an apple knows when to fall from the tree. Maybe this was the only way the story could go.

When she drained the water, the tub was lined with streaks of dirt. Millicent couldn't bear to look at it.

She came out into the living room with a towel wrapped around her hair and another wrapped around her torso. She just stood there, dripping, unsure where to go. She didn't even know if her bedroom was still hers.

Sophie looked up from her guitar, her hazel eyes inviting Millicent to join her on the couch.

"You just have to get through these few weeks, Mill. It'll get better."

Sophie kept saying things like *the passage of time will heal the pain*, and she guaranteed that at a certain point, they would be able to laugh about what had happened. Millicent curled up on the cushion next to Sophie so that their bare feet were touching and stared at the setting sun, which was exploding through the living room window.

"Maybe," she said.

She knew that the intense feeling of being alive that she had experienced with Pascal might never come again. And she was certain that she would never fully heal. She didn't know if she even wanted to. Does healing mean forgetting?

ON THE FIRST DAY that was warm enough to go without a jacket, Millicent drank in the sun, her feet floating
a foot above the Millennium Trail. The energy from the
sunlight vibrated through her body and she had to hold
herself back from breaking into a run. Instead she speed
walked, arms swinging by her sides, phone tucked into
the back pocket of her jeans. She knew she had to do it.
She couldn't hold off any longer.

Millicent rehearsed what she would say to her mother.
She would lay out the story from beginning to end. She
would admit that she had lied, and that she had been
avoiding phone calls from home for so long because she
couldn't bear to see herself reflected in her mother's voice.
Millicent repeated the script in her mind until she reached
the bench closest to the *Nugget* office. It would be fine, she
told herself, a quick call to explain where she had been
over the past few months, and then they could move on.

On the bench, Millicent stretched out on her back,
her shoes on the wood and her knees facing the sky. Her
phone rested on her stomach, rising and falling with her
breath.

The honking was barely audible at first but after a
minute the sound turned into a chorus of deep, throaty
barks. Millicent stretched her neck and tilted her head
farther back so she was looking at the southern sky
upside down, at the V of large, white birds cutting rapidly
through the blue. Tundra swans. It had to be them,
migrating north for the season. So they had returned.
The sharp blows of noise vibrated in her eardrums as the
birds flew directly overhead. Millicent clutched her phone

in her palm, the barks growing fainter and fainter until the sky grew still as a painting.

Her mother picked up on the first ring.

"Millicent." Her voice was pain and relief. "Are you okay?"

Millicent breathed into the phone.

"Millicent?"

It was those three syllables that broke her. She could not talk. She could not breathe. She lay there, staring at the sun that had tacked itself to the top of the endless sky, refusing to budge. Tears ran hot into her ears. Her mother remained silent on the other end, waiting. Finally, with a shaky voice, Millicent began.

Epilogue

TWO MONTHS LATER, THE first official day of summer. Franc's jean jacket hung on his office doorknob. Talk radio blared from inside. Millicent pushed the door open to the smell of cleaner and cigarettes. Franc stood at the window, his back to her. His red carpet had been cut into diagonal vacuum lines. His desk was cleared too.

Franc didn't notice her. He spritzed the window with blue cleaner, placed the bottle on the windowsill and with the same hand wiped the glass clean with a wad of newspaper. With his other hand, he took a drag of cigarette. CBC blared the nine o'clock Monday morning news.

"Franc?"

He lowered the volume on his boombox and turned around. His forehead was slicked with sweat. She wondered if he had been there all night, cleaning.

"Millicent," he said, gesturing to his work. "What do you think?"

She stood in the doorway. "It looks great, Franc. But where is everything?"

There was the sound of footsteps clumping up the stairs. Bryce hovered behind her. He unclipped his helmet and ran his fingers through his flattened hair.

"What the fuck is going on?" he asked.

Franc stubbed out his cigarette. "I'm leaving."

Millicent forced an awful laugh that sounded like she was choking.

"It's not a joke."

"Franc," Bryce said in a teasing tone.

"I'm going out to the fishing camp with Charlie for the summer. His whole family is going. Cousins and aunts and uncles." Franc sat down behind his empty desk.

"A protest," he said, meeting Millicent's eyes. He picked up a stapler, turned it over in his hands, frowning. "Anybody want this?"

"What about the court case against the government?" she said.

"These things take forever," Franc said. "Won't happen until fall. We'll be back by then."

When Bryce spoke again, hardly any sound came out. "But who's going to run the paper?"

Franc pulled out a small box from his drawer and rattled it near his ear.

"Who needs five hundred thumbtacks? I mean, Jesus Christ."

"Franc," Millicent said.

Franc opened the box and absent-mindedly pricked one of the tacks against his thumb.

"Who do *you* think will run the paper?" he said.

"We're folding?" Bryce asked.

"Oh, c'mon, Bryce. Have a little more faith in the old *Nugget*."

Bryce dropped his panniers and his helmet on the carpet and folded his arms over his chest.

"No," he said. "I can't run a newspaper."

"You can."

Bryce leaned his head back against the doorframe and closed his eyes. "I can't," he repeated, as if in physical pain.

When Franc started to laugh, he couldn't stop. Millicent had never heard this kind of joy coming from his body. It was like water seeping from a dry well.

"Not just you," Franc said when he found his breath again. "Mill will help. It's easy. Just pay the bills when they come in, and—"

"But, what bank, like," Bryce stammered.

"And leave at least half an hour for layout, before the paper goes to print. Don't let the advertisements, ever, manipulate editorial content. Business will come knocking at your door, saying they'll pay for a full-page colour ad for a whole year, if you just write a little article about how great they are." Franc shook his head. "Never ever fall for it. I don't care how in the hole the *Nugget* is. That will ruin us." He paused, then added, without a hint of irony, "Oh, and spend time on the headlines. We all know it's the only part of the newspaper anyone reads."

With that, Franc reached for his pack of du Mauriers in the back pocket of his jeans, struck a match against the box and then took a drag, forgetting, it seemed, that

Millicent and Bryce were right there, watching him.

"Really," he said after a few moments. "Get to it, kids. Paper is not going to write itself."

ONCE THE CROCUSES WENT to seed, the lupines bloomed. The stalks with their delicate violet petals grew on the banks of the Yukon River, in garden beds and from the cracks in the pavement. The tourists returned in swarms. They parked their RVs at the back of the Walmart parking lot. They rented canoes from the shop next to the *Nugget*, wobbled into the boats, steered themselves into the current and floated down the river, watching the riverbank slide by: the old log cabins buckling in on themselves, red foxes lurking between stands of trembling aspen, owls skimming through golden air.

After the lupines, the wild roses seduced the town with their musky, sweet scent. Wild sage grew from the top of the clay cliffs. Juniper bushes down by the river. Then the fireweed flushed deep red, signalling the end of the short summer. Once the nights filled with stars again, the tourists fled back down the Alaska Highway.

Bryce kept Franc's office tidy. He even bought an aloe plant to try to get rid of the cigarette smell, but the office still had an inextinguishable essence of Franc, like he was lurking in some dark corner, like he had never left for the land at all.

With Bryce as editor, it was Millicent's responsibility to write the entire local news section. Some mornings, before he had any copy to lay out, Bryce would pace behind

Millicent's desk and ask if he could help her with anything. When she said no, she had it under control, he would give a small nod in a half formal, half proud kind of way.

Sometimes when she was working on deadline, she heard the sound of a throaty engine and she knew it was Pascal's bus; the very sound of the diesel engine had distilled into her bloodstream.

IT WASN'T UNTIL THE gift shops closed for the season and the streets of Whitehorse emptied that she saw him.

His bus was parked across the street, outside the liquor store on Second Avenue. He was leaning against the back doors, scrolling on his phone, waiting for something. Millicent felt her entire being collapse in on itself. A carefully stacked house of cards, gone in a second. Was he waiting for her to come out of the building? After all these months? After all the strength she had gathered in order to leave, to be alone and stay alone?

No. A young woman with a volcano of red hair came skipping out of the liquor store with a six-pack under her arm. She couldn't have been older than twenty. He took the cans from her, set them on the pavement and drew her into his arms. They kissed. He twirled her like they were on a dance floor.

Part of Millicent wanted to run down the steps and out the front door. She wanted to grab the girl by the arm and coax her away from him. She wanted to tell this girl with volcanic hair that she didn't have as much control as she thought. She wanted to tell her that if she stepped into the bus, she wouldn't be able to get off, not for a long time.

And yet, as Pascal and the girl tossed their heads back in childish laughter, and Millicent found her way back to her body, she watched the scene like any stranger would. Like it was love. Like this is all there is.

Acknowledgements

WRITING A FIRST NOVEL is an exercise in patience, perseverance, luck, blind faith and most importantly, community. I could not have written *Rabbit Rabbit Rabbit* without the help of so many brilliant writers and editors. Thank you to everyone who supported me through earlier drafts (and there were *many*) of this novel.

To Gil Adamson, who believed in this novel before I had even finished the first draft. Your wisdom and love throughout this whole process has been nothing short of astounding. I will never be able to thank you enough.

To Allison LaSorda, whose deep friendship and keen editorial eye throughout this process kept me going. You are such a light in my life.

To my University of Guelph MFA peers, for loving so hard and believing so deeply in the writing life—Marcia Walker, Mahak Jain, Sarah Feldbloom, Ana Rodriguez Machado, Jessica Popeski, Rebeccah Love, Khalida Hassan, Simone Dalton and Andrea Perry.

To my MFA professors for your insight and belief in earlier drafts—Catherine Bush, Michael Winter and Russell Smith.

To all the wonderful writers who acted as first readers—Buffy Cram, Bruce Kirkby, Lana Pesch, Rami Schandall, Becky Blake and Christine Fischer Guy.

To my mentors at the Banff Centre for your deep thought and time with this manuscript—Caroline Adderson, Marni Jackson and Romesh Gunesekera.

To the Yukon, for inspiring this story and helping me become the adult I am today.

To Dorothy Thomas, for your generosity in sharing your Gwich'in culture with me.

To my agent, Samantha Haywood, for taking me under your wing.

To my editor, Douglas Richmond, and the whole staff at House of Anansi for believing in this story and making it so much better.

To the Canada Council for the Arts and the British Columbia Arts Council for gifting me the time to write this story.

To the Sander-Greens, for being the best family anyone could ask for. Truly.

To my mother, Helen, who read and copy-edited many drafts and was always cheering me on.

And finally, to my partner, Murray, and son, Oskar. Thank you for all the support and love. There are no two people I would rather do life with.

© Allison Seto

NADINE SANDER-GREEN grew up in Kimberley, British Columbia. After living across Canada—in Victoria, Toronto and Whitehorse—she now calls Calgary, Alberta, home. She completed her BFA at the University of Victoria and her MFA at the University of Guelph. In 2015, Nadine won the PEN Canada New Voices Award for writers under 30. Her writing has appeared in the *Globe and Mail, Grain, Prairie Fire, Outside, carte blanche, Hazlitt* and elsewhere.

NADINESANDERGREEN.COM

@NSANDERGREEN